SHADOWS ON SIDEWALKS

JAMES GRADY

PEGASUS CRIME
NEW YORK LONDON

This is dedicated to driving
from where we were to
where we hope to be.

SHADOWS ON SIDEWALKS

Pegasus Crime is an imprint of
Pegasus Books, Ltd.
148 West 37th Street, 12th Floor
New York, NY 10018

First Pegasus Books edition May 2026

Interior design by Maria Fernandez

Library of Congress Cataloging-in-Publication Data is available.

ISBN: 979-8-89710-123-8

10 9 8 7 6 5 4 3 2 1

Printed in the United States of America
Distributed by Simon & Schuster
www.pegasusbooks.com

"Sex and politics and murder is the way to go if you want to get people's attention."

—Bob Dylan
September 4, 2020

1

She swayed into the Chat & Chew at 10:07 that September Tuesday small town morning *before*. Midnight hair brushed the shoulders of her white blouse. A dark blue skirt flashed smoothly tan lean legs from her perfect knees to her big city high-heeled shoes that step-step-stepped straight toward me.

The bell above the door *dinged!* when she walked into the only full-menu eatery left on Sidner, Montana's Main Street. That *ding!* vibrated me. Stirred lust/guilt/fear in the Big Shots—eight middle-aged married White guys ruling a table by the café's picture window on our world between eras of plague masks.

I sat alone at my table.

Faced the door *because*.

Besides the Big Shots and me, the only other customers were two tables of passing-through travelers. A fiftyish wife's eyes stabbed her husband as he ogled the surprise vision. The eyes of a his & hers tourist couple of my and mystery woman's Millennial generation stayed locked in their cellphones.

The Old Farts' customary table of Boomers sat empty. I'd chauffeured my aunt and four others of that crew to the assisted-living Evergreen Center where my mother was bedded with casts on her broken legs and left arm from falling down her basement stairs. She needed care far beyond what her *come-back-to-town-to-help* son could provide. Mom'd never been part of the Old Farts, but they loved bringing their coffee klatch to her senior citizen invalid's bed, catching her up with town gossip and sharing *'remember when'* and *'we're still here'* humor.

Now a dream woman slid into the chair across the table from me. Dark eyes whirlpooled between black eyebrows and high cheekbones. A clean jaw led to a trim neck down to two undone buttons of her white blouse and the rise and fall of her breaths. She smelled of musk perfume and maybe marijuana.

She wore someone else's diamond rings on that finger of her left hand.

Out from her ruby-lipsticked smile came her magnetic husky voice: *"Hi."*

Out of me came: "I didn't think so."

Blink.

Her laugh held a stream of real humor. Other currents I couldn't name.

"So what *are* you thinking?" said this black haired beauty.

"I hadn't gotten that far yet."

"*Naw*, word in town is you never stop thinking. *Crazy*, but he's ours, he's . . ."

She let it come out like a TV newscaster: *"Local hero comes home."*

"Then in walks a stranger."

"The classic movie."

"Don't buy a ticket or click its stream. I'm just the guy sitting here."

"Nobody is ever *just the guy sitting here*. Besides, I know what—who I see."

"Maybe your eyes need a little help."

"They've got Google."

"Screens only give you what they want."

"You'd be surprised what my fingers find. And you're *'just the guy sitting here'* whose first novel got turned into a movie. That only happens *in* movies."

"We're all in some movie," I said. "Mine's been lucky. What's yours?"

"The one that got me this far."

"*Who are you?* This town, my table. *Why are you here?*"

She broke away from my gaze to give coffeepot-carrying waitress Elly a respectfully polite *'No thanks'* soft shake of her head.

Shot me with her dark eyes: "I'm here for you."

Smiled: "We want you to come to dinner. I'm Mrs. Ronald Zane."

My breath took that in. Let it out.

Told her: "Mrs. Ronald Zane. Is that who you are?"

She didn't blink.

"He and I aren't friends," I said. "I only know him by sight and . . . reputation."

She shrugged. "No matter. While you were growing up, he was growing out. Left, but kept in touch. Then came me and us coming back. Kind of like you now."

"Coming home isn't coming back."

"And coming to his—*our* place for dinner tonight won't kill you."

"Are you sure?"

She gave me *'I dare you'* eyes.

"So," I said. "A command performance when you—or is it *he* says?"

"You know how marriage works."

But I didn't. The closest I'd ever come to being wed was a lost year of absurd unrequited love for a blonde woman who called us best friends, smiled when I paid for our hangs and let me drive her wherever she wanted.

"We'll see you at 7:00," said someone else's wife. "Plenty of time to visit with your mother. They'll probably drug her out by the eight o'clock TV shows. What else better do you have to do? Stay home alone with your screens? Nurse a beer and listen to some bartender's playlist of songs that don't strike a chord for you?

"Besides," smiled those ruby lips, "don't you want to know what a guy who has millions and *more* wants with you?"

That *more* lay like a beating heart on the table between us.

Mrs. Ronald Zane stood with a *see you later* smile.

Said: "You know the house."

Swayed away with her quivering moon hips.

The bell above the door *dinged* and she was gone.

I calmed my heartbeats.

Picked up my cellphone.

Paid my tab.

Walked out to Main Street at exactly 10:33, the Officer in Trouble radio code I learned riding with DC's Homicide Squad.

Smelled invisible smoke from coming closer wildfires.

Looked east—the direction she had to have swayed or I'd have seen her going past the café's window. Saw struggling retail stores amidst the ether of cyber sales. The Roxy movie theater featuring a movie long available on home screens. A bar. A pawn shop. Empty *used-to-be* family businesses validating my dad's hero Springsteen's whitewashed windows of broken American dreams.

I turned toward where sunset would light the town.

Parked across the street sat the dark wedge of a Tesla Cybertruck.

What overwhelmingly cruised that prairie town that 21st century morning were vehicles akin to those driven by decades of American generations after World War II. Family ferries. Weathered sedans. SUVs. Pickups of various grandeur and gumption. Summer parks motorcycles near the Tap Room or the Lowdown where youngbloods go to tap their screens to be seen while they search for *maybes*. And while fine sedans from Detroit or Hiroshima might roll down Main Street on that Tuesday, in Sidner there was only one Tesla Cybertruck.

Everybody knew that *who*:

Queen Dee, widow of the last man to strike it big in the oil fields north of town, a reclusive loner whose first rig came in just before she let him knock her up. She was fifteen. A quick ahead-of-the-law wedding ring, a miscarriage, then a few more until many years later, she finally gave him an heir named Ronald.

As in slow-walking, smooth-talking *Mrs.* Ronald Zane.

The dark Tesla Cybertruck with its sloping-back windshield crouched across the street near the bank the Zanes owned a chunk of, diversification being one of the moves Dee made when she took over the family ways and means from her killed husband.

Legend has it that she and baby Ron brought her husband's lunch to an oil rig on the prairie that he was working alone. Drove up just in time to see a drill chain snap free and whip around his neck/jerk him straight up the derrick. His body fell to the platform. Nobody could have heard that *thud* over the *boom-boom-booms* of black gold pumping out of our earth to kill it. Dee dragged his body into the back seat of her car. Shoved it in there with the strapped-in car seat holding their kid. Drove into town. Didn't waste time with a stop at the hospital. Drove him straight to the funeral home and herself into her Queendom.

Now she held the steering wheel of the Cybertruck like facing eighty was triumphant personified as she gazed through its slanted windshield toward me.

Everybody knew that wedge of darkness vehicle cost more than the combined annual incomes of any two American middle-class families.

That was the point: *Everybody knew.*

And its rear cargo box caged any soul who couldn't afford to escape.

The dark wedge slid out of its parking place, parade-paced east on Main Street past me. We locked eyes. Dee gave me a nod of her shellacked silver head.

I walked the other way, west, past a boutique named Prairie Smiles.

Locals called it 'the P.S.' The P.S. was the only place in town that sold touchable books, along with arts and crafts, plus counter service of brewed coffees. I usually scored my caffeine there, relaxed in its *aches to be Paris* atmosphere, but that morning, the Old Farts' foray to my mom's had landed me in the Chat & Chew.

Now I tapped the bulletproof glass door just past the P.S.

Got buzzed into Last Chance Guns.

How Cody stayed in business baffled me. There were already four times as many guns as people in Sidner, and while he'd maybe pay his utility bills selling ammo, I couldn't believe he made a living from the pistols in the locked glass counters or the cowboy movie lever-action rifles, the duck-banging shotguns and the deer-dropping scoped bolt action long guns, the high-tech military style weapons posed in their rack like twitching commandos.

"Like pussy or cock, everybody always wants what they ain't got," Cody once told me when I asked how he kept selling guns. "Besides, out here, a lot of folks think it's all gonna go batshit any day now."

"What do you think?"

"Batshit came to town long ago."

Batshit had hit everywhere by that autumn of 2024.

Bullets dropped ten people in a mass shooting at the Super Bowl parade in Kansas. No word from the Wizard Of Oz on whether Dorothy was hit. More wars than the count of all my fingers raged all over the world, leaving bomb-blasted children crying for their dead parents and vanished futures. Tornados killing hundreds of people had been slamming my U. S. of A. since February. Hurricanes were a-comin'. Taylor Swift's *The Tortured Poets Department* broke the record for most streamed album in a single day and Pulitzer Prize winner Kendrick Lamar's mega-hit song accused a rival rapper of pedophilia. LA evacuated truckloads of citizens from out-of-control climate change wildfires—the smoke I smelled came from forest fires machine-gunning the Rocky Mountains west of town and in Canada. Louisiana's governor mandated that the Ten

Commandments be displayed in every classroom and fuck America's official separation of church and state. With the two of them bracketing Queen Dee in trips around the sun, the current eighty-one-year-old white haired president bumble mumble lost his shit on global TV while debating his seventy-eight-year-old orange-haired convicted rapist rival.

Touchable newspapers lay on the glass counter housing Colt 1911 .45s and snub-nose revolvers for scared grammas. Cody subscribed to three black-ink-on-processed-trees newspapers. Sidner's local six pages weekly booster came out on Thursdays. The thin daily newspaper trucked up after midnight from a Montana "big city" nearly two hours' drive away announced that autumn morning that it was "fully transitioning" to its online edition on the coming 2025's New Year's Day. *The New York Times* lying open for Cody's gaze took nine days to get to him via the US mail and that morning headlined that artificial intelligence now zapped through governments, industries and "daily human services" all over the world.

That headline made me blink.

Remember the *Terminator* movie released in George Orwell's prophetic *1984* year starring an eventual Republican governor of California as a cyborg-killing machine sent back from our future ruled by exterminating-humans AI promising: *"I'll be back."*

Once I asked Cody why he didn't just go online for what he wanted to read.

"I've got enough algebra on me," he answered with no hint of irony about the ultra-modern cellphone never more than a heartbeat away from his grab.

Then I asked him how it felt getting *'all the (*real*) news that's fit to print'* so many days after it had been reported.

"If you learn what people were thinking *before* and pay attention to what's happening *now*, you get a shot figuring what's *next*."

Cody stood a shade over my six feet tall. Clipped his hair too short to grab. Now his sniper eyes read buzzed-in me:

"What happened?"

"I'm not sure," I said. "I met Ron Zane's wife."

"Ahh," sighed Cody. *"Lana."*

He grinned: "Back in town not even a week and already courting trouble."

"What do you know about her?"

"She keeps it tight," said Cody, whose only *long time out of town* came somewhere for the Marines that he never talks about. Just like he never talks about his occasional *ghostings*. "You'd already left home when Ron came back from his hot-shit days in LA with her in tow.

"Her, *Lana*, word is they were Montanans who met up in Hollywood where she was trying to be an actress, landed a role as his *Mrs.* instead. Don't know why, but *major White boy* Ron makes sure people know she's *Indian* blood."

Didn't want to know/had to ask: "Does she . . ."

"Fuck around?" said Cody. "You'd think so because she can't be liking what she's got. Lot of people think *maybe*. Nobody knows for sure and for real. So," he said, "you thinking of taking that shot?"

"They just asked me to dinner tonight," I said.

"You wanna borrow a gun?"

"I think I'm fine."

"Really."

I looked around at the shop he bought with money from where nobody knew, not even his *friend since fifth grade* me. Racks of rifles. Counters of pistols. Stacks of bullets waiting to zing. Righteous America decals and posters, including the giant red, white and blue banner stretched along the wall behind the register:

THE RIGHT OF THE PEOPLE TO KEEP AND ARM BEARS SHALL NOT BE INFRINGED.

"You ever get shit for posting that?" I asked.

Cody's voice chilled: "When I'm lucky."

His canyon eyes met mine. I didn't blink.

"See you later," I said. "I've got to go stop a murder."

My rental car was parked back beyond the Chat & Chew. Getting there walked me past that bell-dinging door as it spilled out the Big Shots headed back to their money machines. I polited my way through their posse and past the haunted Roxy. Didn't look back. Felt their eyes on me walking away.

My ride drove me around the east end of Main Street, up the hill past the former city hall turned "Visitors' Center" where nobody ever came. I motored past our house where the voices and visions first started swirling in my skull.

Drove around the block dominated by a *repurposed* tan brick, two-story former hospital. Parked outside the glass doors of the Evergreen Center. Marched inside to rescue the Old Farts' coffee klatch from my mother before somebody got killed.

They were all glad to see me walk into that healing room—especially my aunt who'd been keeping the peace and the party going around her older sister trapped in a hospital bed with white casts on three of her limbs.

I shuffled the party out the door to the green-carpeted, cream-walled hallway shaft to the elevator that smelled like pine disinfectant.

Told them: "I'll be right there. The car's unlocked. Go on. Settle inside."

I closed the door behind them.

Mom lay propped up in the bed. Pulleys raised her two casted legs. Her casted left arm lay on her hospital gown. Nurse's aide Irma had brushed Mom's snowy mane before the coffee klatch arrived. But after visiting with those invaders, Mom's white hair looked like she'd been whipping it back and forth at a rock concert.

Now she whispered to the world: "I gotta get out of this fucking place."

"We *gotta* do what we can with where we're stuck."

"You little shit," she said. "That sounds like something I'd say."

"I paid attention." My eyes checked to be sure the door was closed.

She caught that: "What's up?"

"What do you know about the Zanes?"

"What about them?" Blinked a mother's guess: "*Her*."

"The whole lot of them."

"They're not our kind."

"I'm not our kind, Mom. I've never been anybody's kind."

"Just because you got bigtime, don't go high-hatting."

"I wear what I got born with 'n' what I earn."

Mom's harsh look announced we were done talking about the Zanes.

But I wasn't.

"Them not being *our kind*," I said: "Is that why Dad quit managing the Roxy back when I was a freshman in high school?"

"The theater got sold. He got a better job than working for her."

"And?"

Mom saw me waiting. Knew I wouldn't let it go. Sighed.

"Was her," she said. "Queen Dee. Your dad, he said she didn't give a shit about movies or what the Roxy was. He cared about all that. Like you. For her it, it was just one more piece of Main Street under her thumb."

Smiles of pride brightened our faces as we sat in a room with Dad's ghost.

We heard muffled voices outside Mom's second story windows.

"You better go," said Mom.

"Don't worry, I left the car windows rolled down."

We laughed. I gave her uninjured shoulder a gentle squeeze. Left her room.

Made it four steps away from the first floor's door to the fresh air sunlight when from behind me came an unknown woman's voice:

"Jim! Hold up!"

Turned, saw a business suited, couple decades older than me, brown haired woman striding toward me. I remembered her, and her name was . . . was . . .

"Mrs. Gage," she said.

"Of course."

We didn't shake hands.

"Look," she said in a private voice in that public hallway, "I have to tell you that even with your mom's Social Security, Medicare and her supplemental private insurance program—not the best in the world, let me tell you, they're all a rip-off but she probably got what she could figure out and afford . . . Anyway, her bills here are making her come up short, dip into her savings and . . ."

"Don't worry." I faked a smile. "My sister and I have her covered. Sis is the business whiz. Just let her know what Mom and you need. I just write checks."

Flashing through me came: *For how much longer can I do that?*

But I kept my smile.

She sighed with the relief of having done more than her job. Of being human, not just a cog in some corporation's cash machine.

Let me walk out into the sunshine of *sure I can*.

I chauffeured the Old Farts to where they were still lucky enough to live as free as infirmity, income and the irresistible let them. Last one delivered was my aunt, who lived in a square brick cottage on Knob Hill, the southern prairie wall for the glacier-carved valley holding the town and the railroad tracks that birthed it after my ancestors arrived to claim land won from the Crows by the Blackfeet who then lost it to cavalry blue coats. My aunt leaned across the front seat of my rental car. Patted my hand with a *good boy* smile and a kiss on my right cheek. Walked up the sidewalk of her widowhood.

I sat there in that ride I'd rented at the big city's airport when I arrived to relieve my older sister, who had two kids, an artist husband and a Chicago exec's career in a glass skyscraper she couldn't desert to "be there" for our broken-bones mother after the crisis stabilized. Remote work triggered in the first Trump-era plague now didn't work for Boss Her. Because my gigs are in my skull and laptop, it made sense for me to take over for the weeks of Mom's recuperation. A silver airplane flew me away from my movie-sale-afforded, DC, three-story urban townhouse where I rented out the two mortgage-covering lower apartments and perched my sparse loner's life in the loft.

The rental car's steering wheel turned away from the curb in front of my aunt's cottage of bricks. I knew where I'd end up going. I made myself wait.

You've gone back to those roads where you came from, right?

To drive past your ghosts.

That vacant lot is where you went to grade school.

There's the doorway of your first kiss.

The house where your high school crew hung out in the basement with video games while your friend's parents upstairs pretended not to know you were stoned on something besides the pills RX'd for kids whose adults could afford to give their beloved children such 21st century chemical channeling.

There's where the cops sirened you over one night. Gave you a ticket for busting through a stop sign even though you were innocent. They didn't care. They had a quota. You were a teenager who had to learn The Way Things Are.

There's the house where Glasses Girl who sat in the back of the class lived.

You never connected, face-on or in-screens. Now you realize you know nothing about her while you drive the streets of your shared small town yesterdays when you thought you knew so much.

That morning I headed west through the blocks of Knob Hill houses both shabby and styled. Reached the gravel street I'd shoveled for the city crew during college summers. Followed it through the iron gates of the cemetery. Drove past a homemade white-plank cross leaning over fresh gravestones. Its crossbar bled the black, hand-lettered scrawl FUCK COVID. Past graves of "my people" gone long before karma coalesced me into being. The car paused for me to give my father's gravestone a nod, settle its weight in my bones.

The car took the long way out of the cemetery, through blocks of houses, turned left down Knob Hill until my windshield heeded a stop sign where the city street hit the two-lane blacktop highway that ran through town. To the left, that road ran under the overpasses of a four-lane interstate thoroughfare for cars and trucks headed up to Canada or down through America.

Across the two-lane blacktop highway, freight trains filled tracks, huge rectangular cargo carriers, some with sliding doors open for Woody Guthrie hobos. A few of the boxcars were gray under that vast blue sky. More of them reddish brown. But mostly I saw dozens and dozens of freight cars exactly the same, colored gold and logoed with huge black letters:

CHINA TRANS . . . CHINA TRANS . . .
CHINA TRANS . . .

Gotta go clickety-clacked through me. *Go now, go now, go now.*

U-turned the car. Drove back up the hill to the street where I grew up. That life had been spent six blocks to the east. I turned west.

Yeah, I "knew the house."

And now I drove past it like a starstruck teenager hoping to catch a glimpse *of* but not get caught being obvious *about* even while dying *to be seen.*

Calling Ronald Zane's house a mansion was wrong, but that long-slung, horizontal lair perched on the edge of the hill overlooking the west side of town qualified as where money lived. Because the house faced the wondrous northern horizon of the town, what I saw from my car was the back of the house where flat stones led to a red wooden door. The lawn looked freshly mown and I knew he'd never done that. The trees growing on the street property line held September golden leaves and when they got blown off by the winds that ruled Sidner most days, he wouldn't be the one to rake them up. I couldn't see through the windows. The garage door was rolled down. The driveway held three parked vehicles:

A new SUV. A sleek German luxury machine. An older American sedan.

My rental car crawled past all that as slowly as it dared.

Rolled through blocks of memories spotted with signs sporting slogans for the *tick-tick-tick* coming presidential election. Those signs came from righteous anger or fervent hope. So many of the souls who posted the signs were right that they'd been wronged but wrong about who and what would make things right.

And all of them—*hell, the whole town!*—were justifiably angered by the hip 'intellectual and cultural elites' on both coasts who prattled anointed *virtuous* speak and who'd coined the mocking term "flyover states" for where/how/why my hometown hearts lived.

I rode back to the white cottage with a blue roof where I'd grown up. Parked out front. Sat at the kitchen table I'd adapted into a desk for my laptop, chargers, a couple yellow pads, a last-century black moleskin journal.

For the umpteenth time read yesterday's email from my New York literary agent who told me not to be discouraged by pre-publication reviews and online zaps of my new novel even though we both knew those sniper shots were death notices for that labor of love and perhaps for my life's dreams.

Spotify slid me into a *clong*—one of those music moments when what you're hearing snaps into a cosmic soundtrack of what you're living. That then & there *clonged* with a song by the rockers War on Drugs about not living here anymore. That was true. That was also a lie: Some places never let you leave.

I made a tuna fish sandwich. Drank a glass of Mom's milk before it went sour. Twittered—excuse me: "X'd"—and Insta'd. Filled an hour playing a video game. Told myself that I *obviously* really did need to shower again.

Drove two blocks to park in front of the Evergreen Center and deliver Mom's snail mail—envelopes of *pay me* or *give us* plus a "Here We Go!" reminder for a wedding on Friday that my aunt had already hooked me into. Watched my mother bitch about her dinner tray. Left her staring at the TV above her bed. Popped a second breath mint. Got in the rental car and drove. Drove slow and strong to that house. Right on time: 7:00 on the dot.

The car door slammed behind me. That big blue sky let me inhale the green of new mown lawn. Musky gold prairie. Smoke from coming-closer fires.

I refused the doorbell. Chose my strong knock on the solid red door.

That blood wood slab swung open and there stood the homeowner.

"Jimmy!" he said with a smile like a slashed saber.

"Ronny!" I said and stood where I was.

"Of course you came," he said. "I knew we could count on you."

He stepped aside.

I entered.

The red door closed behind me. Locked.

Ronald Zane.

He'd swirled his dyed hayfield hair around his skull. He was taller than me. Heavier with a body molded with barbells or machines, not manual labor. He wore a green golf shirt. Khaki slacks. His dyed tan TV handsome face seemed surgically tight. Thin lips opening for his words revealed perfect white teeth.

"This way."

He led me through the entryway with framed paintings—none of which featured cowboys like my great-grandfather or a lone steer near a barbed wire fence, the usual subjects of art on the walls of Montana homes.

The front of the house spread out like a slice of apple pie. A curved wall of windows opened to a view north across the town: Over the train tracks almost a mile away. Past the giant pink factory where I'd gone to high school. Past there to a prairie-hills horizon ruled by the Coyote Hills.

"Coyote" as pronounced the Montana way: "*Ki*-oat."

In any other geography, call those thirty-miles distant hulks *mountains*, but not out there in a landscape with westward views of the Rocky Mountains sixty miles away. Those three hills rose like blue guardians of the northern horizon. To my right outside the picture window, East Butte lay on the golden prairie like crumpled socks. Middle Butte rose like praying hands. West Butte sprawled on the horizon like the number 9 laid on its back like a stretched out and waiting lover.

Her husky voice behind me: "West Butte is the best."

The wall of window glass filled with a translucent vision of her.

I turned to see her flesh.

Walking toward me. Stepping down the levels of this living room pit. Black shoes with stiletto heels. Tan legs led up past her knees to the hemline of what a defense attorney would argue was "a simple black dress." That dark soft sheath curved around her hips to a V of flesh between unbridled heavy breasts. Her dark eyes locked on me as she stepped closer. Those tensed wide thick lips hid secrets within their ruby glow.

"Spare us," said her husband. "They're just piles of rocks, right, Jim?"

"Not if you know how to look."

My answer filled her eyes.

"Oh good," said Ronald. "You two will get along just fine."

My eyes turned to him. The wall behind where he stood held a giant original oil painting of tycoon-suited him. He saw my blink, preened.

"Lana, darling," he said. "You haven't offered him a drink."

"I'm fine," I said. Kept my mind clear. Let her off the hook.

"Well later she can share one of her smokes with you. The smell annoys me and the high bores me."

Booming male voice coming closer to us: "Who would dare bore you, Ron?"

The new man walking into the living room pit was between Ron and me in age with his dyed black hair styled akin to ancient history's Elvis Presley.

He shook my right hand with a firm grip I knew how to *gung fu*.

Ronald said: "Meet my cousin."

The cousin kept his grip and I let him: "More than just a *cousin*. Terence Ewing, Ron's personal and corporate lawyer, even though he's a terrible golfer."

"Who wins every damn time," said Ronald, and I just knew he cheated.

Cousin Terence smiled at me: "You'll be pleased to know that everyone at Barb's Ribs was impressed that we've got you over for dinner tonight.

"Barb's Ribs," he said again, the best place in town for dinner, though hell, there were only three other city-limits choices besides the vending machines at the truck stop. "That's what we're having for dinner. I picked it all up."

And deliberately told 'everyone' about us, I thought. *Why?*

The four of us stood in a socially distanced square. The wall of windows to my back. Black-dress Lana beside my heart. Her husband facing hers. Next to her husband, lawyer Terence watched me with courtroom eyes.

"Well, Jim," said our host Ronald, "why don't you tell us about—"

"Why the hell am I here?" I snapped.

Heard a sharp intake of breath from Lana. Kept my eyes on the two men.

Ronald smiled: "I told you he's perfect! Gets right to the point. Plus, despite what some people say, I know he has the smarts and the guts and the . . ."

His self-validated smile widened.

". . . the *hunger* to know he wants to, he needs to say *yes*."

"What are you talking about?" I said. "No bullshit."

"No bullshit, *James*. And we won't tolerate bullshit from you. *Any* bullshit."

"You'll get what I give you. What is it you want with me?"

Lana breathing hard.

"What I want," said Ronald, "is what we all want, all of us, yes, dear?"

Lana blinked more like a *deer* in the headlights than anybody's *dear*.

She whispered: "Yes."

Her husband Ronald sighed. "I don't think he quite believes you."

The woman with midnight hair stood tall with the inhale of everything she had. Her husky voice reached my core as she said: "Yes. I want it. This. Him."

"It's technically more complex," said Ronald, "but truly quite simple.

"I—*we*—want you to fuck my wife."

2

Thundering hearts.

Gunslingers eyeing each other from the four corners of that box of time.

"What?" I yelled.

Heard Lana's husky whisper: *"Be careful."*

"Now, now," Ronald told both of us, "I thought we'd have a drink, then over a plate of ribs, I'd lead us into *what's next*. But *quicky, Jimmy*, you jumped the gun. Learn to be patient. To trust me. I'll get you there."

"You're not taking me anywhere."

He sneered: "You're already here."

Hyperawareness vibed me in that sunken living room with its wall of windows filled by the Coyote Hills. There was a fireplace where you could toss your novel nobody liked or burn evidence. Beside it, cousin/lawyer Terence swayed like a hooded cobra. Between me and the red door stood blond golf Viking Ronald. Lana stood trembling out of everyone's reach.

Ronald grinned at her.

"*Lanny*," he said, "while I give our Jim a tour, go to my study. Fetch the legal documents about the money and such."

Terence raised his lawyer hand. "I'll get the—"

"You get the ribs out of the oven," said his cousin. "This won't take long."

Ronald jerked his head. The black-dressed woman he'd belittled as *Lanny* climbed the three steps out of the sunken living room. The sway of her moon hips.

"Isn't it great to watch her walk away?" said Ronald.

"Of course," he added, "we all have our own motivated *appreciations*."

Lana turned left at the top of the landing, down a hall, gone.

"We go this direction." Ronald gave me his back, led us up those ledge steps up from the sunken living room, turned us right down a shadowed hall.

He leered at me. "You must admit this is far more interesting than whatever you click on the apps like Tinder to link you up with *un-huh, un-huh*. And don't worry: This isn't any kind of *throuple*. What we all want is just you and her. And *no*, we don't want to watch."

Ronald snapped his fingers.

Recessed lights illuminated that hallway.

I spotted what I hadn't noticed when I came through the red door.

A framed, poster-sized, blown-up color photo of her in a wasteland.

Only *not her*.

She was the center of five sexualized women dressed in a movie scene's explosion of Hollywood characters—skimpy-shorted, ripped-bloused cavewomen *and* starship troopers in strategically torn battle uniforms. That photo caught her warrior's on-guard pose. The curve of her ass. Her straining breasts.

Past the blown-up movie still, carefully at eye level and close enough so you'd know they belonged together, hung a glass-framed document.

The website called IMDb—the Internet Movie Database—is *the* data archive of every film ever made, every director, every actor, every screenwriter

—or at least, *much* of cinema's history. My IMDb page showed me as "novel by" for the movie, but missed crediting me for three episodes I wrote for one of that streaming era's fictional TV network cop shows.

So much for my place in history.

That wall held the framed screen-grabbed IMDb page for Lana LaBuff.

An empty blue rectangle waited beside her name. Successful Hollywood players filled that space with a photo. Blue and black fonts linked the artists to the films where they were due credit.

This is what eyes staring at that framed screen-grab saw:

Lana LaBuff . . . . Slave Girl #7, Planet Nine
. . . . (uncredited), corpse in massacre, Terror Streets

Empty inches of blank white space waterfalled from those two credit lines to the bottom of the framed screen-grab.

Ronald's warm breath filled my ear:

"They say a picture's worth a thousand words."

"And you make sure everybody sees her *never-happeneds*."

His hand tapped a file folder on a table below his display of her.

"Everything you need to know is in here. Her physical two months ago. She's clean and completely vaxxed. She's got one of those inserts so don't worry about her skipping pills. High school diploma. Her tribal registration. A DUI she only did a day in jail for. She had the 'just seventeen' card to play. Back in LA, she punched a man in a bar. Dropped him. He dropped the charges. He was a manly man, humiliated. A transcript for one year of college where she never learned much of anything except *draw-ma*—you see where that got her."

His fingertips stroked the manila file folder.

"Nude photos. Disclosures we owe you. Color printouts. They're not very good. She was dead-eyed and like, *no pizazz*—and she claims to be a professional actor who cries or cums on command!"

He saw me *not* stare at the file folder he held down.

Caught my eyes on the closed red door.

"No one will believe you," he told me. "Our three testimonies against yours. Terence and my successful businessmen reputations against yours as somebody who makes a living telling lies and fancy tales—and *no*, that you used to also be an 'investigative reporter' won't help. 'Fake news,' *Jimmy*. Fake news."

He was right and he knew it. My heart pounded and he knew it.

"Go on," he said. "Leave. Drive away."

Leaned close enough for me to kill.

Whispered: "Leave her. With us. Alone."

My chest heaved. Couldn't draw a full breath.

Click-click-click came her stiletto heels closing in on me.

And him.

She stopped. Stood there with another manila file folder in her hands. Stared between us at the file folder on the hallway table.

Ronald took the file she held. Left that other file on the hallway table.

Proclaimed: "Let's eat!"

He strode between Lana and me like we were irrelevant.

She followed him. I trailed her to the dining room and a table set for four. White paper plates. White paper napkins. Plastic silverware. Regal wine glasses waiting for their red fill from the pricey bottle of pinot noir standing beside an aluminum tub of warm ribs smelling of maple syrup barbecue sauce. Carryout tubs of mixed-greens salad stood further down the table, unopened and forlorn.

"Darling," proclaimed Ronald, "this looks absolutely perfect!"

I tensed myself against his coming leer at Lana.

He turned lawyer Terence's face up for their deep kiss.

Like that.

Those two men preened.

"You see, Terry and I are *kissing cousins*." Those two men leered over their secret joke. Ronald brushed Terry's cheek. "Makes it easy to explain us to this *judgy* town. Here in Sidner, 'everybody knows' *poor Terry* lost the love of his life in a car crash in Alabama. A blonde with big fucking tits who *officially* became the angel he can't let go of."

Ronald grinned: "Sell a glitzy legend and nobody challenges your lies."

He set the file folder beside the paper plate at the head of the table. Pulled out that chair. Settled into its throne. Spread his arms out wide for us to sit.

Terry smirked as he claimed the chair to our host's left.

Lana kept her head down as she dropped into the chair to his right.

Walk out. Run. Leave this damn table. Leave . . .

I sat down beside her.

Ronald gave his paper plate to Terry.

"Before I get everything sticky," said Ronald, "here's yours."

He passed me printed-out pages of prose from the manila folder.

Terry plopped a smear of barbecued ribs onto the white paper plate.

Passed the plate to Ronald who placed it in front of him. Ripped a chunk of meat and bone from the mess. Chomped into it with his sharp white teeth.

I set the papers that I'd been served on the table beside my empty white paper plate without those documents getting scarred by my DNA or fingerprints.

"Give me the highlights," I told the barbecue-smeared face of Ronald Zane.

Told, not *asked*, and he knew it.

We both ignored the lawyer sitting at the table.

"We're giving you what Terry calls *boilerplate.* A *don't-ever-tell* NDA—Non-Disclosure Agreement. All the smart CEOs, Hollywood stars and influencers have them now and the smartest ones of them get NDAs from whoever they've fucked, so you see, all of that's pertinent to your case."

"I'll never sign away my rights to write and publish!"

Ronald beamed to his lover/lawyer: "I told you so!"

Turned his winner's smile to me.

"I—we," he said, "added a 'get out of jail' clause for you. You deliver what you promise, and then when it's all over, you can write what you want.

"Personally," said Ronald, "I might love some celebrity story about all this. Though be careful: I have a herd of lawyers besides Terry to stampede you into dust even if you tell everything exactly the way it is—*was*—and not what I say. Money trumps facts. But if you're careful, maybe me being the star of notoriety . . . Well, being any kind of star beats being just another moon."

He fluttered his hand in a consciously nasty mocking cliché of the LGBTQ: "And what-*Ev-a* with your *nov*-els. Who cares about *what might have been*?

"Right now in the real world," said that boardroom businessman, "focus on what's in front of you. That's a contract you gotta love:

"In exchange for what *we* decide is a 'credible and demonstrable pattern of behavior' regarding the par-*tay* of the first part with the par-*tay* of—"

The lawyer interrupted: "That enumeration may—"

Ronald said what sounded like: "Shut up, *Ter-Ter.*"

As in *Terence.*

Who did what he was told.

Ronald laid the gnawed bare barbecued rib on his now no longer white paper plate. Rogue barbecue sauce stained both his hands.

"Here's the deal," said that man with a face smeared like a mad clown. "It's my mother," he said. "The bitch just won't die."

He leaned toward me: "You know what I mean."

Blink, and I envisioned killing him as he invaded the hospital scene that brought me back to my hometown.

"Well of course you really don't," he said. "Your people never had money. Until you, but that was always penny ante, and now, mostly gone."

I gave him nothing.

"We thought Lana would be enough," he said as he gave Terry a smile. "I mean the bitch was already seventy-two—

"—*Mother*, I mean," he said. "Our other bitch here seven years ago was twenty-seven. Makes her three *depreciated* years older than you, but still a bargain."

Ron shook his golden head. Tightened his pink face: "Some of us still haven't gotten the bargain they deserve."

He leaned his meat-sauce face across the table toward me. His voice tightened as his green eyes drilled me with *The Way It Is*:

"Mother craves a dynasty to carry on her *taken* name.

"*But fuck me NO!*" cried out Queen Dee's son. "I'll never let a dime of what's mine go to some *spawn* like she did so she could groom *it* to get rid of me! Fuck her dynasty. *I'm* her dynasty, and I say *fuck her!*"

He got his breath back: "Like I'd ever want to fuck any woman."

Lover/lawyer Terry chimed in: "We thought we had that beat when we signed up Lana. We thought the obvious fuckability of her would make the old woman assume it was just a matter of time before her grand-heir would arrive on the scene. We thought back then that Dee'd naturally terminate forthwith."

"But the bitch won't die," said her son Ronald. "Fifty fucking years of me not celebrating who I am because she hates people like us for *bullshit* prejudice."

He shook his head.

"You think she'd change with the times," said her son. "I mean, the *consigliere* for our White House pick was gay-as-hell Roy Cohn!"

I scoffed.

"Roy Cohn persecuted his own kind," I told the room. "He didn't care about who were 'reds' or 'Commies' when he investigated and savaged folks to keep drunk-ass Senator McCarthy famous in the 1950s. 'Enemies of America' labels were a distraction for power grabs, revenge and a way to keep his personal enemies under his thumb. Then he became a fixer for the Mafia in New York."

"History is only worth what it gets you now."

Ronald sneered. Nodded his head at Lana. At me.

"Besides," said the son of Queen Dee, "the deep down reason she hates people like Terry and me and other gay men is she can't woo them or put them under her thumb with sex—*she still thinks she's got it at seventy-nine!*

"And now," said Dee's son, "Momma ain't getting what she want from our history. She's antsy about the lack of breeding results. *The baby blues*. When Momma gets blue, she gets nasty. I know she's scheming how to rip me off to fund something besides a baby for these small-town eyes because she wants them to see the *slut* they call her will keep winning long after they're gone.

"I'm done waiting for what's mine," snapped Ronald. "I'm sick of not being me. I'm tired of being stuck in this damn nowhere town where I never belonged. I'm sick of seeing those damn Coyote Hills you two think are so special.

"So we're changing our little improv show we've been playing successfully for seven fucking years and you two lucky small town lights get to be the stars."

Kept my voice lean and steady: "I work my own stories."

That got a shared smile from the table's two secret lovers.

"How much longer you think you're going to get to do that?" said Ronald.

"Don't you love the Internet?" he said. "When this is all over, I'll send you a link. Terry and I. Black vests and leather chaps. Brilliant. You won't recognize us. We wore masks—black leather, not Covid. We *so* know how to do that."

He took a long sip of his glass that Terry had filled with red wine.

Left a reddish smear of barbecue sauce on the lip of the glass.

"*James Traven*," said Ronald. "Small town boy wonder. You probably did OK from the movie sale of your first book nobody I care about would ever read."

"*Wait*: You *care* about other people?"

"*Well*," he drawled. "But back to you.

"I lived in LA. I know Hollywood accounting. I bet lots of your due royalties never get through all that. And while you're a '*New York Times Bestselling Author*,' that was the paperback with a cover of that *gorgeous* actor in the movie.

"Plus, a credit check by our bank confirmed you paid off your student loans in one snap, not like everybody else in your *fucked-from-birth* Millennial generation. That had to take a chunk out of your Hollywood sale.

"And now, according to the Internet, your fourth novel is about to bomb."

"Don't believe everything you read online."

"Believe this: What we're *all* banking on is that you're desperate to keep writing. Keep doing what you told some interviewer is what keeps you alive. Your exact words were: '*Like a cross between sex and a heroin addiction*'."

Ronald sucked barbecue sauce off his fingers.

"*Mmm*," he said. "Have I got a fix for you.

"Now you don't need to worry about being a loser. We're giving you money you don't have to earn by going back to some road crew or as some gig-working keyboard clicker just so you can still work nights *shooting up* your dreams."

Deadpan, I said: "What more could anyone ask."

"Precisely. And *precisely* for you means $200,000. Upon delivery."

Cousin Terry added: "That's seven times more than the annual median income in this damn heartland town. You could probably stretch that to four or five years of big city economic freedom with a few side hustles. Time enough to write a book the critics won't hate and maybe, who knows, Hollywood might love."

"Plus the sex," said Ronald the husband. "I know you're *up* for that."

The woman in the black dress burned with me.

"You have to fuck Lana," said her husband. "Fuck her enough to let it be . . . a discovered, credible 'secret.' Something Mother won't be able to ignore or fix or deny or let stand to tarnish her own fucking whore legacy."

Breathe deep. Settle in the now. Move from your center.

I turned to my left to ask Lana: "What do you get out of this?"

"Free," she whispered.

Ronald waved his hands like a symphony conductor.

"Nothing's ever *free*. There's a *total fault for her* adultery clause in our prenup. She fucks, she gets kicked out on the street and, in my mother's eyes, gets kicked out of the *glorious* Zanes with no more than a one-way ticket back to LA.

"Then *legitimately* I'll be *temporarily* out of fatherhood contention. Broken hearted. I'll ride that *boo-hoo* until *Queen Dee* finally fucking drops dead.

"What won't show up in the divorce is Lana's on-delivery transfer for $200,000—a salary bump—or should I say *hump* for her."

"We choose our own words in America."

"*Really*," he drawled. "Well, whatever you two choose to call it, that transfer in an offshore account ought to be enough to slide her over to her next John."

He shrugged. "Or *James*, like you."

We four sat there in barbecue sauce smells.

"This seems to be a lot for you to digest, Jim," he said, "though God knows why. I mean: *Hubba hubba!* and *Ca-ching!*

"So why don't you go absorb this tremendous opportunity. Leave the file with the legal on the table, we can't let you take that. You can take the pictures from the file on the hallway table.

"But both you two crazy kids better know the clock's ticking. This project had better be over and done by . . . let's say . . . no longer than it takes for Jim's mother to get her casts off. Plus, my *mother dearest* could drop dead anytime. If that happens before she's seen my divorce locked down and kept her will sane, then . . . Well, then both of you lose. You'll have nothing worth buying.

"The clock is really ticking for you, Jim. You're my easy first option.

"But there's other ways this can go. If you don't get back here *tomorrow* to sign the papers and say yes by around sundown, 7:00 on the clock, then *fuck you* and *fuck off*. You'll be just another lost-out loser."

3

Lana whirled off the chair, spun away from that table. Her rush rocketed me after her. We left the two assholes sitting where they were. Didn't look back.

I caught up with her in the front hall as she kicked off those black high heels, bent over, hips curving up to my eyes as she pulled on a pair of well-worn white sneakers. Looped a small black purse on a gold chain around her shoulder—

—flashed me a crazed leer: "*You coming?*"

The red door slammed closed behind us.

4

Hollywood calls that conspiracy of light and location "*magic hour.*" The sun sinks below the horizon yet its illumination remains. Shadows vanish. A clarity of vision is born for the camera and discerning eyes.

That magic hour lit a woman in a sensual black dress and scruffy white sneakers striding away from a residence of riches as a man in black jeans and a short-sleeve blue shirt hurried after her. Caught up to her. They walked side by side on a cracked sidewalk toward the end of the block where the sun had gone.

"We're right where they want us to be." Lana shook her head as we walked together. "Right where anybody looking out their windows can see."

This was the last block on the western end of First Street. There were homes for moms and dads, for kids. A tricycle waited on a front lawn across the street. A dog barked inside some house.

"What happened back there?" I said—to both of us.

"What's gotta work," she replied—to both of us.

Walked us with no chosen direction beyond rage.

"Did you ever make some *oh so gutsy* move?" She shook her head. "For me, was going to be a year or two at most. Then gone with enough severance to get my sister through high school off the Rez with Mom.

"Grace, my baby sister, she has to watch every step and live in fear just because of who she is and where she is. I won't let her become a *disappeared* or *dead, destroyed, damaged* like . . . like so many other of the *just Rez women.*"

"Come on." I led her across the last street in town, out of the neighborhood, onto a prairie plateau where the city road crew kept a ten-foot-tall gravel pile. I led her around that mesa to its west side facing across a deep gully to the rolling away wide prairie. None of the town's windows could see where we stood.

"It's just us here," I told her.

A night bird screed and made me a liar.

"I don't know what to call you," she said. "I heard him say *Jimmy*."

"That's the kid they told me I was. My parents. My big sister. Grown-ups in my life. A nice kid. Too dreamy. Gets too intense but reins it in. *On The Spectrum*. Refuses to take pills but does what he should. Or at least doesn't get caught."

"Is that who you were?"

"Is anybody ever who they say you are?"

I stared at the woman in a chic dress and dirty white sneakers with the breeze blowing her black hair around her shoulders.

"You're not anybody named *Lanny*. I'll never call you that."

"Ron loves to cut somebody's name to cut them down to their place."

"Their place in his glory," I added.

Waited a breath before I spoke.

"Is your name really Lana?"

She blinked in the wind.

"You're an actress. Did you change your name?"

"They wanted me to. Not *Lana*—my last name, *LaBuff*, that was the problem they said. The marketing opportunity, they said. The low rent agent, a producer: They wanted me to be more '*genuine Native American*.' Some *re-brand* so casting directors would slot me for *visible* inclusion and diversity in the end credits. Feel virtuous. Cover their asses from discrimination cancellations."

She shook her head. "We *brand* people now.

"*Still*," she added. Shook her head again.

"*Lana Morning Star*." Her face hardened. "I refused. That would have been denying who I am *and* my blood. Would have been me building new chains for us."

The breeze gusted.

"And my hair," she said as she brushed strands of it off her eyes. "They told me to keep it black and long. 'You know,' they said, 'like it's supposed to be.'"

"For an Indian," I said.

Deliberately used the old term instead of Native American or Indigenous.

She got that. Got why I did it. A smile flicked her red lips.

She nodded toward the western horizon where magic hour would vanish.

"*There.*" She pointed. "You can see it there."

Blinks of light so distant they fit in the palm of your hand.

"That's the prison," she said. "The private prison."

I'd driven past its football fields of chain link fences, barred warehouses and poled spotlights just off the highway to town every time I'd come home.

"There's big money in locking other people up," she said. "Write laws the right way. But let the proper people get the best lawyers—and judges. Then supply and demand paid for by regular taxpayers makes the dollars roll.

"You should hear Ron and Terry sell the line that 'private enterprise' can do anything cheaper and better than 'the government." Hell, without the public roads and water pipes the government built and maintain for it, without tax breaks and payoffs from public money called '*incentives*,' that prison would never have come here. They needed a bond issue. Convinced enough voters in Sidner that the prison would save this town's economy. All you have to do is drive down our broken Main Street to see that lie.

"And now . . ." She shook her head. "Guess what? DC big bucks lobbying means that our prison is one of a couple dozen who have a 'population guarantee.' The government pays tax dollars to make sure our private prison has income for having a 90 percent occupancy—no matter how empty the cells are."

The smoky breeze blew our bare arms.

"I don't know most of the *sort-of* legal shit Ron and Terry do," she said. "I know the Zane family companies for prison stuff wanted 'minority ownership interests.' That was one reason they brought me to town."

Lana laughed. "Hell, I'm probably on the line for some kind of fraud, but they'll never get nailed. Not guys like them. The boys up top never take the fall.

"But *me*? Or *you*?" Her reddened lips smiled. "You know that story."

She looked away from that fading-light horizon.

Turned to the north, where the hour blued the Coyote Hills.

Took a heartbeat. Two. Faced me full on.

Snapped open the black purse hanging by a gold chain from her shoulder.
Pulled out a lighter and a well-rolled joint.
Slid the joint between her crimsoned lips. Flamed it to life with a snap.
Her exhale brushed around me like a cloud.
She held the smoldering joint towards me:
"So am I doing this alone?"

5

Prison lights on one horizon. Our eyes on each other.

"We're already stoned from all this," I said. "Might as well get straight."

"Is that *Jimmy* talking?" she said as I took the joint from her red nail polished fingers. "Or now is it *Jim*?"

The drag I took on the joint started easy, ended searing my lungs.

Rushing out with my exhale cloud came: "Took until sixth grade to realize I wasn't *Jimmy* anymore."

The cloud inside my skull tingled.

"Or at least I didn't want to be." I passed her the joint. "Sylvia Jackson. Golden hair. *Little Jimmy* wasn't who I wanted her to see when she looked at me."

"*Of course* she was blonde."

"She was the smartest kid in the class," I said. "Her family moved to Ohio."

Lana took a slow drag on our joint.

"Plus, there were 'The Guys.' *Jimmy* wasn't a name for us. We were going to be wild and run the streets and run our own lives. After . . .

"After Queen Dee bought the Roxy and my dad quit being the manager, the crew and me were just like a ga-jillion other guys our generation. We were going somewhere standing still. Basement nerds. Video games. Junk food. Illegal dope. When I wasn't with them, I devoured novels. Light novels online. Kindle. iPad. Library books. There was something in those novels that made more sense than what '*everybody*' said was going on in their *posts* and *feeds* or out here."

She blew smoke. "Plus you jerked off."

Just . . . *said it.*

"Who didn't?" I took the joint from her fingers. "We learned how to *stone.* How to score. How to download porn. How to get drunk and clean up our puke in Joe's basement so his parents wouldn't know."

The joint's glowing ember warmed my fingers as it burned down.

I took a hit knowing there weren't many more coming.

At least, not from that fire in this magic hour.

Rode the swirl and let the words come out.

"My folks thought all the clicking they'd hear from my laptop was homework or playing video games. My crew knew I was gaming out stories, but that was just who I was, that's *Jim.*

"Or *Traven,*" I said. "I'm one of those people who gets called by his last name. Didn't choose that, it just keeps happening."

Blinked. Rode the tick-tock. Handed her the joint.

She took it: "What about the guy from the gun shop everybody says you're best friends with? Is he from back then, or . . . ?"

The ember of the joint glowed as she toked.

"Cody. He was and he wasn't in our crew. Welcome, but he was out there on his own. Like we all were, really. Like you must have been. But he . . .

"We got each other," I said. "We both knew we were going to have to go our own crazy way or die trying.

"*Jim,*" I said, "*Jim* was me being one of Albert Camus's true rebels. Not just saying *no* to what I got, saying *yes* to who I chose to be. Cody, he is that, too."

"You grew up with him being some kind of hero—Cody, not Camus."

"You keep using that word, *hero.* Back in the café. Out here. Wasn't like that. Isn't like that. Sure isn't me, then or now. Cody and me, we were just two of those people who thought that they were the only ones all alone in the world.

"But we were wrong. Everybody's all alone in the world. More so now that we're trapped alone in our screens. Unless you get real lucky. Unless you find some flesh and blood who gets you beyond any site's '*match.*'"

She faced the Coyote Hills.

I didn't know if she was looking away from me or toward them.

"Maybe I keep talking about heroes because I know the other kind," said Lana. "Slowing down in a car behind you. Standing in the hallway. Sitting across the café. Coming out of your screen. Waiting in the office where you gotta go.

"Though *yeah*, there's my mom busting her ass to keep my sister and me alive. People working every day best as they can without hurting anybody else. Trying to do some kind of right while staying not wrong. Most of them invisible to 'the media.' Nowadays, they're the closest to heroes we can hope for."

The light was perfect.

She handed me the joint.

Settled absolutely still.

Lana stood tall—on point, like a ballerina, eyes closed, mind open. Whirled in her white sneakers and black dress. Her reddened hair swirled. The dance of her *now* on this oil-smelling plateau hiding behind a gravel dump.

"That's why we have novels," she narrated as she twirled like Taylor Swift singing her own ode. "Songs. Paintings. That's why we have Broadway and Hollywood. That's why I wanted to work creating someone who wasn't me. Not to *be* a star. I wanted to *feel* the stars that shine on everybody. To see. To show. To breathe hope for *what is* by creating *what isn't* but what could be and should be. Everybody, we all need *make believe* to show us *what's real*."

She swooped up to me and froze like a gypsy statue.

Her eyes nailed me through a sideways V mask of her fingers.

A deep breath filled her.

Proud confession steeled her voice: "And all that lets a few of us be our crazy. People like lucky, lucky you."

She took the joint from me. Took a last drag.

Tossed its dying ember to the ground near our feet.

I shook my head: "How did those two find you?"

"They threw a party in Beverly Hills. They made up some phony film production company. Went online and zapped every casting agency and every agent they could find. Said they wanted to host an event for 'fellow Montanans in the industry.' Such obvious bullshit but Hollywood runs on obvious bullshit."

"And genius," I said. "Dreams. Savvy. Talent. Guts. Blood, sweat and tears."

"The only genius I met was on the screen or couldn't book a gig. And I had to face knowing that there was no genius in my mirror."

"We all have to face that."

"But the show must go on. The agent who kept me on her rolls because I was 'diverse' didn't figure I'd get work from meeting that week's '*new players in town*,' but if they were going to be *somebodies*, she wanted an *in*. So I got an invite. I wasn't on the forklift schedule at the warehouse 'fulfillment center' or for an acting class. Finished my shift at Starbucks. Used that bathroom to wash my pits. Changed into my roommate's stolen-from-a-TV-show's-set, *oh-yeah* dress. Walked through a Beverly Hills store for trophy wives. Sampled perfume. Showed up to at least score finger food for dinner."

Sunset streaked black hair with a crimson hue in the cooling air.

"A party like that is the kind of social stage Ron and Terry dream of starring in, so their secret strategy made sense.

"But evidently not to Lily Gladstone, the up-that-Montana-highway-to-Browning-born star. She wasn't at that party. She didn't get the Oscar for *Killers of the Flower Moon* like I thought she would. Maybe audiences don't like stories about how things were and are even if they're set in fiction.

"I don't know if Ron and Terry had both scams in mind that night, or if meeting me flashed the 'minority' lightbulb in their heads. They'd already decided they'd need an actress and that one who knew the setting for their scam would be best, hence that 'fellow Montanans' bullshit. There I was, two for one. Got a *we'll call* chat. Then they hired a PI. Hacked me. Knew about my mom struggling to put food on the table and keep a roof above her head. Knew Grace was in fourth grade. Knew my career was rotting in the California sun."

She shook her head: "What do you grab onto when your dreams let go?"

"Reality that works," came out of stoned me.

She shrugged:

"I *got it*. What they were trying to do. The part for me. Knew I was down-bound without their deal. Figured two years, like they said. All I had to do was live comfortable in the kind of small town I'd left. Cash my checks to send dollars to my mom and sis. The deal was *no fucking*. None of us wanted that. No *on the side* sex for me either. That was back when they thought Dee would die any second and didn't want her paranoid about whose genes were in any baby bump."

Her sloppy grin scowled in magic hour.

"Ron gets a thrill out of parading his beautiful Hollywood wife in front of the downtown guys," she said. "Makes him more powerful. Envied. And the joke's on them. Gay him laughing at them the whole time. So the deal includes me costumed for and acting the part. I wear the war paint and I wear it well."

A car horn honked somewhere beyond the gravel mound that hid us.

Like a good reporter, I led with a truth: "I can't figure why Ron picked me."

Lana said: "Because I told him to."

6

Lana said: "It has to be you and me, or me and murder."

"I'm too stoned for that joke," I told her.

"Not a joke to me."

"Cut it out, Lana. *Murder?* I know and write about that for a living."

"I'm working on not being made dead."

"Is that what you're doing here?"

"That's up to you. That story Ron and Terry concocted about how Terry lost the love of his life in a car crash? The whole world bought it. A few weeks ago, the two of them started reminiscing about that scenario. How well it worked."

"And you think they're . . . casting you as *The Next Blonde*?"

"Before they made up their minds, I had to convince them that getting me fucked was more fun for them and less risky than murder."

"Blink of an eye."

"What?"

"Murder happens in the blink of an eye. That's what I learned when I rode with the cops. Figured I better feel the facts to find the truth in fantasies screaming in my skull."

"Get out of your cloud. Murder happens all the time, all around you. Blink of an eye or long and slow—like the coal company czar who didn't give a shit about his miners so they died trapped underground or coughing black lung."

"Yeah, but somewhere along in that tycoon's life, he knew or he worked hard at not knowing what he wrote on the budget lines. That was the blink."

Lana shook her head: "We're really stoned."

"Why did you do that to us?"

"Like you said, where we are, we need to be stoned to see straight."

"This whole thing. *Us fucking*. All your idea."

"I had to. My sister. My mother. My ass in a car crash. All those costs gone for Ron and Terry. A story that Queen Dee would believe."

"That's some complex bullshit."

"They're guys who love being clever."

"And you being made a *gone blonde*: How could that be worth it to them?"

"*Really?* Don't you—"

"Never mind. I saw bodies dropped for less than a dime."

"This is about lots more than a dime," said Lana. "Seven years ago, my deal was $50,000 a year plus expenses, a $5,000 increase each year—there were only going to be two. Maybe three. But now I'm up to $80,000 for this year.

"The Zanes love their money. Oil pumping out of the ground. Stocks. Their private airline that got Congress to order new regs to put competition out of business. The private prison with government guarantees. Local businesses here, though hell, they only keep the Roxy theater open as a tax write-off."

"How did you get them to go for this crazy idea?"

"Next year, I'll be up to 85K plus expenses. In a divorce, if there's no adultery or other 'major violation' by me, the prenup gives me a lump sum equal to the total I've already been paid. That's nearly half a million dollars. Plus, who knows what I could spit into a public record or testimony. Forget criminal stuff, I could make them a joke and really piss off Dee. What that would cost Ron makes what I negotiated for you and me not much more than a bad day on Wall Street."

She shrugged: "A car crash would be cheaper, but luckily, more of a risk."

"Why did you pick me?"

"Had to be you."

"Just what every man wants to hear."

"You're not just a man, you're *James Traven*. You're a big name in this small town. Ron needs to be a Big Man. If *Ronald Zane's* wife is going to fuck around with anybody, it better be with somebody who's got weight, not just some regular Main Street guy or gandy dancer off the railroad crew. Plus, you won't be sticking around, and that's another 'public' reason for me to go, too."

"I'm . . . flattered."

"No, you're fucked. And not by me."

"Is that who I am?"

"Who you are—who are you? *James* on your books, *Jim* in these streets?"

"I've been coming home to this small town at least twice a year for all seven years you've been here. The county fair and rodeo in July. Christmases. I heard about you. My aunt and mom gossiping. But I never saw you in these streets."

"I'd always hear when you were coming to town. Lay low."

"What?"

"You were a dreaming nobody like me, but one who made it. You'd either be somebody who wasn't worth what he got, *or worse*, you'd be worth all that."

"I'm just me."

"There's a lot of *just* about you, *James*."

"James is the person I got to be and wanted to be. 'Got to' means 'I had great luck to get to' and 'I've got to honor that luck.' Plus never forget who I am, *Jim*, and hell, even *Jimmy*."

"Maybe now all this means you get to *be* all three of you in one."

"I'm more about what I've got to *do*."

"So what are you going to *do* about this?" she said. "About us?"

"I'm working on that."

"Me too, *Jimmy-Jim-James*. Me too."

Lana shook her head: "Did you ever feel like you're just walking through life playing a role you never got to choose?"

"All the time," I said. "Then I started saying *yes* to who I was—*am*.

"But hell," I added, "sometimes I still feel trapped."

"I thought being smart was what I was doing here," she said. "But I've been stuck in a seven-year prison term. And now I've gotta get out of this role, or one way or another, it's going to kill me."

"And tomorrow comes our sundown."

"But now it's still light out. We're here. We can see each other."

Magic hour faded. The Coyote Hills darkened to ominous hulks. The prison lights grew brighter. A passing-through train blew its lonesome whistle.

Her burning palms cupped my face so I couldn't look away from her.

"This one time," she said. "This last chance. This *yes*. This one is just us."

We folded into the electric river of her ruby kiss.

7

Two men leaned against the grill of a maroon SUV parked at a "tourist attraction" *pull-off-the-two-lane-highway* road sign east of Sidner that September night. Stared at the vast midnight sky twinkling a thousand points of silvery light from faraway stars that might already be dead.

The maroon SUV we leaned on was Cody's.

His denim shirt over a T-shirt hung open for a bulge on his right hip.

His eyes scanned the empty dark highway running past us.

My parked car waited on that graveled turn-off.

Our town was a faint glow beyond the rim of its valley wall to our right. Crickets chirped in the musky dusty prairie hay and tumbleweeds beyond the barbed wire fence behind us. Other rustlings. Maybe rattlesnakes. The last of that year's mosquitos hummed by every now and then, too experienced and smart to risk a slap of Cody's quick hands. They weren't sure about me, but why take a chance this close to the first frost when their life's work would finally be done.

The breeze from distant forest fires brushed our faces and made the table-sized, hung-from-chains wooden "tourist information" sign groan in its frame.

That weathered red sign had hung there since our parents were the first kids living with the Doomsday Clock of nuclear war that would wipe humans off the face of the earth. The sign's title read: "*The Oily Boid Gets The Woim.*"

The story carved in that wood told how a pioneer days' railroad clerk randomly left an empty box car on the sidetrack in a prairie valley. Named the place *Sidner* after himself. The railroad clerk later blew his brains out, but the sign doesn't mention that. History must be useful. The sign proclaimed our town here in what 20th century cartographers and 21st century tourists call "the Big Empty" was actually Somewhere Important because of its resourceful *early birds'* discovery of lakes of oil hidden under the golden prairies north of Sidner. *Yeah*, the same pools of black gold that decades later still pumped killer CO-2 into the air and power into the bank accounts of Ronald Zane and his mother Queen Dee.

A freight truck rumbled past us from left to right, east to west, from where we were 700 miles and eleven hard driving hours to Seattle and the mythical ocean. The truck's yellow dragon eyes showed it where to go and showed us its coming: closer, closer, *whoosh*-gone. No horn blared to show the beast cared about us.

My scruffy black leather jacket flapped open in the breeze.

Cody said: "It smells like a bullshit con."

"I know."

"How much of all that do you believe?"

"Believing isn't the problem. It's what to do."

"I keep telling you," said Cody with a shake of his head: "You're supposed to write about this shit, not live it."

"Sometimes our *supposed-to's* crash into our *get-to's*. Or *got-to's*."

Rumble whine, the shine of headlights over the rim to our right, then up over that rise topped a freight truck bound 1,500 miles and twenty-two hours from the town of Sidner in its rearview mirrors to windy city Chicago.

"*Got-to* ask yourself," said Cody as that dawn-bound truck rumbled past: "Is the *she* you'd get out of all those *watch-outs* worth it?"

"Won't know that without meeting her."

"So who will you *be* after whatever you *do*?"

"Don't know that either."

The taillights of the eastbound truck winked away in the night.

Maybe that wheel-steerin', gear-shiftin' driver was rolling to Chi-Town, but then further *back east*, 700 miles and eleven hours *more* away from my sister Katie's safe family to the loft in DC where I lived and was the one clicking the keyboard birthing fantasies while dreaming of *who*.

Cody looked down to check his luminous analog-hand Navy SEAL watch—the kind anyone could buy online then if you didn't have another way to get one.

"Coming up on tomorrow," he said. "You either bust their play with one of your own or back away."

I said nothing.

"Don't hang on a cross somebody else builds for you."

I said nothing.

"You don't know what the hell you're going to do," said Cody.

Car headlights topped the rim—

—turned off the two-lane highway. Spotlighted us in its bright headlights.

Cody stood calm and steady in front of his vehicle in that land of the free and the home of the brave.

The new car parked. The headlights winked off.

Parking lights and flashers appeared.

Cody said: "Keep your hands in plain sight."

I knew that already and they were pressed on my black-jeaned thighs.

The new car's engine turned off. Emergency light flashers kept blinking, red slashes low above the ground in the black highway night.

That driver's door *wunked* open.

Darkness obscured the big man who climbed out of the car.

Came his deep gravel voice: "You doing OK here, Cody?"

"All's cool, Sheriff."

No cherry top on his car. A spotlight on the driver's side. No badges painted on the doors. No official insignia.

He carried a black gun on his cop's belt. Rambled close. Faced me. A jowly fiftyish face with earned gravity.

"Ross Fenton," he told me. "I'm the big badge around here."

The sheriff shook my hand like he didn't give a shit if I thought I knew how to *gung fu* his bear grip. He let me go one heartbeat into my knowing I was had.

"And I know you," the lawman said. "You're Mary Traven's boy."

"Call me Jim."

"Well, you call me if you get up in anything I need calling for." He grinned. "Everybody knows the law's number.

"So what's up, guys?" said the big badge. "Car trouble?"

"Memories," said Cody. "I lost my virginity in the back seat of my old man's car parked right here out in the open. She had something to prove. Who was

I to say no. You two are the only ones I've ever told. You don't get to know her name."

Both Sheriff Tom Fenton and I sensed Cody was telling the absolute truth about back seat sex. I didn't know if the sheriff bought that truth as *why* we chose to meet up here after two hours of restless pacing made me call Cody, who rendezvoused us way out here where we could see who could see us.

The badge said: "Hell, Cody, there's nothing I wouldn't believe about you.

"Well," he said, "that takes the *what's going on* wind out of my rollin' out before turnin' in. You two take care now. Get home safe. *Cody*: Good to see you. *Jim*: Good to meet you. See you around, long as you're in town."

He got in his car. Drove away. Left us alone in the night.

"How is he?" I asked when those red taillights were gone.

"Sheriff Fenton? He does the job he got elected to do."

"Is that law and order? Keeping the peace? Or is it justice?"

"Day by day," answered Cody.

"Is he his own man?"

"Let's hope you never need to know. We don't want to handle that."

And he meant that. All of it. *We*.

Cody said: "My guess is that now you *don't* want me to caravan with you down to the airport tomorrow to turn in your rental car."

"There's too much going on here to worry about that now. We'll do it later."

"When you get your phone out of my glove box," he said of my turned-off device he made me give him so we could talk outside its range, "there's a Glock. Locked and loaded. Two backup mags. A couple different holsters."

He felt me shake my head:

"The slinger I'm facing in these streets is me."

"Times change," said Cody.

"Yeah," I said. "And thanks. But I'm not there."

We stood in the moonlight by a road out of town we weren't going to take.

His eyes stared through me as he said: "*Yet*."

8

Darkness ruled my childhood bedroom.

My hand picked up my cellphone from the bedside table: 5:27 A.M.

Less than fourteen hours *until*.

I padded to the kitchen. Turned on the kitchen faucet's *whoosh* to fill Mom's teakettle. Put it on the gas stove's burner—*whumped* blue flames. Went to the bathroom like you do after you wake up. Refused to look at my phone.

Whistling steam. Dark coffee grounds Katie bought at the P.S. on Main Street, along with the glass coffeepot plus paper coffee filters. Big sis, always taking care of things. If she only knew.

Dawn came as I pulled on sweats. White socks inside black *gung fu* shoes. Didn't look at my phone as I carried it outside and down the back porch steps.

Nobody'd put the lawn furniture back on the gray cement slab my dad had called *the patio* that, given the long hours he'd worked, was an architecture he created but seldom got to use. Best laid plans and the slabs they leave behind.

Had to do it:

I checked the cellphone I'd linked to hers on that gravel flat on the sunset side of town. Now my screen said 5:57, coming up thirteen hours *before*. No messages.

That *Taiji* practice was a joke. My mind ran wild like a crazed monkey. Three rounds of half-assed form and I retreated to the windowsill where my phone stood sentry: 6:27 in the A.M. I set its timer for three minutes of standing in *Huang-chi*: feet shoulder width, arms soft and slightly raised, spine straight up to heaven and down to hell, a *no-mind* contemplation that that morning wasn't.

The cellphone timer *dinged* like a bell above a café door.

A steamy shower. I shaved in that rain I made. Water and whiskers swirled down the drain by my bare feet.

I wore the same black jeans. A maroon shirt. Sat at the kitchen table with a cup of microwaved coffee and still-drinkable milk from the refrigerator. Tapped my laptop. No emails that mattered. Enough memory left for what's to come—tomorrow captured in what yesterday can do.

Mom's antique radio tuned to the local AM station announced new forest fire alerts. No new *major* viruses. Melting arctic ice. The radio played a country & western song about a knife-walkin' woman whose man done her wrong.

"Gonna be a mite chilly out there today, folks," said the radio DJ.

And *like that*, it was 8:41 on that September Wednesday morning *before*.

Wearing my black leather jacket, I stepped out onto the front porch.

"*Hey, Jim!* How you doin'?"

Debby Petersen stood in front of the sagging house she rented next door and beside a curb-parked car that was older than her two kids on their way to grade school. Debby's hair needed brushing and her grocery store cashier's smock hung crooked, but her daughter and son had clean and fed faces.

I walked down the front porch steps, told this single mom who'd been two years ahead of me in high school: "I'm doing OK."

"And your mom: how's Mary doing? She was hangin' in first day I stopped by. I keep trying to get over there to see her, but the kids and you know."

"I know."

Her son stared: "I can see me in your sunglasses."

"My name's Courtney," said his little sister.

She pointed to her big brother: "He's Brett."

"What's your name?" said Brett.

I said: "What do you think it should be?"

The kid shrugged.

"*Jimmy*, *Jim*, or *James*?"

He shrugged again.

"Yeah, me either."

His mother blinked like I'd watched other people do over the years when I let something slip that I shouldn't have said out loud.

"Sorry," I told Debby. "It's already one of those days."

"Tell me about it!" Her chipped-lipstick smile forgave what she didn't know.

Mark it as 8:44 when that family chugged away from the curb. I got waves from the mom and sis in their old car while the boy tried to look hard and made me again remember Dad's favorite Springsteen song.

The front door to the institution caging Mom was just a block and a corner-turn away, but I drove there. Parked in front for a quick getaway. Didn't take the elevator: It could get stuck, trap my tick-tocks. Jogged upstairs to Mom's room.

She was there.

Of course she was there. Why wouldn't she be?

Propped up white-casted legs, white hair around her face. She was smiling up at the fortyish nurse's aide Irma, telling her: "You're too good to me."

"*Ennh*," said Irma with a Latina lilt, "if I'm not good to you, you'll take it out on our other folks here. I don't want anything bad to happen to any of them."

"Well what about me?"

"You can take care of yourself."

Both women laughed as I glanced at the clock on the wall: 9:04.

"Look who's here!" said my mother.

"I told you he was going to come, didn't I?"

Irma was stout, with a mother's hips for a son who my mom told me walked with America's army in some foreign wilderness of land mines. As she left, Irma told me: "She's doing better, but needs to *do* better."

I helped Mom eat her breakfast of black-peppered scrambled eggs, cold toast, green honeydew melon and orange cantaloupe slices, cups of pills and weak tea. The TV above her bed pattered a morning talk show.

Then I fibbed like a conniving teenager: "I'm going to go get a cup of real coffee downtown, come back. Can I bring you anything?"

She said something about a chocolate donut but I was already out the door. Ran down the stairs. Hustled out of that place. Pulled my car to the curb outside the Chat & Chew as my phone screen read 10:01.

No one walked Main Street who I wanted to see.

Ding! went the bell above that café door as I made my entrance.

"Well, hi there, guy!" called out my aunt from the Old Farts' table.

Six faces checked me out from the Big Shots' table.

A fortyish lawyer for wills and wants. The fiftyish multi-millionaire owner of a trucking company that absorbed its rival after my father retired as its manager and that this transport czar chose to keep in his hometown, keep dozens of jobs here instead of rolling his life to a more luxurious center. A balding accountant who worked with my sister to file Mom's taxes. Katie said he gave her a cheap rate. I didn't know the other three faces but I sensed they knew something about me.

"Come on over here and take a load off!" came to me from a man at the Old Farts' table. He'd been my high school football coach. Let me suit up for varsity games even though my only skill on the grass gridiron was wobbling up after getting smacked down. His wife sat across from my aunt. Next to her sat a graying crew-cut widower who'd beaten cancer twice so far.

"So what's going on?" said the retired coach.

"Just thought I better check on you guys, make sure you weren't getting into any trouble," I said, standing beside their table.

"Oh hell, don't worry about us," said the coach's wife. "You're the one who comes in here and sits down with trouble—or so we hear."

One day. One day and the word, *some* word, was out in this small town.

"Trouble's not my style."

That got a good laugh.

I turned to my aunt: "I was just up to the Evergreen. Mom seems OK. Thought I'd catch you all here, let you know."

The Old Farts' smiles said they bought how that might be true.

Waitress Elly waddled toward me, a steaming glass pot of brown liquid in her hand: "You want a cup, hon?"

"No, thanks, I gotta go."

"Well, hell," said Elly, "on your way, do me a favor? Take breakfast over to the Tap for Gary to give to Dale?"

And oh yes, sure, *ding!* out the door from where who I'd come to see wasn't.

A hot white Styrofoam box filled my hand as I walked across Main Street to an open doorway in a flat-faced tan brick wall with a chest-high window. A red neon sign glowed in that glass:

THE TAP ROOM

As soon as I walked through that open door, my eyes still blinking from the outside sunlight to that dimmed interior, a man's voice yelled: "Mirror Man!"

Mirror Man: The name of my first novel that far bettered itself as a movie.

That tavern's owner stood between the bar's mirror with its ranks of bottled liquor and the scarred wood for customers' beers, shot glasses and bowls of peanuts waiting to be cracked, shells dropped to the floor. Gary was as old as my dad would have been. His salt and pepper hair was curly, his smile quick.

There was a couple about his age perched on barstools behind celery-swirled Bloody Marys. The woman was named . . . Donna. We smiled, nodded.

Further down the bar slumped a rumpled, torn-coated man with stringy hair and stubbled cheeks. His twitchy eyes looked up from a cup of coffee poured from the *get-it-your-own-damn-self* urn near the beer fridge.

"It's Nick Traven's kid!" he called out. "Helluva good man, Nick. Helluva."

"Thanks, Dale," I said.

My dad in college had protested the war soldier Dale'd survived.

A half dozen empty barstools past Dale—around the bend of the bar where you'd sit if you needed to watch the door—perched a woman my age. Cropped brown hair. An *I dare you* face. A Bloody Mary sentried her bar space.

Gary said: "What can we do you for, Jim?"

"Delivery." I put the white Styrofoam box that smelled like bacon near Dale.

"About time," said Gary. "Any later, you wouldn't get your tip."

He leaned closer over the bar.

"Here's your tip," he said. "Remember to watch your step but don't worry 'bout crunching no peanut shells on the floor, they're there to get swept up."

All I could do was smile. Wonder what all he meant. What he knew. I knew he felt obligated to watch over me: I was Nick Traven's kid, grown up or not.

"As for you, *Dale*, get started on your breakfast here if you want a beer when the noon whistle blows."

"What if I ain't hungry?"

"Not my problem. You want a beer, you eat your breakfast."

Dale grumbled. Reached into the Styrofoam box, picked up a white plastic forkful of . . . *yes*, scrambled eggs. "Hell, put it on my tab."

Everybody in town knew Gary and the Chat & Chew zeroed Dale's tab.

Hell, even with his vet's disability and Social Security, Dale couldn't afford to leave the crumbling house his folks left him for someplace like the Evergreen. Not that he'd ever go somewhere else than the bottle or his family home to die.

Dale held the white fork holding yellow scrambled eggs in front of his face.

Paused.

"Hey, Nick Traven's kid," he said. "You a writer, books and stuff, yeah?"

The forkful of eggs quivered above the bar as he listened for my answer.

"Yeah."

"You wanna write about somethin'?"

Everybody has a story. Some people need to tell you theirs. Need to be heard by someone who's supposed to be able to make sense out of what they say.

"I always write about something," I told Dale.

The trembling white plastic fork clung to by yellow eggs owned all the eyes in that bar except Dale's faraway twitching gaze.

"Hey," he said. "You know what?"

"*Ah* . . . No."

The eggs gotta fall off the fork!

"You know what we got out of th' Vietnam War that ended forty-nine years ago?"

The white fork trembled. The yellow scrambled eggs shifted.

"Nam," Dale said as he had when he was nineteen, patrolling that jungle on his way to a Silver Star and a Purple Heart for two missing fingers on a hand that never knew a wedding band and knew far too many glasses, a leg that dragged, a scar that pulled his face out of alignment. "Sixteen years of war in fucking Nam. Fifty-eight thousand-plus guys like us on the Wall. You know what we got out of all that?"

Dale's whole body is closing in on itself with trembles!

"What we got out of all that was . . ."

Dale paused like he forgot his thought.

Eggs trembling!

". . . was me," said Dale.

WHUMP!

A glass pounded on the scarred wood down at the end of the bar.

The chopped-hair woman my age slammed her glass on the bar again.

Eggs trembled on Dale's fork.

The chopped woman raised her glass:

"*Iraq and the Stan, motherfuckers!*

"Come home," she said, and I knew she had. Officially.

She chugged what was left of that Bloody Mary. Signaled for another.

Dale pulled the white forkful of scrambled eggs toward his mouth.

Everyone held their breath.

And . . .

Not one fleck of fate escaped Dale's gotta-do bite.

Gary kept his eyes on Dale working through the bacon and eggs in the white foam box as he said: "You want a cup of coffee, a beer or somethin', Jim?"

"Thanks, but I gotta go."

"Most guys go *after* coffee."

He and I laughed me out the front door.

Two cars of nobody I wanted to see cruised past me as I waited to cross back to the other side of Main Street. None of the maybe thirty parked cars lining both sides of that main drag garaged at a money house on the west edge of town.

The picture windows of the Chat & Chew showed me who was in there: The Old Farts. The Big Shots standing to leave. Waitress Elly. Nobody else.

I was halfway across the road when the dark car rolled toward me. Knew before I saw through the windshield that the driver was Sheriff Fenton.

Cops make innocent people nervous and guilty souls tense. The innocent know their secrets include dreams they must keep locked up. Outlaws know what they broke free and hope they can save their ass.

That Wednesday morning, I stood my ground in the middle of Main Street in my hometown. Gave the law a smile, a nod.

The big man behind the unmarked cruiser's steering wheel sent a nod back. Gave me eyes that said he saw me. That he was watching.

If he checked his rearview mirror after he passed, he saw me *not* looking at him as I finished crossing Main Street toward the P.S. curios shop.

She wasn't in there either. I shared smiles and small town greetings. Recognitions that we were all there. That we all mattered. Got two café au laits to go. Carried them outside. Cody buzzed me into his store at 10:19.

"Thought you could use this." I gave him one of the specialty coffees.

He took the warm paper cup in his steady hand. "What could you use?"

"There's what I can use and what I need," I said.

Made my long ask.

He said *yes* and *how*.

Said: "You still don't know what the hell you're going to do, do you?"

The clock on his wall above the racks of rifles read 10:21.

"I gotta get back up to check on my mom."

"Sure. That's what you've *gotta* do."

He buzzed me back out to the real world.

Sipping from my paper to-go cup was *obviously* why I slow-walked back to where my car was parked—*not* that my eyes were seeking who wasn't there. I paused with my hand on the car's door. Stared at the daytime-closed Roxy. The marquee and posters in glass cases on the theater wall advertised one of that era's comic-book billion dollar "superhero" franchise movies where costumed protagonists saved the world and themselves until the next blockbuster sequel.

Never been my kind of story.

My watch read 10:37 as I parked at the curb in front of the Evergreen Center. I shuffled up the sidewalk to the glass doors. Pushed my way into that warehouse of the worn-out and waiting-for. Dropped my empty coffee cup in the trash near where nurse's aide Irma sat behind the counter.

Irma gave me a smile, an approving nod: I'd come back. Not everybody did.

I took my time and took the safe stairs: less than nine hours left to kill.

TV sounds drifted around me as I walked down the green-carpeted, white-walled hallway that smelled of must, pine-scented disinfectant, and—

—and my mother's room door was open.

Health care protocol for patients' comfort and sanity mounted a concave mirror near the ceiling by the TV and above a window to the outer world so when patients looked toward their feet—or in Mom's case, her casted and suspended legs—they could simultaneously glimpse the outer world, the TV screen, and in the mirror, see who entered their room. Or who didn't.

My image curved in the mirror above my mom's eyes.

She shouted: "We got company, Jim!"

Sitting in the visitor's chair beside Mom's bed: *Queen Dee.*

9

Deirdre Zane turned like a teacup in that saucer of time.

Her silver hair was shellacked like a crown for the British matriarchy. Her surgically smoothed, pink powdered face turned up the voltage, lighting her green eyes and lifting her glossed pink smile. She wore what used to be called a *professional woman's suit* that made her birdlike body seem less frail.

White cotton gloves. She wore white cotton gloves. Like for a garden party. Or a funeral. A wedding. A princess's wave from atop the back seat of an open convertible in a Fourth of July parade down Main Street.

Or like for hiding fingerprints.

"There he is," she purred as I entered, posted between my mother trapped in the bed and the visiting royalty. "We were just talking about you."

Mom snapped: "Not me!"

"You know how it is." Queen Dee's sideways glance projected charity for the old and the infirm onto my mother who'd contradicted her.

"Actually, *no*," I said. "How is it?"

Dee leaned back like she was waltzing me on a dance floor. "Hearing what's going on. With friends. Family. Famous sons."

"My new book is out," I said. "You can buy one. Hell, buy a bunch for gifts, friends and family. Make it a Traven Christmas."

"I'm sure it will be quite lovely. Maybe I'll take you up on that idea. My son doesn't read anything. That's what he has his lawyer Terry for. And while your novel no doubt has some good sense in it, those boys are all about dollars."

She waited.

So did I.

I glanced at the clock on the morning wall above and beyond Dee: 10:47, still a little more than eight hours left *until.*

Her *until* wouldn't let Dee wait: "The 'sense' I said was like in *dollars and cents.*"

"Oh," said Mom from her bed, sarcasm that made me proud: "I get it now."

"I'm so glad for you," purred Dee. She smiled at me. "Perhaps I'll give your book to my daughter-in-law. She likes fictions."

"Don't we all," I deadpanned.

"I'm a facts kind of lady," said Dee.

Came a raspy male voice in the doorway: *"No shit."*

10

He was a withered, wrinkled old man. Decades-old khakis held up by suspenders over a tan shirt.

His splotchy face sagged. Grayed strands of once flaxen hair straggled across his head. His owl-eyed glasses focused on Queen Dee.

Mom yelled up at the mirror mounted above her head: "Hell, look who's here! Come on in, Mike! Let's make it a party!"

My mother hated parties. People come close. Breathe on you. Tell you things you don't want to know or got nothing to say that's worth hearing. Can't believe anything anybody says. The person you want to see never comes.

But sometimes what you hate might be what you need. Or can use.

Queen Dee rose from the visitor's chair. Turned her back on Mom and me to paint her face with polite as she said: "Hello, Mike. Good to see you."

"You ain't been looking," said the old man.

"Well," said Dee, "I obviously know right where you are."

"Bet you do."

Queen Dee gracefully turned and swept her palm-up hand toward me.

"Do you know Mary's son?" she said.

"Nice to see you, too, Mike!" shouted my mom to the mirror. *"Where you been since I been in here?"*

Mike's foggy glasses filled with the woman tethered to the hospital bed.

"Heard you had company," he grumbled. "Figured I better check it out."

Queen Dee turned to me: "You remember Mr. Jodrey here, don't you, Jim? He ran the hardware store my late husband owned that I then kept running."

Mike said nothing.

Dee looked at the woman trussed-up in the hospital bed.

"*Mary*," said Dee, "so good to see you doing so well. You're so lucky to have Jim here come home to help out when you need him."

A cock of her silver head and savvy smile shaped her face as she said: "We'll have to figure out something to keep him entertained.

"Who knows," she said: "Maybe he'll get another *wonderful* book out of it."

Mom snapped: "You better believe it!"

"I do," said Dee. "But—now that Mike is here to keep you company—I have to borrow Jim. I need his help with something heavy in the car."

My mom and I locked eyes in the curved mirror.

"Don't worry, silly!" Dee told the woman she'd known for decades. "I promise I'll send him right back up. And you know I always keep my promises."

She turned to the owl-eyed old man.

"Mike," she said with a polite steel smile. "As always."

Queen Dee gave me a regal smile, a *follow-me* with her white gloved hand.

11

I walked the nursing home's green carpeted hallway beside silver-haired *grande dame* Dee. Felt like the two of us were on a conveyer belt.

A frail wispy woman in black shuffled towards us from the end of the hall. She stopped us with a trembling hand.

"Have you seen my mother?" said the wispy ninetyish woman in black. "I can't find her anywhere."

Dee said: "I haven't seen her, Carrie. Why don't you look down that way?"

Carrie blinked and for a moment—just a moment—something besides confusion flickered in her eyes. It floated away. She shuffled down the cream-walled hallway toward the way we'd come.

"I'd rather be dead than like that," said Dee.

From up ahead, I heard the elevator *ding!* Its doors slide open.

Laughter carried a trio of senior citizens around the corner from the elevator toward us: one man in a wheelchair, one woman working a walker, one handsome gray-haired man keeping his steps in time with his friends.

They maneuvered to one side of the corridor while we claimed the other.

Dee awarded them a smile: "Hello."

Mumbled polite replies followed us as we walked on by.

Dee led me around the corner at the end of the corridor—

—darted back to look around the corner to be sure the trio was not close.

Darted back, whispered to me:

"Smell that? Places like this, they're full of it. The old people smell."

Old people.

Like her.

Like my mom and my aunt.

Like the two *older than my kin*, East Coast Baby Boomers suit & tie White Guy presidents whose faces emoji'd the raging politics of America then.

Dee's white glove pushed the black button on the wall. The elevator doors slid open. She strode into that box. Pushed the button to keep the doors open.

I walked inside. Leaned against the opposite wall and stared at her.

Her white-gloved finger pushed the button for FIRST FLOOR.

We waited. The doors closed. The floor dropped our feet with the big down.

Dee said: "If you can't smell me from over there, come closer."

"No thanks."

"You already know my scent. What *I* choose. Lavender."

My slight smile showed awareness and revealed nothing.

"You've been gone a long time, Jim. But you're not the forgetting kind. You know how things work here in Sidner. That's why you're suddenly becoming so friendly with my son. And the rest of my family—*yes*?"

I didn't think she expected an answer. Didn't get one.

"You know how children are," she said. "You have to keep an eye on them. Make sure they and their little friends don't screw up or fall down."

Whunk went the elevator, shuddered us to a stop.

"Gravity rules," I said.

"Not if you can afford the right machine."

Rumble went the elevator doors as they opened.

She smiled: "After you."

Her gaze burned me as I stepped past her, out of the box and into the Evergreen Center's front entrance hallway.

We flowed side by side toward the double glass doors of the EXIT.

No one waited behind the check-in counter by the doors. From inside the glass-walled dining room to our left came a blur of blue medical scrubs:

Irma, scurrying to catch us.

Calling out: "Excuse me! Mr. Traven! Jim!"

Irma's respectful smile put Dee at ease as we stopped to listen to her.

"I'm sorry, and I'm *really sorry* to be so rushed, but Mrs. Pellet *way* needs her bath 'n' I've got to take out the trash before the city crew gets here 'n' Paul, he broke his leg and we were already short-handed but now, *now Jim*, I know Mrs. Gage, my boss, the administrator, she'd want me to, needs me to ask."

Irma took a deep breath, let it out: "Can you drive a stick shift?"

"My dad insisted on teaching me and the road crew—"

"Oh, thank God!" said Irma. "Do you know what tomorrow is?"

"Ah . . . *yeah*: Thursday."

"No—I mean, *yes*, but it's the first of the month. October first.

"Every first of every month, we take residents who want to go up the cemetery. Some like to visit the graves. Leave flowers. Carrie wanders around looking for her mother. Paul keeps an eye on her *but not anymore*, not *now*.

"That what, that's why we're hoping we can get you to drive the bus.

"Not much of a bus," she added. "More like a long van. And you drive stick! They can't spare me. Already down one nurse and two aides. And there's no room in the budget for anybody to take Paul's place when he's out hurt. So . . . So could you volunteer tomorrow? No pay, but would you, *please*: Will you drive the bus?"

Dee laughed.

"Imagine that," she said. "We were just talking upstairs about how Jim here needs to find something to keep himself busy and out of trouble."

Irma told me: "I already asked your mother. She thinks it's a great idea."

"See, Jim?" said Dee. "How can you say *no*?"

"With a different *yes*," I said. "I've got work."

"Oh, writers like you can always work where and when you want," said Dee.

Every author who ever bled ink wanted me to punch her.

I *obviously* directed my words to Irma: "If you and my mom and these folks here need me, *yeah*, I'll drive your bus."

"That's great!" said Irma. "See you tomorrow just before ten. Out back. But right now, sorry, I've got to go. It's not just Mrs. Pellet who needs me."

"So," said Dee as blue-scrub Irma scurried away, "you're the kind of man who can be counted on. I like that. And I like how you knew to step up for me."

Dee glanced past me, down this floor's cream-colored corridor. I turned to check out what she saw—

—stared into the faces of a couple I went to high school with as they slow-walked one of their mothers or maybe a grandmother toward the dining room.

Our hometown. They stayed. I left.

They gave me a nod that said they recognized me. Their faces knew who I was with. I nodded. Gave them a smile. We all walked on.

We're all minor characters in someone else's story.

I hit the waist-high silver pad to open the glass doors.

Led Dee out to the morning sunshine of only about eight hours *until.*

"Did you know that I chair a family foundation?" she said. "A marvelous tax write-off. Bottom line, it doesn't cost me a thing. Hefty dollar honorariums for speeches from elected leaders who vote the right way. Plaques and prize money for public servants who run the rules and regulations that keep things working as they should. We pass on dollars donated to us by like-minded people who want to be discreet about who they support. Just like we support other foundations that have a more active role in current affairs and with those new finagled things your generation knows all about. Websites for regular people to trust. Patriotic spokesmen and 'influencers' on that Facebook thing and Insta-something and Snap-whatever, plus Tweeters and Twitters and Twatters, Tickers and Tockers—and all other people who keep things on track for our great country."

"Who's '*our country*'?"

She gave me her primly pink smile.

Slowed our walk to a stop as we reached the parked cars lining the curb outside the Evergreen Center.

Where was her Tesla Cybertruck?

"We've given hefty grants to artists from our foundation," Dee told me. "You've probably seen the . . . fascinating oil painting of Ronald hanging in that house where he gets to live. That was a particularly generous grant to support a young artist from Wyoming. Doug *Something.* A nice young man. Nervous. We don't see him around anymore."

Her white-gloved finger rose into the air as if to mark an epiphany.

"*You know,*" she said, "we should give you a grant for your next book. A large chunk, I would say. And maybe some sort of . . . 'continuing endowment.' We've done that before for certain very smart people.

"*Probably,*" she said, "all you need to do is tell me a good story. *A proposal.* One that works for me. So that I know what's going on."

Her white gloves opened a pocketbook in the black handbag she carried.

Tucked a business card in my maroon shirt's heart pocket with my phone.

I didn't break her arm.

Her minted breath warmed my face as she purred: "Make sure I keep up with what you're seeing. Thinking. Doing. As a supporter of the arts. And you."

"I work alone."

"Don't we all. But we all need to get along to go anywhere good."

She led me up the street toward a parked curbside, ordinary compact car.

"Sometimes discretion is the best way to go." She pulled a key fob out of her purse, clicked it so the lock *thunked* on her covert machine. "But you know that. The kind of books they tell me you write. Spies and killers and such."

"Don't believe everything *they* say."

"I'm very careful about what I believe. And do."

She opened the driver's door on her unmarked compact. Slid behind the steering wheel. Clicked her seat belt.

"So what's the heavy thing you said you needed me to help you with?"

"You can shut my door," she said.

"*Naw,*" I said. "I think you've got it yourself."

Turned and walked toward the Evergreen Center's glass doors.

Heard the car door slam. The roar of her engine. Crunching tires.

12

"What the hell was all that?" asked Mom for the third time since I'd come back upstairs to her room and found her there alone.

I'd pulled the door closed. Wanted to do more, but the locks on the unit doors in a place like that can only be worked from the outside.

Only—*of course*—for the residents' own safety.

The visitor's chair where I sat smelled like lavender.

"Which part freaks you out most?" I said. "Queen Dee or Owl Eyes Mike?"

"He's always been just another pissed-off old man," said Mom. "But what in the hell was he taking on Dee for?"

"Seems like they've known each other a long time."

"Hell, we've all known each other a long time." Mom shook her head. "He would have been . . . Yeah, he was younger than her. I remember him back in high school before me and after Dee'd already married-up to what's-his-jerk."

She shook her white hair.

"I remember that and the sounds of rock 'n' roll coming out of my folks' car radio. Three cool Black women in glittery silver dresses singing: *'Baby, baby, baby.'*

But I can't for the life of me remember what I had for dinner last night."

"You're getting old, Mom."

"So the hell are you. And then came Queen Dee. She just started in talking."

"About what?"

"All the usual shit you say to someone in the hospital. How are you. What do the doctors say. This room ain't so bad. *Yada, yada, yada*. She was starting to slip in *this* and *that* about you. Questions I didn't answer and couldn't have if I'd wanted to. Then you showed up."

Mom stared at me: "She didn't say nothing about *her*."

Then watched me sit as still and silent as a Buddha.

Finally said: "Don't know if I should tell you this or not."

"But now you gotta."

"Your . . . that Lana, she's friends with Halle up at the library. And Halle thinks the world of you. I worked up there with her back a ways. You know her."

Since those *back a ways* days, but I knew I had to let Mom tell it.

"Halle's proud as hell you writing books on the shelves up there. Makes *can-do* real for the kids. Just like Adele's boy playing football down at the U. He'll go pro if he doesn't get busted up too bad. Hope he don't get his brain crushed.

"So Halle knows Dee's daughter-in-law. I wasn't gonna tell you, but since you're no doubt going up to see Halle, say *hi* like always, figured's better for you to know what you're walking into. If you weren't going before, you sure as hell are now. Besides, you're taking back the books on the dresser she brung me when she visited back in the hospital. Get her to give you some more for me.

"Over there," said the woman chained to a bed. "My purse on the dresser."

I obeyed her command. Took the four short steps to the nursing home bureau. Picked up the targeted purse. Turned and started back to give it to—

"What are you thinking?" snapped my mother. "Is your head in the clouds or something?"

She jangled her cast-wrapped arm: "Like I can do anything with it?

"Reach inside," she said. "My pocketbook."

I pulled out the decades-old scruffy red leather, holdable in one hand ID, credit cards and cash carrier.

"Take the dimes 'n' pennies 'n' such for the fishbowl."

As I snapped open the wallet, she added: "Leave the quarters. I hear there's a vending machine downstairs 'n' you never know."

There was only one quarter. *Remember that*, I thought. Her wallet also held two fives, one ten and three—no: *four* one-dollar bills. I snapped the wallet shut. Dropped it in the purse, put the purse back on the dresser. Picked up the library books Irma and others read to Mom because she couldn't hold them with one hand. Slid the designated coins into my black jeans front pocket.

Mom grumbled: “I never got my chocolate donut.”

“Sorry. Next time.”

“So we hope, right? That we all get a *next time.*”

A siren blew over the town. One long wail that stopped. Several such wails would summon Sidner’s volunteer firemen to risk their lives. Lone whistles blew for the 10:00 P.M. curfew for minors. And blew daily at noon.

Like now: seven hours left until.

13

Six hours to go.

One o'clock found me sitting behind the steering wheel of my car parked at the curb outside the Evergreen Center. Engine off. Window rolled down.

Four plastic-covered library books lay scattered on the car's shotgun seat.

I knew one of the authors, a Philly Black woman who was many rungs above me on the ladder to deserving a Pulitzer and who would argue that I was wrong about that. I thought about texting her a picture of her book on the car seat. But what would I say: '*Look what I found on my way to blowing up my life*'?

I left my phone in my shirt pocket.

Rumbled the car to life.

Pulled away from the curb in front of the Evergreen where Irma'd brought me a lunch tray "on the house" as appreciation for driving the bus to come. Then she "had to confess" that the meal was actually a send-back from Warren who'd eaten too many of the homemade brownies from his granddaughter. I couldn't tell you what a single bite of that salvaged lunch tasted like as I forked it down.

"You eat what you get," Mom'd said.

"Yeah," I said. "And what you take."

Nobody said anything about *deserve*.

The car's open window let in the smoke-tinged, earthy scents of autumn. Fallen leaves skittered on the sidewalks of Sidner.

I circled the block that held the Evergreen Center. Slowed my drive past our family house with two giant blue spruce trees my father'd planted in the front yard four years apart when they brought first Katie, then me home from the hospital. My folks knew they were never going to leave the town where they'd been born and come back to after Dad left college.

Katie's tree rose taller and more like a screen-saver beauty than mine. Hers towered over the east side of the front lawn and rose into our dawns. Mine swayed on the west lawn, scruffy and facing into the relentless wind.

Nobody was home next door. Debby stood on her feet behind a counter tallying other people's groceries for eight hours a day. Her kids did time inside a public school and then at an aftercare center she paid to shelter them so she could earn money for their food and their thrift store clothes.

I should have turned left at the corner. But I headed west into the smoky breeze. And *yes*, I was on First Street. And *yes*, that was *where*.

Off to my left rose a hill topped by a castle with a silver roof flying an American flag. The fortress's four levels of sandstone bricks and huge windows let in sunlight. The castle was a rectangular architecture of function and form, the county courthouse built during my grandfather's youth by President Franklin Delano Roosevelt's triumphant put-ordinary-people-to-work strategy to use *bubbling up from the ground* rather than *trickling down from skyscrapers* economics to save the country from that era's Great Depression.

The windshield showed me the street ahead.

Two vehicles parked off to the right side of the street by a vacant lot between houses. The machines were grill to grill.

The pickup's popped-all-the-way-open hood faced my coming like a great white shark about to take a bite out of the fish-gray sedan's engine compartment spread open to say *Ahh*.

Cables linked the two machines like touching tongues. The white pickup's hefty woman driver was jump-starting the dead battery of a guy grinding the ignition of the gray sedan. The vehicles' "57" license plates showed they were from this county. I nodded to the hefty woman standing in the street as I drove past. She nodded back. The gray sedan roared to life. An ordinary Wednesday made better for somebody by someone else in an American small town.

I turned left. Passed the two-story Methodist church where our parents sent Katie and me to Sunday School to learn religion. They figured their children needed to learn that language and those links to get by in this world. The church spire had loudspeakers that every Sunday blared organ hymns picked by the preacher's cellphone—algorithms curating heaven.

Again I turned the car left, the house of that God shrinking in my mirrors.

Pulled into a parking spot reserved for the county library.

Growing up as video games, online manga and light novels filled the screens in our house, going to the library felt like a big deal. Not a download. A real deal. A touchable, smellable experience. I'd wander from the kids' section through the science fiction shelves to the mysteries and thrillers. Scope out the shelves for the wizard series that captivated my generation with tales of obvious heroes and villains. All that along with the movies washing over me in the Roxy's seats and out of the family's TV in the era when it finally came alive with brilliance even as cellphone screens captured our lives, plus being an innocent bystander trapped in my dad's 'sound system' replays of Bob Dylan, Richard Thompson and *Broooce!* Springsteen, all that electrified the stories swirling around in my skull.

"Oh my God, Jim, hi!" called out librarian Halle as I walked into that sunlit box shelved with dreams, desires, designs. She was only a bit older than me but years deeper into what Sidner called maturity—a home, a family, someone to fall asleep next to at night and get up with to face the next what's-coming day.

Out of nowhere, a big *wonder* flashed through me:

How much sex do married couples really have?

Didn't ask Halle.

A classic no-water fishbowl sat on the librarian's front desk. The glass fishbowl held a handful of random coins. A handmade, palm-sized, scissored white paper sign scotch-taped to the fishbowl held green ink letters:

DONATIONS FOR OUR LIBRARY

I dropped my mom's coins in the fishbowl.

Dropped what little change of my own was in my pockets.

Knew that these days, plastic and clicks rule 'legal tender' for payments.

Librarian Halle and I sat at a small table in the back office with its view of the checkout desk and stacks of books waiting to be reshelved or repaired. Talked of this and that. Halle said she'd ordered two copies of my coming novel "because everyone here will want to read it," both of us knowing that was near to false. She asked about my mom, handed me three new novels she'd picked out for her.

I said: "Have you had trouble with scared haters censoring your shelves?"

"Thank God, so far no." A slim chain around Halle's neck lay on her sweater to hold a small gold cross. "But I hear rumbles. Did you know they're now going after Margaret Atwood's *The Handmaid's Tale*? A great story about women in a fictional world fighting for freedom and they want to censor it and call this 'a free country'! It's like Orwell and Big Brother saying words mean only what they say they mean and—*And they want to pull those classics off the shelves, too!*"

Halle shook her head. Gave me a grin as hard and grim as a saber.

"What I did," she said, "what I've done, is put one crucial book like those propped up and standing tall as 'feature of the week' over there."

She nodded to the prominent glass case museum of remembrance for arrowheads and artifacts from governments who ruled this stretch of earth before my family and others arrived, the Blackfeet, the Cheyenne, the Crows, the Nez Pierce, along with medals, photos and a burial flag for America's "Greatest Generation" soldiers who fought and beat Nazis and fascism in World War II.

"A wildcatter on an oil rig up north just picked up Steinbeck's *Grapes of Wrath*. Today I'm putting out Sinclair Lewis's 1935 novel *It Can't Happen Here*."

"Let's hope not," I said.

"Let me know if they come after you or this place.

"And let me know who 'they' are," I added.

"Evil has a lot of faces." Halle sighed. "Faces hiding behind lies and smiles. And more money than we got in the fishbowl."

We stared off into tomorrows we didn't want to see.

Blinked back.

"So what's going on?" she said.

"I met Lana Zane."

"Isn't she something? You know, she spends a lot of time up here. Takes out a lot of books, but she also got her husband or that foundation thing—"

"That Dee runs, right?"

"Well, that's who signs the checks. Lana gets them to pay for Give a Kid a Book day every year. And she helps JoEve's Saturday story hour for the little ones. Picks up the tab for snacks like bananas and apples and *boy* do we gotta watch out for that! Nut allergies and such. Lana found some 'non-allergenic protein bars' online that she gets shipped straight here. I don't care for the taste, kind of like . . . cardboard, but some of the kids, those protein bars and the cheese sandwiches Stacy Maynard makes—*You remember her?*—some of those kids, I think that might be the only Saturday lunch they get."

Halle shook her head: "We're so lucky."

"Yeah," I said. Said it again: "*Yeah.*"

"Hey!" said Halle with a subject changing smile. "Guess what's coming up?"

My face showed nothing.

"Halloween!" said Halle. "I'm already helping a few kids after school with costumes so they have something to wear so the other kids won't stare. We're going to have an after-school Trick or Treat party here. Ghost stories. Regular snacks plus some 'safe' candies. Lana shows up to help pass out the goodies and read a story. She dresses like a witch."

Like she'd just thought of it, Halle said: "You should come! From what I hear, you'll still be here. Your mom's casts might not be off by then."

The librarian said: "I wonder what your costume will be."

Like the Evergreen Center, the library in my sagging hometown used an old-fashioned analog clock on the wall to keep track of time. A red second hand swept around a circle of black digits equal to the number of Jesus's disciples.

My glance past where Halle sat showed me the time: 2:03.

Less than five hours to go.

I picked up the books for Mom.

Told Halle: "I've got work to do."

14

Inside the home where I grew up with Katie as our folks watched.

The leaf-skittering wind of that Wednesday afternoon blowing past the kitchen's picture window framing the backyard where us kids used to play.

Me at the keyboard of my laptop open on the kitchen table.

Muckraker, motherfucker.

That's who I was. That's who I am.

A one year out of college fellowship for investigative reporting at an online national news machine. Slotted into DC. While the other fellows scrambled to uncover Insta- or YouTube-worthy celebrity or castle scandals like Watergate, I rode the cops' streets with press credentials as my badge.

Weeks' worth of police ride-alongs, each of the three shifts, four-to-midnight being the best. Scout cars with uniforms. The Vice Squad where a human-trafficked street prostitute bet me "a Benjamin" she'd fuck me before I left the force. The corporatized corners of Narco. Homicide, the last line.

Yeah, I knew cops who I wasn't seeing were deep into cruelty and crime. But the cops I rode with cared that somebody from the civilian world got it *right*. Knew the stomach-twisting fear of *not* knowing. Gunfire by a school. The *'No!'* wail of a bullet-broken mother. The rush of a Code Three/Shots Fired/10-33 Officer in Trouble, sirens-and-red-lights responding cruiser you're riding as every fiber of your being screams: *'Go! Go! Go!'*

And there I was. Learning truths from our touchable streets.

Two ways to investigate.

Go out to find what's there and hope you recognize it when you see it.

Go out hunting for what you think you might find.

And while worthwhile investigative reporting requires *going out* street time and the feel of human hearts, your keyboard is step one.

I had targets.

Queen Dee. Son Ronald. Cousin Terry. Their foundation. The prison. Their bank. My haunted Roxy movie theater. Lana LaBuff *nee* Zane.

I had 240 minutes *before.*

Conventional wisdom in 2024 claimed that *'you can find out anything'* in that ether of the Web and Dark Web, social media like Facebook or Instagram *or-or-or*, plus YouTube and its copycat sites.

But remember my IMDb link? A hit on a search engine is just that: maybe accurate and factual, maybe even true, but just a hit.

Googling furiously, I found:

Ron and Terry smiling in a sports page photo of a team golf tournament in one of Montana's "big" cities. They took fourth place.

A news story in the daily newspaper for the city ninety miles away where the airport was: A state environmental office lamented its sudden loss of budget to oversee Zane Petroleum Industries' compliance with a court order to curtail dumping toxic chemicals into the alkali flats on the prairie north of Sidner.

Queen Dee popped up two pages of Google results, including a story from nine years earlier when she won Montana Businesswoman of the Year. This story I found 141 minutes before my deadline noted that was the last time the title would be awarded by the Chamber of Commerce that was "transitioning" to "gender-neutral awards."

Corporate filings for the parent company of the private prison on the edge of town showed a major stockholder was a current member of the United States Senate. I scrolled pages of links about lawsuits, regulatory fines and outrages like sick inmates left to die alone in their cells in private prisons scattered across the country. Found a list of businesses with contracts for "construction, maintenance, supplies and services" for Sidner's prison. Most of those neutral-named businesses linked to the same address as Zane Enterprises.

A *New York Times* story confirmed Sidner's prison as one of thirty-one private penal institutions guaranteed in their contracts a "90 percent occupancy income" that an industry spokesman claimed was "only fair" to the corporations. If we became better people, if crime went down, "so that the shareholders wouldn't suffer," the taxpayers had to pay for empty cells.

A picture in the local weekly newspaper showed Dee and Ronald smiling as lawyer Terry presented a foundation check to a shy angel of a man identified as the Wyoming artist Doug *Something.*

I clicked on a story from the daily newspaper in the state capital of Helena.

The photo showed Ron and "his bride, Hollywood actress Lana LaBuff" hosting a reception "for their Helena friends." She posed like a pro beside a preening Ron. The prose noted "the bride's mother and younger sister of the Northern Cheyenne Reservation" were in attendance. As no doubt were smooth talkers. Movers and shakers. Backroom bullshitters. Hall whisperers. Wankers and walk-it-through'ers who stalk public castles like state capitals for whoever pays. All such "friends" got to see the new titles the big bucks White boy from the small town of Sidner painted on his résumé with Lana's red lipstick.

I didn't have time to check all the dozens of civil and criminal filings linked to Ronald and Dee and Terry's names and Zane businesses, the list of which kept growing as my clock kept ticking, but I scanned a summary of an odd post-verdict filing about how a victorious Zane enterprise that was awarded a $1 million settlement plus legal fees had, *allegedly*, padded up the services of attorney Terence Ewing to outrageous levels. That made me wonder if Terry'd cut himself a little *sumthen'-sumthen'* on the side.

A three-year-old local newspaper photo of the library's Halloween party showed Lana dressed as the perfect witch: conical black hat, a spooky costume beyond any "simple black dress," greenish makeup and dark lips that couldn't hide their smile in their character's scowl.

Thus, what I'd been told about her by a human source was now confirmed by trustable online data.

I leaned back from my screen. Checked its battery icon: 41%. Still probably enough memory left for what was coming, but I deleted some old files anyway. I closed the laptop. Plugged it in to a charger linked with an extension cord to the wall socket closest to the picture window where time blew past in the wind.

The black hands on my mom's wall clock pointed to 5:43.

Seventy-seven minutes left *until.*

I needed more human sources for whatever was out there that I needed to know. And like in many investigations, my best (so far) source, Lana, was hip-deep in whatever malice and malfeasance I needed to find.

My cellphone lay on the table. Its battery read 100%. I pulled out the charger cord, entered my security code, swiped and tapped, held it to my face.

Heard the buzz.

Heard the click.

Told the person who answered: “Now.”

15

Four of us sat around a kitchen table as afternoon became evening.

The red door into that house of lies was locked.

Lana sat by my side. She wore around-the-house clothes: Torn blue jeans. A gray sweatshirt. No makeup. I felt her breath. Her gravity.

Across from us sat Ronald and Terence wearing sweated-through golf shirts and the scent of flowery sunblock.

Three stacks of legal documents sat between us:

Lana's original prenuptial and services required deal.

The conditional exit package for her outlined to me the night before.

The contract with my name.

"You surprised us, Jim," said Ronald. "We figured you'd run out the clock before making your move. But here we are, forty-seven minutes left. Terry and I had to rush back from the country club to make us all smile."

A gold ballpoint pen lay beside my contract.

Lawyer Terence said: "We're glad you've agreed to the terms."

"No," I said.

Lana fully looked at me for the first time since she'd opened the red door.

"The paperwork is clear," snapped Terence. "You've read it all. While we can't let you take it to a lawyer here and there's no time for you to zap it to some hotshot back east, you're a 'professional wordsmith.' You know what it says."

"What it doesn't say, too."

The lawyer said: "If it's not on the page, it's—"

"What's *not* on the page counts. I get the deal. I'll probably sign the deal—now that I've seen the pages for her, for me. But we're not taking your terms."

Lana heard my "we."

Said nothing.

Ronald's brow wrinkled. He was *annoyed* headed to *angry*. But I knew the unexpected action had him intrigued.

"We'll all take the bottom lines we sign for *what*," I said, "but she and I decide every *how*."

Terence snapped: "The deal is—"

His client/cousin/lover shut Terry up with a raised hand.

"So," purred the husband who wanted to pay me to make him a cuckold, "tell me about your *how*."

"No," I told the room. "She and I haven't decided on that yet."

"Well," said Ronald as his cousin seethed, "time is of the essence.

"And," he said . . .

Then I knew I'd been right. He'd been planning on controlling everything.

". . . there are necessary restraints on your timing."

My expression gave him nothing.

"Tomorrow night is the annual country club banquet. You're not invited. My supportive wife must be at my side. Appearances and such."

"The wedding," whispered Lana.

"Ah yes," said Ronald. "Day after tomorrow, Friday. Another dreary event I won't get to go to with just the one I love. Though he'll be there, too."

A smile mollified Terry's seething face.

"What can one do?" said Ron. "A man in my position has responsibilities."

He leaned across the table to graciously explain the situation to me.

"A bank teller is marrying the young stud who's been sitting at the desk on the floor pining for her ever since she got there. His father is the president. The young stud's holding down his own second fiddle chair until his father retires. As chairman of the board, *Mother* will be attending the wedding, and as vice chair, where she goes, so do I. And that means *we*, doesn't it, *dear*."

An order, not a question, to Lana.

"But actually," said Ronald, "since *your* mother was supposed to go to keep your aunt company—the girl is shirttail related to you like half the rest of this damn town—well, your mom is in casts, so . . ."

He shrugged.

"You already checked the guest list," I said. "Schemed this out."

"I know the cards I play. That wedding works with our coup. *Mother* will get to witness for herself the farce we're creating. All you two have to do is act like there's an attraction between you two that's real and going somewhere."

Lana spoke for the first time since we all sat down.

"And after that?" she said.

"We'll let them know," I said with my eyes on our two would-be puppeteers.

"Well," said Ronald, "you two can talk about that later. Now we've got to build the drama. Set the stage.

"*I know!*" he said. "We'll all go out to dinner tonight. Barb's again. It's the most public place. We have to let your . . . relationship show it's growing in spite of the poor husband whose loving trust is about to be betrayed."

Ronald spread his hands wide.

"My mother has eyes all over this town," he said. "We have to give her the right show to see."

My heart closed around the secret of my morning with Dee.

I told her son: "You already made the dinner reservations."

"This is my town. I don't need reservations. Plus, there's always space.

"Now go pretty up, Lana," said Ronald. "Look like somebody who Jim here would want to fuck."

"I'm going as I am," she said.

Her cold dark eyes saw my proud smile.

"*Ehh*," said her husband.

Lawyer Terence clicked the gold ballpoint pen. Pushed it toward me.

Two copies of that contract. I signed them. Took one for myself.

"Well then," said Ronald. "Here we go."

16

Dinner was absurd.

Lana drank two single malt Scotches on the rocks. I matched her, though alcohol has never been my thing. Ronald and Terence drank martinis.

Murdered animals sizzled on our plates.

Barb's Ribs was a huge restaurant built for better times. There was a bar. Out from it spread a serving floor with tables. Booths lined the walls. Doors out of the dining room led to a "casino" where coffin-sized computers designed as video poker and slot machines with whirling lights and sound effects legally spun away pensions and paychecks of dreamers who sat pulling levers and pushing keys as if the courage of their flesh and pleas to heaven mattered instead of algorithms. Rare were the moments when winners' bells carried out to the dining room where big screen TVs hung high on the walls to show sports, talk shows, flashes of a dominant politically biased network that admitted in a court case they were an "entertainment" not "news" endeavor. Those mute TVs flickered over everything.

Ronald waved to the few occupied booths as we four followed the hostess/waitress/busser to the table he insisted on in the center of the dining room. Ron kept calling new arrivals to our table for uncomfortable chitchat. He'd mention who I was even though most everyone knew. Someone in those trapped groups usually asked about my mother before they scurried away from our center stage show.

Our table's sounds were Ron's pronouncements and Terry's admirations. Lana and I sipping our Scotches. Slicing our meals. Silently praying to get the hell out of there.

Ronald *loudly* insisted on picking up the check.

Lana and our two co-conspirators had driven to the restaurant in Ronald's SUV. I'd followed in my rental car.

Now the four of us stood by our parked vehicles in the parking lot outside of Barb's Ribs. There were maybe ten other vehicles parked there.

But we stood alone on that packed sand in the evening light.

"Well, kids," said Ronald, grinning at Lana and me as he paraphrased my father's favorite movie. "Here's looking at you."

He ushered her into the back seat of the SUV. Drove her away with them.

I watched the taillights disappear.

Wondered if she'd looked back to see me standing there.

Fuck magic hour.

Sundown bled the sky.

I was on the turf where I was born. The place that raised me as I ran toward who I was. The place I'd come from and gone so far from and couldn't leave behind even if I tried. This was my hometown.

But now it wasn't. Maybe never had been *mine*. A place carved out of space and time by thousands of souls like me. None of us have a full claim on where we're from or what it means to the ever-expanding universe of nevermore.

Darkness weighed on me as I drove streets where ghosts of *used-to-be* drifted amidst beasts of *here-now*. Homes with windows ruled by rainbows of TV assaulting those trapped inside. Political lawn signs poked in scruffy lawns. Old cars junked in driveways. Too-needed-to-be-junked cars parked at curbs. A bumper sticker proclaiming *unto-death* fidelity to poverty-inducing firearms. A tipped-over aluminum garbage can clattered and wobbled near the mouth of a potholed alley. A dozen houses sported Realtors' signs, twice that many with "For Sale by Owner" posters. An American flag hung outside for the night at a house that didn't know or didn't care about accepted protocol for Old Glory. A sagging peeling-paint wooden house sported a *Don't Tread on Me* flag like those carried by cop-killing terrorists who'd stormed America's Capitol three years ago. Houses with broken windows and busted-down doors. Flickers of cigarettes in their shadows. Fading flames from meth heads. I imagined powders of opioid or *f-j's*—*j* for junky, *f* for *fentanyl*, for *fucked*, for *fatal*.

Fewer than thirty cars lined that night's Main Street flowered by the red neon sign for the Tap Room, hues for two other bars and the neon marquee of the Roxy theater. No one walked the sidewalks.

Main Street led me to the viaduct bridge over the railroad tracks. Pigeons lived under that bridge—cooing big city refugees hiding from prairie hawks.

The two sides of town meant something more when separate grade schools waited on either side of the train tracks. That ended by fourth grade for me when all of us grade schoolers were "consolidated" in one building on the north side near the pink high school. That same consolidated classroom space now also contained what used to be called junior high into middle school.

That night I drove off the viaduct through twilight toward The Big Pink.

Everybody goes back to their old high school—even if only in their mind. That's where we started to emerge. That's where we fought being submerged.

Me and my high school crew became scrappers who got out of town, Cody to the Marines, the rest of us to universities or colleges to build lives somewhere that wasn't just where we came from.

Our big pink high school had been built way, *way* back when World War II hero Dwight Eisenhower was president. That general had a brilliant strategy for saving America from communists and Nazis and polio. From flying saucers. From horrors that back then only noir novelists and science fiction writers imagined.

Republican Ike's genius plan: Educate everybody—*everybody*. Equally. Free of any religion's chains, unlike many Muslim countries. Make all America's children as smart as they could be so our everyone could be savvy enough to handle the world of atom bombs, crippling plagues, climate shifts and concentration camp barbed wire fences.

And it worked. Not perfectly, but for a while. For my parents' generation.

My dad liked to brag how two Nobel prize contenders in science came from our town. Plus there was a poet in his class who got published in *The New Yorker*.

But dollars, not dreams, ruled America's new education system that night.

I drove toward The Big Pink as darkness rose to the sky. Security lights beamed bright cones of light toward that two-story pink-walled fortress where I'd served time. This was the last of September. A Thursday night. School was in session. The parking lot held a few cars. A big yellow school bus.

The students who'd answer the ringing bells in that big pink high school the next morning were like millions of other kids in small towns and big cities.

Well, except not like in gated communities and big city neighborhoods where rivers of money washed the streets. The teenagers who lived there never worried about food or shelter. From their competitive parents' preschool enrichments on, they were labeled and ladled beyond-the-basics as algorithms and correct society indicated. They had the best equipment. RXs. Top teachers. Tutors. Orchestrated 'life experiences.' They got prepped for The Tests. They got help writing college application essays to show how independent and original they were. They got onto prestige college conveyer belts to the mega bucks jobs and pedestals of power. Forget about President Ike. They did all that in a system of meritocracy for those who could afford it.

Plus, across the country were the "home-schooled" and "religious schooled" kids where obedience and believing *whatever they were told* was more important than facts and truths, "educational systems" that were nudging their way into taxpayer funding even though they were not freedom-of-thought public schools.

My headlights bathed the pink walls of my high school as I pulled into the teachers' parking lot. Stopped. Put the car in Park. Let it idle.

I rolled down the driver's window.

Yelled to the pink fortress: *"Kick their asses!"*

Turned and drove home rumbling over the train tracks.

I parked out front of our house. There was a driveway on the east side of the house that ran back to a garage that made the border of our backyard. Katie'd moved Mom's car into the garage.

When I showed up with my rental machine, I felt like I should keep the driveway open in case Mom's car needed to flee.

Debby Petersen's car sat at First Street's curb a few yards west of where I parked. I saw lights on in her rented house. Wondered if she'd put her kids to bed. Wondered if she'd find enough rest for another hard tomorrow.

Walking up the stairs and sidewalk between the dark shrouded pine trees planted for Katie and me felt as old as time. I stood on the front porch. Opened the front door. Stepped inside.

Something's wrong.

You feel it. You sense it. Your jungle genes scream.

My heart thundered.

The dark hall held me with my back pressed against the closed front door.

Shadows filled the house where I grew up, a geography of furniture and walls and doorways I could once walk with my eyes closed. But that was back when I was a boy and boogeymen were just my imagination.

Smells filled me.

The dusty gray carpet I should have vacuumed like sister Katie told me to.

The dying flowers from a Get Well Soon vase sent to Mom's hospital room that had been too big for the surfaces in her Evergreen Center room.

The whiff of Scotch on my breath.

Sweat dampening my maroon shirt.

I had no weapon. No backup. No partner. 911 or Cody meant taps of the cellphone in my shirt pocket—sounds that would betray my moves.

A switch on the wall just out of reach would snap on the hall light.

That would let me see the living room.

That would make me a clear target.

There are no certainties. There are only strategic decisions.

Snap! went the light switch I flipped on as I hugged the side of the hall.

Shapes of living room furniture made clear. Glass shelves with pictures of our family. The hall to the left led to Mom's bedroom and my boyhood lair I'd reclaimed. Off center to the right waited the open door to the kitchen. The back of the house. The stairs to the basement where Katie's pink bedroom and the laundry room were. The stairs Mom had fallen down.

Listening. Hearing nothing. Feeling stillness. Sensing . . . disturbance.

I feinted toward the kitchen—rushed left to the bedrooms and bathroom. Snapped on that hall's light and ducked back without getting shot. Charged in! Bathroom clear. Spun into Mom's room and threw open her closet door—clear. Crouched back through the hall to my bedroom, feint/charge—nothing on the bed, and the closet door, the cubicle a boy could imagine housing zombies—I jerked open that closet door with its full-length inside mirror and found no one.

Back to the living room where no one had run out the front door.

Pause. Hold still. Press your back against the wall next to the open door into the kitchen. Wait. Wait. Wait.

I rushed around that corner, snapped on the kitchen light.

No one stood in that corridor between the sink and the refrigerator and stove. No one stood way back by the table in front of the picture window.

My laptop: Pushed out of place. Its screen open but dark.

The yellow pads with my notes shoved around and flipped through.

The black moleskin journal with poems far enough along to write down, snatches of prose, thoughts that often weren't as good the next day as when I saved them:

That black journal lay pushed face-down and open on the table.

On the table was the bar of hand soap kept by the kitchen sink.

I snapped on the light above the kitchen table.

Revealed what the soap'd smeared on the picture window to the night:

WhORe

17

Cody stared at the invader's graffiti as he stood beside me in the kitchen. He'd insisted on checking the whole house with me again. Checked the garage. Opened the trunk of Mom's car. Went through all its compartments, did the same with my rental. Made sure both vehicles were locked.

"Remember growing up here when nobody used to lock their doors?" I said.

"*Remember when* ain't where we are now."

He'd acquiesced to me not calling Sheriff Fenton: That would put the law in my business that I didn't want anyone to know. Would take away my control.

"Control," said Cody. "Is that what you've got going for you?"

Silence was my answer.

He listened to me say that no hacker could have fired up the opened laptop without my security code. Plus, there was nothing incriminating in there. Yet. The Google searches from before dinner. Emails Russian or Chinese digital eyes had probably already seen. Porn visits that were tame, perhaps one—*OK, two*—clicks to kinky, but not perverted. Short stories I hadn't been able to sell. The draft of a novel that hadn't fully revealed itself.

"The raid's not what they *got*," said Cody. "It's about what they *can*."

He didn't need to tell me to lock my doors.

Check my six and be careful going around corners.

The Glock he'd brought rode my right hip since he'd materialized through the front door. Felt like a weight nailed to my bones. Felt heavy.

Felt like it almost wasn't there. Felt terrifying. Felt good. Felt familiar and so fucking real.

We stared at that crime-kissed pane of glass to the night.

"The obvious question," he said.

"*Who.*"

"Yeah. But not just *who* wrote it. *Who* is it talking about."

18

On the bus.

On that bus the next morning meant me getting up at dawn. Checking my cellphone. Checking the Glock holstered on my bed table.

You pick up a gun, you've made your choice.

Now you have to figure out how to live with that.

On the kitchen table waited the *sure it hadn't been hacked* laptop. The yellow pads that *sure*, had ink scrawls from my Google searches, but didn't reveal the *not much* that I knew. The black journal's poems written and waiting that revealed *only* that I keep trying to capture how it feels being alive.

All that plus the black holstered Glock lay on my family's kitchen table as I drank coffee without the milk in Mom's refrigerator that had finally soured. I consumed the online '*news today, oh boy*',' including a story about how the secret police in one of America's foreign allies had locked up a novelist/journalist. The charge was "sending subliminal messages" in his prose. That sixty-something family man sought truth in his fiction as a novelist and fought to keep fictions out of the truths he reported as a journalist.

My gun sat on the windowsill beside my cellphone with its countdown clock *ding!* like a café's come-on-in door while I did *Taiji* and let the soft functions in the form remind me how to break an arm, crush a larynx, rocket an aggressor into the oncoming rush of a bus.

The Glock waited on top of the toilet tank while I showered.

I got dressed.

Watched out the front window as next door's mom and two kids hurried to their dented family car to get to school on time that Thursday morning.

The Evergreen kept its orange minibus parked outside a rear service door. By 9:47 that Thursday morning I sat behind its big steering wheel wearing my aviator sunglasses and my zipped-low black leather jacket.

Faces full of *once was* climbed into that bus.

There was Mrs. Malletta who'd lived up the street. And Roma Aikens.

Up the stairs came my high school buddy Brandon's mom who'd driven across town and moved in with the man who ran the laundromat, a revolution Brandon still hadn't forgiven her for as he and his sister fought to stay with their dad. His mom saw me, walked past with wet eyes and trembling lips.

Behind her marched Owl Eyes Mike who passed by like he didn't see me.

"Well hello there, again!" said spry but wispy Teresa as she followed Owl Eyes Mike onto the bus. She was my buddy Joe's mom, and it was her basement where we all gathered to grow up: Brandon, Joe, Jonah, Neil, Nathan, Lincoln, Alex, sometimes Cody. And me, "Traven."

Two of the residents who Queen Dee and I met in the hall boarded the bus. I knew they felt bad they couldn't bring their wheelchair friend.

Faces I remembered and faces I didn't climbed the stairs.

Three of them asked about Mom. My answers reassured.

A blue-scrub, *not-Irma* nursing aide who looked not long out of high school was the last person to walk up the bus stairs, a slouching journey she made with her pale face captured by the screen of the cellphone in her hand.

No one else in scrubs or carrying an iPad or even an old-fashioned clipboard of authority was waiting to board the bus. I called out to the nurse's aide as she clumped past: "Is that it? Should we go now?"

"Yeah, whatever," was the answer she sent me as she shuffled to a seat.

"OK, then," I said to no one but myself.

Pulled the lever for a pneumatic whoosh of the shutting doors, pulled out of the parking space as I shouted out for everyone to wear their seat belts—

—realized I should have walked through and checked that myself before I started driving. Silently cursed and prayed that my lesson learned wouldn't include the sight of a wailing grandma with a bloody smashed nose and broken dentures from bashing into the seat in front of her when the bus driver slammed on the brakes for *whatever.*

I gripped the steering wheel and drove the bus below the speed limit.

Kept glancing at the big mirror above the windshield that reflected the white-haired scene in the rows behind me and my own tick-tocking face.

Kept checking the two trembling rectangular side mirrors.

Tried to dodge potholes that my old boss of the road crew warned me about when I'd run into him in the grocery store. He'd said the city ran out of budget dollars to fix its streets "way back in July." I dodged what hadn't happened to keep something worse from happening.

My windshield showed me everything as a fantasy fiction saga. *Yes*, I knew these streets. *No*, I'd never seen them so surreal.

What we see depends on how we ride.

I knew the way to the cemetery.

But I had no clue as to where to go after I drove the bus through the open-for-business black iron gates that Thursday morning. I slowed the bus to a chugging crawl over the graveled vehicle paths through that autumn-browning grass field of gray headstones.

No one behind me spoke up with any suggestions.

Everyone probably thought the man with his hands on the steering wheel knew what he was doing and where he was going. They always do, *right?*

Up ahead, two fiftyish women climbed out of their parked car.

Off to the left of the bus as it chugged forward stood a small backhoe.

Off to the far right stretched the fields and plots of graves, the leaning cross of the plague. Scraggly bushes made the far border of the cemetery. Those bushes hid the Coyote Hills on the far horizon. Near a graveled road beside the bushes, a visitor kickstand-parked a motorcycle, swung a blue-jeaned leg off that steed. Gravestones' reflections filled the black face visor on the visitor's helmet.

Over there: a sixtyish man in an old Army jacket stood staring down at a grave where a miniature American flag fluttered.

I spotted a patch of gravel that looked like where I could park and, more importantly, back out of. I cranked the big black steering wheel. The bus bounced over ridges and craters. Amidst groans and whiffs from the jostled old people in the bus behind me came some man's voice: "Ride 'em, cowboy!"

Felt like everybody on the bus laughed.

As the bus braked to a stop, Carrie said: "Does anybody see my mother?"

Pshushh as the lever I pushed opened the pneumatic door to the cool air.

My best bus driver voice announced: "We're here."

19

Off the bus.

The slow parade of yesterdays grabbed whatever 'the old folks' could hold onto as they shuffled down the steps. Two women carried flowers. Passengers walked this field that would soon claim them. Carrie drifted toward where the motorcyclist's black visor reflected her shuffles. Owl Eyes Mike again passed me sitting in the driver's chair. Wandered toward the backhoe.

The nurse's aide who wasn't Irma plopped her butt on a gravestone. Her phone in her hands held her in its thrall while those in her care wandered.

"Fuck," I muttered.

Stepped off the bus.

Floated like a butterfly from one group of seniors to the next. Checked to be sure they were OK and acting smart enough to stay that way. Caught up to Carrie. Turned her thin shoulders so she faced back toward the bus and not toward the gaps in the cemetery fence with glimpses of the Coyote Hills between the autumn-leaved bushes. Her mother wasn't that way anyway.

Then I saw us at our simple human best.

Those strangers who'd been here when the bus rolled up—the man in the army coat and the two middle-aged women and the helmeted motorcyclist—changed how they stood and where they looked, became like volunteer drovers on a cattle drive like my great-grandfather cowboyed on this prairie.

The mourning soldier gently steered two white-haired women around something on the ground. The helmeted motorcyclist gestured for Carrie to search for her mother by the safety of the bus. One of the fiftyish women bent down and picked up Warren's dropped black cane.

My cell phone buzzed with the first text Lana ever sent me:

I'm going to need to get
real drunk at the banquet
if I'm going to make it
through tonight.

I heard the five-beat chirp of a meadowlark as I texted her back:

I'll be thinking of you.
Be careful. Don't drive.

The wind stirred the prairie where I stood. My phone buzzed:

No chance of that.

I texted back:

"Chance of which?"

Shouting across the graves came: *"Who-hoo!"*

The nurse's aide with her butt on a tombstone looked up from her cell.

We spotted the two *whooping* women who'd carried flowers off the bus.

"Hell," said one, "if you can't laugh in a graveyard, you ain't gonna leave!"

The nurse's aide went back to the prison of her screen.

I spotted Owl Eyes Mike leaving the backhoe and walking back to where his contemporaries wandered. Put my cellphone inside my black leather jacket. "Casually" drifted to intercept Owl Eyes Mike's path to join the others.

But the handsome man from yesterday's corridor saw me coming. He left his friend standing in her walker while staring down at a grave that wasn't his. He headed my way and I knew I should let him detour me.

"Hey, Jim," called that handsome man who'd been a champion boxer long before M.M.A. took over. He came home, bought the local radio station with help from his farmer father and a hefty loan from the bank. “Good of you to do this.”

“*Naw*, Gene.” He warmed at me remembering his name. “It’s what we do.”

“Not everybody.”

We let that lay between us on the cemetery earth.

“Speaking of *do*,” he said, “folks here are proud of what you’ve done.”

My face burned in the October sun.

“Gene, I’m . . . that makes me feel ten feet tall and two inches small. I just did what I had to do. And got real, *real* fucking lucky.”

“Maybe, but we’re like everybody everywhere. Give us a little something more than what we got stuck with. Something to cheer for. Somebody from where we come from. Somebody who beats the odds. All that, *well*, that makes us feel good. Feel like all the shit we live in can be worth it.

“Hell,” added Gene, “even if we do think that what you write is stupid.”

Our laughter carried across the field of graves to Owl Eyes Mike heading our way. His foggy lenses turned to sounds that maybe he could not see.

I told Gene: “You must have been a helluva boxer to learn so much.”

He shrugged: “We do what we do.”

My *Taiji* sensed boxer Gene shift into a “casual” pose that wasn’t.

“Speaking of *do*,” he said to me with his eyes unthreateningly on the horizon. “Saw you yesterday in the hall. What are you doing with Queen Dee?”

Kept my eyes on the same horizon as his, my voice steady, casual.

“I was just walking her to her car.”

“Might be careful with that,” said this former Main Street star. “You walk with Dee, you either work *for*, get worked *by*, or get worked *over* by her. With her, you better know where you’re going and how you’re willing to get there.”

An arrow of sparrows fluttered past us.

He turned so I faced his smile: “I better go back to Shirley. She isn’t as good with the walker as she thinks she is.”

My rhetorical sigh said: “Who is?”

Owl Eyes Mike headed toward the bus.

From behind me came a friendly voice: “Hey, Jim! How ya doing?”

There stood a man leaning on a shovel and giving me the same grin I’d gotten when we’d worked up here for his father as teenagers.

Yeah, I was a gravedigger.

Only a few times, but enough to, years later, earn the nostalgic gray T-shirt with a black lettered, crossed pick & shovel patch and logo:

MARTIN COUNTY CEMETERY—EVENT STAFF

Now the son of all that was smiling at me with the guileless affection everyone in town called *'Just Dave.'* A happy man with a hard job as the cemetery's CEO, caretaker, custodian and chief coffin-coverer. Why shouldn't he be happy? He did great work at the sweet executive job he'd taken over from his father, married once and then married better.

"Happy to see you back in town," Dave told me.

"Where else?" I said with a smile like it was a joke.

"Beats me but that's a bone I got to pick with you," he said as we stood in the cemetery. "Hurry up and hook up with some unlucky woman so I'll still be working here when you come to show her."

All I could do was smile.

Owl Eyes Mike climbed back into the empty bus. I was certain he'd shuffle all the way to a back seat where I wouldn't be likely to engage him.

Dave tilted his cowboy hat to keep it on his skull in that October breeze. Nodded toward the earth we'd dug.

"Bet you don't miss working this," he told me.

"I got what it had for me," I said.

Didn't tell him: *And that was way more insight than dollars.*

Dave said: "So you driving the bus?"

"Yeah. And I better get to it."

Before I told the nurse's aide to *literally* get off her butt, help get people on the bus, stand by the door until the last one had safely climbed on board. Before I announced *"All aboard!"* with no authority and every power to do so. Before I herded Carrie into the amidst of her fellow inmates at the Evergreen who gently funneled her into the bus. Before all that, I heard Dave sigh.

"Yeah," he said. "We all got places to go.

"Man," he said with wide open eyes, "the universe. It's so fucking big."

20

O*n the bus.*

Easier driving back as the bus rumbled down Knob Hill. I steered a right on Second Street. Passed the Methodist church. Passed blocks of houses. A mom pushed a buggy on the sidewalk. A trotting dog. The black visor helmeted motorcyclist rode in the bus's side mirror. The bus drove as smooth as silk on warm flesh past the side of the library straight toward—

The Evergreen—*Under attack!*

A SWAT Armored Personnel Carrier slammed to the curb by the front doors. Three unmarked cruisers huddled behind the APC. Blue flashers winking behind grills. A local cop car crouched behind the unmarked cruisers.

I slammed the bus's brakes in the middle of the intersection.

Two black-armored SWAT warriors paced on the packed sand behind the Evergreen where I was supposed to park the bus. They carried military assault rifles. Wore no face masks that *back then* day.

Three SWAT troopers milled on the sidewalk in front of the Evergreen.

Sheriff Fenton and a deputy stood watching SWAT troopers sentinel the concrete in front of the Evergreen's doors.

Where my mother was trapped.

The bus engine roared as I stomped on the gas. Startled *Ohs!* came from the seats behind me. Senior citizens swerving sideways in their seats as I swung the steering wheel through a hard left. The yellow bus slammed to a stop as soon as I steered it out of the intersection with the hope that I'd crashed no grannies.

"Everybody stay down!" I shouted as I stood up.

"Stay in your seats!" I stepped into the bus's metal-floored aisle.

My finger stabbed at the frightened aide. Raced her up front to me.

"Stay here!" I said. "Nobody leaves the bus. Keep everybody calm. Hear shooting, everybody crouch down. This is the lever to open the doors. Close it after me. Don't let anybody but me get on unless they got a big fucking badge."

Her eyes widened: "Wha . . . wha . . . what are you going to do?"

I popped the lever. Whooshed open the doors. Clomped down the steps.

Turned and stared back up to her terrorized face.

The cool breeze of October carried the whiff of smoke—

—but it was only from a distant forest fire—*right?*

My black leather jacket covered me.

Gotta do it.

I zipped the jacket all the way down. Pulled it off. Tossed it into the bus where the nurse's aide almost caught it.

Stood there in my tucked-in, long-sleeved denim blue shirt.

No gun was clipped to my belt or in a shoulder holster:

The old folks' safety and fears first, I'd told myself that morning. *If they saw or brushed against the Glock, they'd freak out and then who knows?*

Besides, I wasn't going to need it with them—right?

So lucky me: no gun to hide from the badges.

My aviator sunglasses went into my shirt pocket beside my cellphone.

I made mine a face with nothing to hide.

Marched toward the cluster of machine-guns and badges at the front door of the Evergreen Center. I held my hands out low like an innocent civilian but out wide and obviously empty like I knew what I was doing.

Mark me twenty paces away from the SWAT crew when a trooper turned and showed the white letters stenciled across his back's black ballistic vest:

FEDERAL POLICE

"Sir, state your business here!" shouted another SWAT trooper.

"Lots."

Made him blink. Made him think. Made him listen.

"I'm the bus driver for the Evergreen. I've got a busload of its elderly residents parked back up the hill there. And my mother is chained to her bed in there. She needs monitoring."

Go for it, I told myself. *Use every bullet you've got.*

"Plus, I'm a press pass carrying writer wondering what the hell is going on."

"What the hell is going on is none of your business!" snapped the SWAT trooper. "We'll tell you what you need to know when we want to."

Neither of us noticed Sheriff Fenton had walked up to us until we both heard him tell the trooper: "You might want to rethink that."

"Klang!" yelled a bald man in a business suit who walked through the small cluster of SWAT troopers surrounding me and Sheriff Fenton. "Stand down."

The man with the assault rifle slung in front of his bulletproofed chest who'd braced me curled back into his armor and stepped aside for Baldy.

Baldy considered the sheriff's steady gaze.

Turned to me.

"We're ICE. Immigration and Customs Enforcement. Executing an arrest."

"With a whole fucking SWAT team and an armored car and machine guns ready to rock? Who the hell are you chasing that warrants or is worth all this?"

"All this is SPORE," he informed me. Then translated that government acronym: "Standard Protocol Operational React and Engage."

I realized even before I heard her sobbing.

Irma.

Led out of the Evergreen Center for senior and disabled citizens where she'd worked for eleven years, her hands zip-tied behind her back, a black-assault-clad SWAT warrior on either side of her blue nurse's aide scrubs as another business-suited, badge-dangling man led the way.

Irma.

Her *in-our-Army* son risking his life for the principles of freedom and justice in some sand-and-rocks political turf beyond the borders of America.

"Irma!" I yelled and none of the ICE guns could have stopped me.

"Mister Jim!" she wept as one of her captors opened the back seat of a federal government cruiser. "I'm sorry! I'm sorry!"

"What can I do?"

"My son, I don't—and Mr. Smith! He needs his pills! Mr. Smith!"

A trooper and business-suited agent folded her into the cruiser's back seat.

"Your mother!" cried Irma as they ducked her head inside. "Tell her—"

Lawmen slammed the car door. *Wham!*

SWAT troopers boarded their armored caravan.

"Where are you taking her?" I asked Baldy.

"Per procedures and warrant," he said.

Said like he was past caring: "It's my job."

Then slumped his way to the command cruiser and off rumbled those steel machines full of men with high tech weaponry and one sobbing woman.

Sheriff Ross Fenton stood beside me on the cracked sidewalk.

We watched the parade roll away on American streets.

The smoky October wind blew. Dust swirled in my hometown.

Ross said: "They'll take her to the Air Force base by where you flew into. A converted warehouse. Bunk beds. Bars on the windows."

The sheriff let that sink in on that October morning.

Then said: "So what would that press pass you talked about say?"

"It might be expired, but the authenticating of me is there."

"Un-huh," he said.

Nodded toward the bus I'd forgotten about: "You need any help there?"

"I got it," I said.

Turned and did that. Parked the bus on the sand just vacated by visor-helmeted machine-gun cops. Helped the nurse's aide guide the shaken passengers off the bus and into the brick and glass institution with apartments bigger than most cells. Ran up the stairs to my mother's room.

"That's not right!" Mom said over and over again. "Irma's good people! She's the heart and soul of this place. Hell, they'll never find anybody to replace her even if there was anybody left in town who wants to come work here. The staff's down two aides and a nurse as it is and . . . What the hell is going to happen to everyone here who needs her help? What's going to happen to us?

"It's not right," she said.

Then cried out: "What are you going to do?"

21

Excuse me," said the man's voice on the telephone. "Who are you again?"

Who he was raced to be revealed as he tried to capture my morning frenzy.

Grabbing my mom's cellphone and charger. *Shit shit shit I hadn't cellphone videoed what I'd seen like a dozen other culture-enraging YouTube posts!* I rushed from her nursing home room to our house.

The kitchen table morphed into the bridge of a zooming starship. Laptop open to multiple windows. Mom's cellphone pressed into service with my keyboards. Flashing between their screens and on my own phone with actual humans. Texting. Talking to a buddy who knows a guy who knows the woman *who*. Begging. Trading on. Cajoling. Alerting. Guilting. Triggering sequences. The fast intros. Pitches to cyber news sites I'd never followed. The *yeah-buts* and the *I-get-its*. *The Washington Post* editor who says it's a long shot but agrees to "see." Working that tentative conditional as if it were a White House press pass and certain-to-publish story. Zapping a woman—we'd realized the only *worth it* personal we'd had was fucking—urging her to use her "influencer" Instagram and TikTok accounts to fight an injustice and emailing an ex-reporting colleague to get an intro to an editor at the paper in the big city ninety miles away near where they took Irma, the paper on its way to e-editions only, but that still hit Sidner front porches every day, me shooting for a backup or to at least up the odds that a *Post* story would get pick-up in this state *where it happened*.

Phone number grabs. ICE Public Affairs. The Air Force base to try and wheedle a direct number to the locked warehouse. The Army division deployed overseas in charge of Irma's son. Immigrants' rights groups—one Montana chapter, one national. Asking questions that let whoever was on the line know their answers might end up on the news their mother watched and YouTube.

And now on the phone, *this guy*.

"Again," I said, "I'm James Traven, a reporter and author from the senator's home state, calling from Sidner, working an assignment for *The Washington Post* and your state's leading newspaper, and our question is:

"*Given the senator's public support of our American troops and his urging Uncle Sam to take better care of our men and women in uniform, what is the senator's on-the-record comment about how ICE yanked the mother of a combat zone Army lieutenant out of her job taking care of Montana senior citizens?*

"The senator's a big fan of senior citizens, too, right?

"*What comment does the senator have about a constituent soldier's mother getting grabbed up by SWAT and shoved into the deportation line?*"

Who the hell knew about the senator's "public support of American troops." What was he going to say? That he *didn't* support America's military?

The man's voice on my telephone said: "How is the senator supposed to comment when he doesn't know a thing about what happened and—This is the first I'm hearing of whatever this is. And he won't get it until I tell him."

"I'm happy to hold the line. We—you and me—we've got a deadline."

"You and me, huh? The press secretary and some sort of *reporter* who writes novels. *Of course* I'm googling while I'm talking to you! If this *is* you."

"Give me your direct email, I'll send you the direct email to my *Post* editor."

Zap her! I thought. *Your email will make the story more newsworthy!*

The press secretary for the inherited money jillionaire, fake conservative of the two Montana senators said: "What's this story to you?"

"What the American people have a right to know."

"Or this is another bucket of alternative facts."

"A fact is a fact, period. Alternatives are fantasies. Or bullshit lies."

"*Gee*, I'm going to have to use that one. Here's your official comment."

His voice took on the tone of a televised press conference:

"*The senator is a fervent supporter of law and order. This is a country of rules. You follow them, you do fine. You don't, our brave men and women of law enforcement will do their duty.*"

"Got it, '*law and order*.' What about *justice*?"

"Goes without saying."

"Yeah. But you didn't—the senator didn't."

"America is for Americans. That's justice."

"Give me your tired, your hungry, your—"

"The damn French gave that to us way back when! We're here now, and—"

The beast in me jumped in before he could end the call: "Mrs. Deirdre Zane here in Sidner is a big supporter of the senator—*right*?"

Silence filled the space between the Washington, DC, office of power and a Montana kitchen table.

Caution filled his tone: "What does Mrs. Zane have to do with this?"

"Nothing as far as I know. Yet."

My phone clicked dead.

Maybe given this push from the *Post* and from a paper back in his home state, the senator's staff might make a call about Irma's case. Then that senatorial notice might create something good for her.

Maybes and *mights*, *coulds* and *woulds*.

My last one vaporized at 4:37 Mountain State Time that Thursday afternoon via email from the *Post* editor: *"Sorry. Too much bigger news. A too-big-to-fail bank crashing because they were SAG—*Stupid. *A*rrogant. Greedy. *A toxic train derailment. Horrors Russian troops did in one Ukraine town. Legislators in four states trying to make it a felony for teachers to say the word 'sex.'"*

I read those words knowing their lethality to my story and yet knowing I'd keep going. Posting online wherever I could to grab eyeballs. Going through with other steps I'd started toward now predictable ends. Not because miracles might happen, but because that's what you do. You finish what you start.

Even if you're just sitting at a kitchen table in the lost American heartland.

Maybe especially if you're sitting at that table.

What the sad fuck else is there to do?

22

Probably I shouldn't have gone to that bar.

Not a Main Street joint like the Tap or the Lowdown. Across the railroad tracks in the part of town that was tough when the town was on its way up.

But that night made me feel like the hell with *shouldn'ts.*

The Oasis.

Long, dark and deep with an empty bandstand. Tables. A bar with wooden stools. The stench of beer. The sweat of ghosts.

The bartender whose name I later learned was Brenda clumped to me like a linebacker when I claimed a barstool wearing my black leather jacket mindlessly thrown on over my blue denim shirt and still no gun. She set me up with a boilermaker—a shot of cheap whiskey, a glass of tap beer that would appall the chic golden brew snobs of my generation.

But this was the Oasis: take what you get, and boilermakers were what my college summer job road crew guys insisted I drink during our after-work payday celebratory visits to this joint back when things made sense.

That Thursday night I sat in the middle of the scarred wooden bar's run.

Waited for the mirror beyond booze bottles to show my skull deflating.

Way down to my left, a tired-eyed couple rested on barstools. Not talking. Just sitting. Looking for better images in the mirror.

Closer to me but still four empty stools away slumped a man with the smell of grease on his gray coveralls. His eyes saw nothing of where the rest of us were.

I'd knocked back the burning shot.

Was drinking cold beer when a *my generation* woman with dark slacks, a blue sweater, chopped wheatfield hair and a hardened face walked in. Plopped herself on a stool around the corner of the end of the bar to my right. I thought about telling her that she shouldn't sit with her back to the door. Didn't. She could see the mirror in her peripheral vision. Saw the rest of us and didn't flinch.

A hundred heartbeats later, in came *him*.

Taller than me. Bulk not bloat. Reddish hair and the bushy beard that was then cool for both Brooklyn hipsters and right-wing shouters who hated each other. His beefy arms showcased tattoos. So did the arms of those Brooklyn hipsters. Sometimes there's more of the enemy in your mirror than you admit.

There and then in Oasis time, Bushy Beard checked his magnificence in the mirror. Claimed a seat between the tired-eyed couple and the greased worker.

Bushy Beard gave the tired-eyed couple a nod like he knew them or they should know him. Nodded to the greased worker who didn't care. Bushy Beard slapped a few dollars on the bar like he had plenty more. Made a point of asking bartender Brenda for a whiskey that wasn't on the shelves he could plainly see. Allowed as how "we ain't good enough for the good stuff," he ordered a rail bourbon and a mug of beer back "but don't give me none of that Mexican piss."

He looked at me and I didn't look away.

Flicked his eyes to the end of the bar and the toughened blonde.

Turned away like she wasn't worth any effort.

Started talking. Loud. With absolute authority. Sometimes he sent his words toward where silent bartender Brenda earned her rent leaning against the back bar. Sometimes Bushy Beard angled his head to the tired-eyed couple. His *"you know what I'm talking about"* and *"the fact of the matter is"* and *"people are saying"* and *"there's no question that"* and other cliché lies pulled polite mumbles from them that he took for confirmation of his wisdom.

He kept cutting glances my way.

I was the stranger in the bar near Bushy Beard's age who could—*should*—appreciate him. And I was giving him nothing. Not a look. Not a nod.

We were both on our second whiskeys when he announced: "That climate change stuff is pure crap. Hell, today was just like October is supposed to be."

He didn't mention that day's news about a white ice chunk the size of this town breaking off the Antarctic shelf and roaring into the sea.

"Science," Bushy Beard told the bar. "What a bunch of bullshit."

Out of my mouth came: "You got a cellphone?"

Kept my eyes in the mirror. Took a sip of whiskey. Nice and easy set the glass down on the bar. Let my shoes slide off the barstool's lower rung to brush the barroom's booze-smelling floor.

The mirror showed a sneer amidst his bushy beard as he dramatically leaned on the bar. Turned my direction: "You talking to me?"

"You're talking to everybody," I told his reflection. "I'm answering."

"And who the hell are you?"

"What difference does it make? You spout off nonsense from fake faces, so you don't care who you listen to. Now, you got a cellphone or not?"

He pulled the latest iPhone out of his rear pocket: "You want me to call you an ambulance?"

I took a pull of my beer.

"Science gave you your cellphone," I told his reflection. "Put up the satellites and cyber you gotta have. Science came up with strip farming to save out here from another Dust Bowl. But when science warns you that now your ass is on the line because of a virus or global warming and you gotta do something logical and smart about that, you say science is bullshit."

Could have left it there.

But said: "You better make up your mind or you're gonna look stupid."

Time froze in the Oasis until he said: "Stupid, huh."

And I heard him make up his mind.

"Whatever," I said loudly, "we're just having a conversation you started."

"Whoever the chicken shit you are, you ain't from around here."

"Born and raised."

"So you say. I say you don't live here anymore."

"Evidently I never left." Gave him what he wanted: "Even if I keep a roof over my head back in DC."

"Course you're from the swamp that's sucking down America."

"You're right about that swamp."

Bushy Beard blinked.

"There's more than 13,000 lobbyists and half that many top dollar lawyers back there getting paid millions to foster or undercut the compromised laws that Big Money got Congress to pass. That's the swamp drowning people like us."

"You know what you sound like?"

"Smart and sane."

"Bullshit. You don't fucking belong here. The boys from ICE. This morning, they took out some wetback crook who didn't belong here. Sent that Pancho back to where he came from. I'm thinking maybe ICE should come after you next."

"Maybe they will," I said as my feet claimed the floor.

I kept my face away from Bushy Beard's glare, an innocence for all to see.

Told all the reflections and ghosts in the mirror: "Nobody better try."

Blur of bulk and beard charging me as I kicked my barstool out of the way.

The first punch came as a right hook to my face. Came faster than my diverting and yielding, his fist slamming my left cheek, spinning me around in the colored-light wall décor of the Oasis—

—spinning back, yielding the space where Bushy Beard threw a video game kick. My arm diverted that swinging-up leg so his two-foot landing wobbled his side to me. I sank into my root to ride my push up beneath his rising balance.

But my *ti-fong* was off. He only bounced back a few feet, hit the barstool the greased worker'd evacuated, landed/whirled to charge me like a football tackler.

I slammed a palm heel strike into his forehead.

He blinked.

I thought I had him set up for a yield and spin as he charged—

—but he slipped/stumbled into me.

We crunched together.

Flew off our feet.

Tumbled in the air like entwined lovers.

Crashed to the barroom floor, on-top me counter-attacking his pounding arms while pulling away from his gorilla—

GZZZZT!

Me flat on the barroom floor beside Bushy Beard. Teeth clenched. Limbs flopping. Can't talk can't scream can't stop my racing heart gasping breaths.

Bartender Brenda jabs her Taser into Bushy Beard's shoulder.

GZZZZT!

Bushy Beard's collapse onto the floor bounces into tingling me.

Brenda strolls around where Bushy Beard writhes.

Comes to where I'm trembling on her barroom floor.

Leans over me.

Her eyes full of glee.

23

You must be feeling lucky tonight," said Sheriff Ross Fenton.

"Do I look lucky?" I told him.

My back leaned against the outside brick wall where the responding deputy'd ordered me to stay.

The Oasis's neon sign, a streetlight on the corner and the headlights of the marked cruiser lit the scene in the night. Maybe forty feet to my left, Bushy Beard shuffled between a chain link fence and the deputy.

The cool October night smelled like beer, dust, and *wanna go home.*

"Yeah," said Sheriff Wade, "I'd say you're lucky. Brenda loves her baseball bat, but she took pity on your sorry ass and used her Taser.

"The question is," he added: "You going to use your luck to be smart?"

"I try to."

I let him see my deep breath. My slump against the bricks where his law held me. Said: "What do you think I should do?"

"You've had a hard day."

"You have no idea."

"That shiner coming up under your eye pretty much tells the story. I thought you knew some kind of martial arts."

"Doesn't mean I'm any good at it."

Sheriff Ross put his hands on his gun belt. He stepped closer. Let his jack-hammer eyes knock the back of my skull against the hard brick wall.

"I was having a pretty good night 'fore I got the call about this," he told me. "Not that you give a shit.

"You come down to the Oasis looking for what? I was up the Evergreen with you. Then there were phone calls I had to take because of you.

"But this is my street," he said. "Way I can walk it tonight, arrest both your asses for disturbing the peace. Lock you up. You two can pay lawyers. Trade charges of assault. Make the folks back in the bar who didn't boogey before my deputy sirened up waste their time witnessing. Sounds like maybe you got some kind of 'the other guy started it,' but don't count on that meaning much.

"Plus, the owner of the Oasis might get rapped for your crap by the state liquor license control board. Then Brenda might lose her job. Ain't nobody in this town wants to lose the Oasis or deal with a pissed-off Brenda."

"What can I do so nobody has to?"

"Drop this," said the lawman. "No charges. No lawyers. You chose to come here. Walked into the Oasis pissed off like that was something special. Now pretend you're smart. Stay away from Darrell there and he stays away from you. Stay out the Oasis. After Darrell signs on, I give the nod and you drive the fuck home 'fore he leaves in his pickup to do the same.

"One more thing," he said. "Forget about your phone or plastic. What's in your pockets?"

I pulled a wad of random dollars from my black jeans. Showed the bills to him. They totaled $78, the remnants of an ATM withdrawal, my nostalgia for the way we all used to pay for what we did.

"Walk it back into the Oasis. Leave half of it on the bar for your tab and your trouble, Brenda's tip. There's a donation jar she keeps by the cash register: *The First Responders' Benefit Fund.* Put the rest of your *heartfelt* wad in there."

Brenda'd already collected my bar bill money *plus* what I'd left beside my beer stein and shot glass before the fight. Said not a word as I dropped the new bills on the wood. Reached for the donation jar before I even nodded toward it.

The tired-eyed couple now vibed an alive-again feel.

Would they rush home and have sex?

The greased worker in gray overalls was back on his stool, a drink in his hand, his eyes again lost in the bar mirror.

The hard blonde who'd sat by the door had skedaddled.

I zipped my black leather jacket and walked back out to the night.

Sheriff Ross stood by his deputy and Bushy Beard Darrell. The sheriff angled his head for me to get the hell out of there and I did as the two lawmen held Darrell there for him to pay his dues.

The rental car whipped backwards out of the angle parking job I'd done, drove away. The Oasis and all it meant shrank in my rearview mirror.

I clumped over the railroad tracks back to the south side of town. Drove up the two-block slope toward First Street. No oncoming headlights in my windshield. A glance down Main Street showed me a dozen cars parked on both sides of the street near the bars I should have gone to instead of the Oasis.

Should've, could've, would've.

The fact that we've all been in that car didn't make my ride any less glum.

Habit flicked on the right turn signal when I reached First Street half a block away from home and sent my eyes to my rearview mirror.

That mirror captured a moving yellow eye behind me.

A motorcycle.

Adrenalized but numb, it took me until I pulled the car to a stop at the curb in front of our house to realize what I'd seen. I whirled out from behind the steering wheel. Stood on the street where I'd grown up. Stared back through the night at the road that had taken me here.

Stared at the corner where no vehicle turned my way.

That night's smoky breeze. The rustling of October's leaves. The purr of a two-wheeler's engine idling around the corner where I couldn't see.

My heart thundered as I stood there alone in that streetlight night.

An invisible motorcycle revved.

Growled away unseen into darkness.

And I knew that from now on, I'd be a gunslinger.

24

That October Friday morning I woke up to face my bathroom mirror's reflection of a half-moon bruise cupping my left cheekbone. My ribs were sore. Crashing onto a barroom floor will do that to you.

Trying not to wince, I did *Taiji* in the chilly morning air.

Wasn't that art's fault I'd failed at its lessons.

Yeah, the Glock was never more than a fast reach away.

By 8:30, I'd checked my 'look' options in the full-length mirror Mom'd mounted on my bedroom's closet door. The Glock rode best and least noticeable in a shoulder holster under my black leather jacket.

At 8:37 I walked out my front door into the breeze of fallen gold and brown leaves skittering on the sidewalk. A bird flapped away from the two pine trees in our front yard. A Boomer's passing car's radio played John Fogerty singing "*. . . I ain't no fortunate son . . .*" as I turned the corner up past the Evergreen.

Forest fires' smoke filled the air as I hurried across the street to avoid Debby's family. The kids might ask about my bruise. The truth needed more than children's eyes to be seen and I wouldn't sell them some lie.

I walked, vibing my street time in DC. In Paris. San Francisco. In Laredo and Mazatlán. Hong Kong and biker bars in LA. Even Chicago where Katie and her family were safe—sure they were. The eyes behind my Ray-Ban sunglasses rode not zen focused on *something* but *Taiji* open to *everything*.

No motorcycles.

No car slowly driving behind me or toward me in a waterfall surveillance.

No *'shoes'* cover team reflected in parked cars' mirrors and windshields.

No glint of a sniper's scope in the Evergreen's windows.

Clatter filled the air as I walked into the Evergreen Center, most of it from the dining room packed by residents with walkers, wheelchairs, canes and two workable feet. No one sat behind the door-monitoring, open-countered office.

In the days I'd been coming, by 8:30 every morning, the breakfast crowd had thinned within a calm scene. That Friday morning showed me waving hands and turning heads. A white-aproned kitchen worker scurried to help distribute lopsided food trays with the business-suited Evergreen director Mrs. Gage.

All hands on deck since Irma got caravanned away.

Elevator or stairs?

There are never perfect choices.

I took the elevator. Preserved my breath and eased my sore bones.

Mom's door was closed. As I pushed it open with a click, I heard her cry out: "Thank God you finally got here! Please, I—"

Then the convex mirror showed her who walked into her room.

"Jim! I—the girls, nobody's been around this morning to . . ."

Then I was standing by her bed.

She saw the half-moon bruise on my cheekbone.

We let out our exhales. Took a breath. Two. Three.

A tear trickled down her pale pink cheek and her lips trembled.

We found each other's hand.

Mom whispered: "We . . . Jim, we . . . I've got to, I need to make you a deal."

"Whatever you need."

"Dinner came late last night, and since then, nobody's been back up to get the tray there I pushed away, don't care anymore but . . . The girls . . . Nobody came this morning to . . . I can't stand it anymore, I . . ."

She took a deep breath.

Let nothing but resolve fill her eyes.

"The girls haven't come," she said. "And . . . My diaper is soaked and I'm lying here trapped in my own piss and it burns, *oh it burns*, and . . .

"And the deal is this: I won't ask you about your black eye if you . . . I know I'm your mother, but . . . If you help me change my diaper, clean up a little, I won't ask you about what you did to get popped in the face."

Whatever was left of normal shattered in me.

"Deal," I said.

"But when Irma comes, ask her to look at your—"

Mom killed those thoughts. Steeled herself. Turned her head on the pillow toward the wall where she didn't have to see me seeing her face.

We got through it.

Then she wanted me to take away last night's dinner tray as much as I wanted to. Both of us needed a break. Some space. Some time to.

The dining room was empty when I walked in carrying my mom's tray but few of the breakfast places had been cleared of dirty dishes. I walked through the swinging doors into the kitchen where a puffy woman cook and a tired-looking dishwasher sprayed water and soap. Left the tray and left without a word.

The elevator took me back up to the second floor. The nurse's aide from yesterday's cemetery stood in the hall fussing over a delivery cart of breakfast trays and last night's retrieved dinner trays.

Gone was the blank face of a screen-mesmerized young woman just putting in her time. She turned to me with determination and a whiff of despair as she blew a stray lock of brown hair off her forehead.

"I don't know what we're going to do!" she said, cementing her belonging to this non-screen real time and place. "Mrs. Gage's trying to hire back Denise. Least she knows what to do even if she maybe did, maybe didn't, steal from the rooms. But *no way* are we taking back Kenny who the sheriff could never prove . . ."

She leaned sincerely to me: "Don't worry about your mom for that. Nobody'll let Kenny come sneaking back into these rooms no more."

"Thank you," I said. "For everything. For this."

She blinked. A sigh settled her shoulders under the weight they carried.

I asked her if she had Mom's breakfast tray. She did. I walked it down the long cream-colored corridor she still had to serve.

I cajoled Mom through her breakfast of cold pancakes, congealed eggs, warm orange juice. Mom counted the pills in the paper cup I showed her. She felt "pretty sure" they were the morning ones she was supposed to have.

We looked at each other.

She made the choice to swallow those pills. I didn't stop her.

Mark it as 10:33 when my cellphone buzzed a text.

I texted back: "Give me 20+"

Told Mom I'd be back around the time the noon whistle blew.

She whispered *thank you, see you, see you.*

Soon as I stepped into the hall, I started dictating a return text to sister Katie in Chicago, telling her what was going on. By the time the elevator let me out back on the first floor—still no one manning the front entrance/exit—I'd zapped the text Chi-Town way. I strode out of the building. Around the corner.

Was halfway back home half a block away when the driver's door opened on the green pickup truck parked behind my rental car out front of our house.

Out stepped Bushy Beard Darrell.

25

We saw each other see each other.

He held his hands out open and empty and wide. He wore a tucked-in-all-around gray shirt and no jacket to cover the nothing that was on his belt.

He saw my hands swinging empty and wide as I slow-walked toward him wearing my unzipped black leather jacket.

A cool Friday morning in early October. The wisp of distant fires in the air.

I circled around the front bumper of my rental car parked at the curb outside my house. My eyes focused on the canyon between my rental car's rear bumper and the front bumper of that parked green pickup truck. Bushy Beard Darrell filled that gap. He held his arms high by his shoulders. His open and empty palms stared at me like an extra pair of eyes.

He yelled: "This ain't me!"

"Sure fooled me." I stepped on the city sidewalk that was the legal border of *mine.* A swollen bruise like a third eye in his forehead made me proud.

"I'm not here for you! I'm not going to do anything to you or do bad!"

"Sheriff Fenton's not going to like you disobeying his orders."

"Yeah, well, he ain't the only boss."

I waited.

He said: "Can I put my hands down?"

"It's a free country."

"For who, motherfucker?" He stepped out from between our two vehicles and stood on the—on *my*—sidewalk. "Here's the deal.

"Phone call pulled me off the job and sent me here to tell you what I told them you didn't *need* to be told. But here I am, and like I told everybody already, you got nothing to worry about from me or anybody coming from me."

"That's the message you got sent to deliver? Who sent it?"

"I'm at the end of the line, asshole. I don't know who sent it. Whoever's got the clout to roll me out here like this."

His gray shirt was some company's issue. Had his name and number patch over the right pocket. I didn't know where he was born. Who his sixth grade crush was. The tomorrow he wanted. He turned to get in his pickup.

"Darrell!"

His eyes and bruise above that bushy red beard glared at me.

"Do you got a motorcycle?"

"You see my ride."

"You seen a motorcycle around?"

"Are you fucking nuts?"

"Yeah. But all this . . . You and me, we're both in the same bar."

"Maybe," he said. "But who gets told where to go?"

26

B*uzz* went the door and I walked into Last Chance Guns with P.S. coffees in my hands and darkness's crescent moon under my heart-side eye.

"You look *fabulous*," said Cody.

"Fuck you," I said with a *'deserve it'* wince.

I told him. Irma. My mom. My close encounters of the Darrell kind.

Cody said: "So, a motorcycle."

"I can't be sure."

"I got that. Do you got any sense of *who*?"

"Well you're not moonlighting, so, no."

"I'll be around now," he said in a voice that wouldn't let me tell him *no*.

My nod told him more than *yes*.

"Did you get what we talked about?" I said.

"You can sling one across your shoulder and carry the rest, or I can carry one so you have a hand free or pamper your hurts."

"I can get home just fine. I gotta check on Mom. But do you have time during lunch to come up and give me a hand?"

Cody ignored the clock mounted above racks of rifles: "I got time now."

27

The steel blue suit Cody loaned me for the wedding was a little tight in the pants, long in the leg and a lot loose in the jacket—

—which was lucky, because that better hid the shoulder-holstered Glock.

Cody's dark blue silk necktie lay perfectly against my maroon shirt that I'd brought over to Debby's house last night before I'd gone to the Oasis. I'd offered her $20 to wash and iron it—a sexist assumption of skill and a logical deduction from how well she took care of her kids. Debby argued that was too much. Countered with $15. We compromised on $25. She used her morning break from cashiering at the grocery store to drive back home, get the shirt to me. Gave me a sad *oh* but no questions when she saw my black eye.

Mom liked the look of me in that suit when I went back to the Evergreen Center. Her bedding looked fresh and her lunch had been delivered.

We talked a lot of nothings for the hour-plus I sat with her. I tried hard *not* to want to leave. Failed. Three o'clock's arrival sent me on my way.

The meal cart parked in the middle of the green carpet in the cream-colored tunnel of that assisted living facility held trays of lunch-leavings piled on for the dishwasher to spray with hot sudsy water.

I was two steps away from that metal cart when a blue-scrub, chunky woman shuffled out of an apartment door, her hands empty.

"Hi," I said. "I'm Mary Traven's son. Is everything settled down?"

"*Ah*, yeah," she said.

Tick tick tick went the clock in my head. *Gotta go, gotta go.*

But tingles up my spine made me sink my *chi* and stay.

My eyes stayed steady on blue-scrub her: "I've never seen you here."

She blinked.

"I mean, I watch out for all the people who help take care of my mother."

"And I gotta get to it," she said, put the cart between us to push it away—

—but I stood in the cart's way.

"Look," she said. "I just started here today."

Blink: "You worked here before."

"I left for a while."

"And your name is . . . ?"

No place for her to dodge. No time to try.

She said: "Denise."

"Welcome back, Denise." I stepped out of the cart's way. Adjusted the knot on my necktie. Strolled to the elevator. "See you around."

My aunt waved me in after I politely horn-tapped the rental car parked at her curb. I slow-walked to her front door.

"We've got to scurry," said my aunt. "Come in."

Led me into a bathroom snapped pink and bright by the switch she threw.

She shuffled me so my left side faced the mirror. Picked up a small tube.

"Bev," I said, "I don't want any makeup."

"Hush," she said from somewhere past seventy. Dabbed cream on her finger. Stroked the dab over the yellow-black bruise below my left eye. "We all need to look as good as we can."

She turned my face to the mirror.

And I saw the clown.

But his left eye looked more human than before.

"Now we gotta go," said Aunt Bev, "or we'll never get a good seat."

The Lutheran church was across the street and down to the corner from my childhood home. The rental car drove me and my aunt back to where I'd started that day—only this time, I parked in our driveway because the curbs on the street were lining themselves with wedding guests' rides.

"Told you so," said my aunt as we quick-walked the long block to the open doors into that version's house of God.

Stained-glass windows glowed on each side of the sanctuary of pews. Vases of flowers stood up front by the platforms leading up to a cross on the altar. I could smell the scent of their roses even in the smoky breeze from outside.

My aunt seemed to know everyone. A wave here, a nod there, a smile. We sat in the middle of a pew three rows from the back of the church. Couples older than me but younger than my aunt crammed the pew on either side of us.

The portly and balding man pressed against my right shoulder coughed. Bathed me with his cigarette breath. His germs. I flashed on the three high-quality plague masks in my across-the-street suitcase.

Organ music played.

I spotted them in the crowd in a pew four rows from the front.

Queen Dee perched on the end of that pew beside the church's center aisle. A royalty hat cupped her shellacked silver hair.

Counselor/cousin/kissy *Ter-Ter* sat to her right, stared straight ahead.

Yes!

I spotted Lana between people fussing in the pews between us. Sitting on the other side of Terry. Her black hair flowed in waves to her shoulders.

What was the expression on her war-painted face? What was she wearing? Had she crossed her legs as she sat in that pew?

Questions and wants tumbled through me. No one could see them on my face.

The shuffling, packed crowd gave me glimpses of Ron's flaxen dome.

The organ chorded.

All eyes shifted to the center aisle.

The organ played standard processional music. Three mid-twenties bros marching down the aisle behind the groom shucked and jived to beats only they could hear. They didn't seem to be imagining the same song. Or maybe they were just bad dancers. One of them wore wraparound sunglasses.

Three bridesmaids in fancy green dresses slow-marched up the aisle with more control and seriousness than their assigned ceremonial partners waiting for them in a line at the altar.

Ooos and *ohs* flowed from the crowd. A kindergarten girl in a white dress tossed flower petals onto the path she walked toward where adulthood waited.

Five seconds behind her came a slick-haired boy her age. He struggled to keep the pillow he carried balanced on his offering arms.

"Aaa-choo!" went the ring-bearer as he walked past my pew. He swooped his right arm to wipe the snot off his face and snapped it away in a mist.

Loving chuckles flowed through the pews around me.

But I saw three different faces flinch at that *oh-oh* sound:

Plague, paranoia, and pain cast long shadows.

The ring-bearer made it to the altar with only one more sneeze.

TA-DAH! came a loud organ chord.

All of us in that congregation obeyed that command to rise.

A woman in white appeared at the doors into the church.

A man who beamed *father* was at her side.

The glowing bride walked toward the altar and her waiting groom. Nerves and joy trembled her lips.

Tears glistened her escorting father's eyes.

She froze when she reached our third pew from the back of the church.

The organ stopped.

The maid of honor tapped a cellphone.

Blasting out of speakers came one of that era's pop music megahits from a woman singer the bride's mid-twenties age. The church filled with a song full of *Un-hun, un-hun*s, a *boomity-boomity-boomity* beat, lyrics of: *"Yeah got it going on, gonna go like I catch, don't call me baby, I'm big time bee-atch."*

The bride broke into dancing to the beat and whirling down the aisle. I knew I'd soon be able to find the production on YouTube and Instagram.

The father of the bride gamely danced down the aisle behind his daughter. Made it to the altar in time for her to whirl and give him a hug, get his kiss on her cheek. He sat beside the Obvious Mother in the front pew.

The maid of honor tapped her cellphone. Loudspeaker music died.

The bride clutched the bouquet of flowers in front of her groin as she stared at the man she'd come here to claim.

The white-robed minister between where the golden cross rose and the happy couple stood. His arms opened wide as he said: "You may be seated."

We did as we were told.

Words from him flowed over the trapped audience. Everything you'd expect. Promises were asked and delivered. Rings slid onto waiting fingers from the cushion held by the little boy who managed not to sneeze. Came the pronouncement and that first married kiss.

The crowd clapped and hooted.

And I clapped with them. Clapped from my heart. My eyes misted.

The bride and groom led the way back up the aisle. Their wedding party crew sashayed behind them—including Mr. Never Takes Off His Shades.

Then each row took its turn to send wedding guests up the center aisle to follow the wedding party's exit, starting with the pews at the front of the church.

Aunt Bev said: "We won't get out in time to see her toss the bouquet!"

My eyes locked on the parade walking up the aisle.

Lana looked from side to side as she followed Queen Dee who was being escorted by her loving son. Their company lawyer walked near the elderly Dee, his arms obviously ready to catch her if she fell.

Lana spotted me through the crowd when she was four pews away.

I knew she saw my pounding heart.

Her black hair flowed on the shoulders of a blue dress. She wore her war paint and wore it well. But she wore it today like it was expressing herself and not someone else's expectations. Her eyes widened as the parade pushed her past me. I couldn't read the line of her slicked red lips.

Then she was gone. Out the open doors to sunlight and smoke from distant fires. Out to watch a bride toss her bouquet.

The Zanes had left by the time my aunt and I walked out of the church. The bouquet had been caught by a stunned woman who already had rings on her left hand. She stared at the flowers as if they had something to say. Wedding guests were opening and closing the doors on their cars, driving away.

"We gotta go," urged my aunt as we walked toward my parked car, but it was me who was setting the fastest pace she could handle.

No motorcycles rode in my mirrors as we drove away.

The giant sign over the doors into Barb's Ribs:

CLOSED FOR PRIVATE EVENT

The parking lot overflowed with cars. My aunt and I parked at the truck stop's graveled lot down the hill from Barb's. We took our time walking up the hill. Were careful not to slip on the rocks shifting beneath our feet. Crossed the road to Barb's turf. The air was chilly. The distant fires' smoke haze seemed thicker.

A band was setting up on a big deck jutting out from the back of Barb's. They were one of those talented *Wows!* shotgunned throughout America's small towns. I knew some of the guys in the band. Had met the pale woman who worked at the prison and sang the band's playlist of classic rock, outlaw country and new Americana with a husky voice straight out of the blues clubs back when racism's segregation ruled my Baby Boomer parents' childhood.

A man on the deck plugged in an outer ring of outdoor heaters.

Lamp poles held other heaters even though this autumn night held no chill.

A stranger held the door into Barb's open for my aunt and me.

The vast dining area of the restaurant had been reorganized so that two buffet tables made the opposite borders of where guests would sit and socialize.

Buffet tables nearest the bar held metal bins of juicy roast beef. Pasta. Vegetables. Rolls. Shrimp unfrozen for the party. Three different salads.

Buffet tables deeper in the restaurant by the back wall of windows and doors leading out to where the band was setting up held desserts.

And the wedding cake.

Waiting.

"Hey, how are you?" said Barb. She hugged my aunt. Gave me a smile. Gave us each two poker chips with her bar's logo.

"After that," she said, "you two are drinking on your own. Knowing you, Bev, you better hope this guy brought his big bucks with him for extra rounds."

Aunt Bev laughed: "Oh, I tell you!"

Whatever that meant, it was enough to let us walk away with grace.

We saw smiles. Heard laughs—a few whoops by where the wedding party of men and women near my age huddled. Two bridesmaids fussed over each other's makeup. Mister Never Takes Off His Shades macked on one of the bridesmaids. She politely watched. People everywhere in the bar stared into cellphone screen portals.

Aunt Bev explained (again) how we were related to the bride as we climbed on stools positioned at one of the tall tables permanently bolted to the floor. A server collected chips for Aunt Bev's red beer and my ginger ale.

"Smart," said my aunt as the white-shirt, black-pants server walked away. "You've already got one souvenir from a night of drinking."

The wedding party filled the restaurant. Men in suits. Women in dresses. Children in whatever *nice* their parents found in the kids' drawers that still fit. Loud chatter. Laughs. Lots of *"Hi!"* and *"Thank you"* and *"Here let me help you."* Some of the clichés from Bushy Beard Darrell floated through the chatter. My aunt wanted to eat right away "before all the good stuff gets gone."

And it was when we joined the line at the main course buffet table that I finally spotted them.

The four of them were locked together in a booth near the back wall's dessert table and the wedding cake. Queen Dee sat facing the front doors of the restaurant and the main course buffet table where I shuffled. Orange-haired Ron sat to her right. I spotted the back of Terry sitting across from Queen Dee in the booth's other free to leave spot. That meant Lana sat unseen and trapped back against the wall in the curve of the booth's horseshoe.

My aunt sprinted around me with a piled-high plate she plopped down on our table as she headed toward the dessert buffet. She gave the Zanes a polite nod.

Queen Dee's burning eyes spotted me across the room.

Two men shuffled behind me in the buffet line.

"Hell of a good spread," said one of the men.

"Well," said the other, "Henry deserves to give it to his daughter. And Rose, she deserves it, too. Gotta be proud of her. Look how well she grow'd up."

"Yeah. Say, you eat at that new Clyde Packers down by the airport yet? You go down to the big city regular."

"Bigger doesn't make someplace better than places like here," he said. "Only time Holly-*weird* or back-east people see us is when they look down."

"Sad truth is, you kinda got that one right. Course a herd of them bought up big houses in ski and hip spots like Bozeman. They click computers on their kitchen tables if'n they even have to work. Now folks like you and me can't afford to live where we grew up and busted our asses working."

They shuffled a few inches further down the line with all the rest of us.

I was at the steaming silver tray of raviolis when they started talking again.

"Yeah," said the man who was closest behind me, "that Clyde Packers place: I don't like to go there."

"Why? It's a good chain."

"They . . . you know . . . They got a Black guy who runs the place."

"Ahh . . ."

"I mean, one thing he's a dishwasher, right? But the out-front boss? Makes me uncomfortable—or what do the kids call it now: *triggered*."

"Ahh . . ."

"*I know, I know*: We're supposed to say *African American* now. Sorry."

I stomped out of the line. Didn't look back. Didn't want to see who they were. Didn't want to know. Didn't want to end up throwing punches. Didn't want to have that fight crash into the wedding cake.

On the way back to our table, full plate in my hand, librarian Halle spotted me, waved and grinned. That eased me enough to send her a smile.

My angle of retreat gave me a clear view through the crowd into the Zanes' booth. I saw Ron. Saw him see me.

As I shifted through the crowd, I heard a different man's voice say: "*Know it's rough and no way is it fair. But things'll turn around. You'll get through this.*"

His friend replied "*Yeah*" like they both believed it.

I reached our table before Aunt Bev, switched our drinks on its circular surface and sat on the stool she'd had so I was facing the wedding cake.

She made no comment about that.

Her eyes and smiles skimmed through the crowded function as she carved the steamy slab of red meat on her plate. I'd take bites to keep her company.

"Glad to see your friend Cody isn't here," she told me.

"What? Why?"

"Well, *you know*: He had a thing with the bride, Rose."

"What are you talking about?"

"See what happens when you leave town? You miss out on what goes on."

She slid a forkful of juicy meat into her mouth. Finished the bite. Then said: "And I bet he never told you either. Cody's like that. Keeps his secrets."

"How the hell do you know about that . . . *whatever*?"

"Family knows." She stared right at me with that message.

Let it sink in.

Said: "Rose isn't so quiet about things. The thing with Cody was over weeks before our groom finally got to start up with her."

She waved to where I then looked. Saw waitress Elly from the Chat & Chew wearing church clothes as the gray bearded manager of the truck stop handed her a drink and they both toasted us.

The ginger ale I sipped in reply felt too weak to convey my sincerity.

Black screens filled ten of the twelve giant TVs positioned high on the walls. The two screens positioned above the bar played loops of photos and short videos. Bride and groom each got their own screen, streams of their lives played

MOS—not the military designation of personnel's occupational assignment, but Hollywood's *"mit out sound"* coined by a German film director long before my generation got the birthing doctor's spank into life.

Sound faded as I watched the celebration of a wedding that wasn't mine.

Two groomsmen slow-mo lunged into sweat-slapping high-fives.

Two my-generation women hugged.

A mother bent over to console her glum-faced, thigh-high son.

Somebody else's husband bumped into somebody else's wife, a back-to-back collision at the buffet line that turned them around to see *who*, see *what*, their mouths letting their MOS laughs spraying out over the plates of food they held.

Librarian Halle stood with a couple who had their backs to me.

Barb's husband Gary—who'd made his Tap Room into the heart of so much of what was right about this town—joked with wedding guests as Social Security–age him helped out his wife's business by busing dishes to the kitchen.

Bride Rose led her groom from booth to booth, table to table. Her face glowed with joy and hope and duty. He beamed like he couldn't believe all this.

Rushing in on me came a waterfall of sounds. Clattering plates. Waves of overlapping conversations. Laughter. A guitar tuning up on the back deck outside where the sky'd turned gray. Thunders of my heart: *now, now, now.*

"Let me get you some more cookies," I told my aunt.

Walked away before her reply.

My eyes targeted the dessert buffet. The wedding cake. *Closer, closer—*

"Hey there!" called out Ron's voice from the booth to my left and I turned, dramatizing the visible lie that I hadn't expected that. "Get over here, say hi."

Queen Dee smiled up at me from her place at the edge of the booth.

I walked over to stand in the center of their horseshoed attention.

Lana glanced away from me as she sat in the back of the booth.

Ron said: "You remember my mother, don't you?"

"How could I forget."

Queen Dee gave me a nod. "What a pleasure, I'm sure."

"Whoa!" yelled her son. "Hell of a shiner you got. What did you do?" He answered his own question like he'd used the line before somehow, sometime, with or about somebody else: "Run into a door?"

"I've been running into doors my whole life," I said. "Then through them."

"Well it's a good look for you, *Jimbo*. Reminds you to be careful."

Cousin Terry slid out of the booth to my left: "Join us. Sit a spell."

Those two men and one old woman who shared Zane blood stared at me.

Lana's brown eyes focused on the white-clothed table.

My choreography kept my unbuttoned suitcoat from swaying open. I slid over the booth's leather cushion until I sat with Lana on my left. Terry slid back into the booth. Trapped me in there. Shoved against me so I had to slide closer to Lana. Our warm thighs touched. Our shoulders pressed together. I kept my left arm down so she couldn't feel the shoulder-holstered gun.

Ron said: "So what'd you do that ended up with you looking like this?"

"Worked out an understanding."

"How does the other guy look?"

"Like he gets it."

Terry said: "It's important that both of you understand *what's what.*"

Lana and I both knew who Terry's "you" really was.

Queen Dee said: "James, I'd love to hear about your marvelous life."

I nodded to the lucky couple swirling past their waiting cake toward the outside patio where the band seemed ready to play: "This is their day."

Dee said: "Every day is what we make it."

"*Hey,*" said her son. "*Lana*: You two haven't even said *hi* to each other."

He turned to his mother: "You should have heard the two of them when we all had dinner the other night—and the night before that, too. Babbling about books and movies, TV shows, all that kind of stuff none of us give a crap about."

Ron grinned at Lana and me.

"What's the matter, you two?" he said. "Cat got your tongue?"

He leered like he was only joking: *"Here pussy, pussy, pussy!"*

Lawyer/cousin Terry dropped reins on his *best friend*: "Now don't go getting all wild and crazy on us here, Ron. We don't want us just having fun to take away from all of us paying our respects to two loyal employees."

Like I didn't know, Terry said: "The bride and groom work at our bank."

"I hope that's good for them," I said.

"Now I've got to go," I told the table. "I promised cookies to my aunt."

Ron said: "Promises need to be kept."

"You're right." I let my pause sink in. "About that."

I turned my body in the crowded booth to move Terry who sat between me and standing up to walk away. That pressure pushed me against Lana.

Her soft inhale made me tremble.

I slid out of the booth.

Ron said: "But you're not leaving, Jim. We'll see you later, yes?"

My feet were back on the public space outside the Zanes' horseshoe.

Lana's anxious eyes met mine for the first time since I'd reached the booth.

I said: "I'm sticking around."

Queen Dee slid out of and up from the booth with an easy grace her peers at the Evergreen would have envied.

"I feel like something sweet, too," she said, put her hand on my elbow to direct me past the wedding cake toward the far end of the dessert table.

She waited until our alibi of getting desserts for the meal we'd been given had taken us as far away as possible from the horseshoe booth. Other wedding guests socially distanced away from where we put cookies on small white plates.

"Your foolish bruise seems to be healing," whispered Queen Dee.

"You!"

She gave me a regal pink smile.

"You made Darrell come see me this morning. Make sure I knew he was under control."

"No need to thank me. But it wasn't *actually* me."

"So you ordered someone to push his button. How'd you know?"

"This is my town," she said, like that was all I needed to know.

"I told you: I'm here to help you. Protect you, even. Or whatever."

"Or whatever? So you can maybe push a different button?"

"Like what we talked about when I visited your mother. How's she doing up there at the Evergreen with all the problems they're having?"

The small white plate of cookies in my hand rose between us.

I gave the queen my coldest smile: "Enjoy your . . . desserts."

Walked away.

Crossed that crowded room to my aunt, who took the plate of cookies from my grip, set it on the table, looked at me and said: "Should I ask?"

Strum of a guitar and the rolling rhythm of drums as the band outside rocked into its first song of the night.

Some wedding guests sat where they were. A few adults were pulled along by the hands of children who they lived to follow. Many souls at this *somebody-else's-wedding* wandered outside to where that music might ease their blues.

"You go on out there now," said Aunt Bev. "At my age, sitting to the beat works best for me. 'Sides, I already either know the songs they're playing or the ones I don't know won't matter much to me now."

I left her alone at our table.

Let the music pull me towards it.

The band played John Stewart's "Daydream Believer" from my dad's era.

I sharked through the crowd toward the outside back porch and patio.

Where was she?

I made it outside as the band played a current country rocker. A husband and wife hit the dance floor out front of the band and their neighbors' eyes.

People I cared about kept stopping me in the crowd to say *hi*. To see how I was. Hear how my mother was in her hospital bed at the Evergreen where Denise was and Irma wasn't. I pushed platitudes as I pushed my way through the crowd. Circled the tables around the dance floor, my eyes searching for—

Lana sat locked in a chair at a table across the dance floor from me.

Terry sat at her right.

Ron sat on her left.

Queen Dee sat just outside their triangle.

I'd missed the classic "First Dance." Now the bride and groom kept turning away from their dancing to take hugs and kisses on their cheeks from people standing shoulder to shoulder in the crowd. The bride broke away from one couple. Reached back to pull her groom onto the dance floor. Raised his arms to circle her neck as the music shuffled them together.

"Two years," muttered the gruff voice of some middle-aged man behind me. "Then the only *touch me* he'll be getting is when she makes him zip up her dress."

A proud father danced with his little girl balanced on his shoes.

Ron spotted me.

That triggered Lana to see me standing across the dance floor from her.

Because this was Sidner, Montana, because brilliance defies time, because it always pleased the crowd, the band strummed into The Way-Back Machine for my grandfathers' Hank Williams: "Hey, Good Looking!"

Ron leered. Grabbed Lana's hand. Jerked her out of her seat and around the table. Spun her onto the dance floor. And *yeah*, his shoes knew how to move.

Knew the evolved jitterbug/cowboy two-step. He trapped at least one of her hands through every spinning twirl.

But I saw every connection he pulled her in to glide into *her* dance, *her* way, held back only *by*. Her red lips barely parted but her black hair whipped through the night air and her hunter's eyes grabbed glimpses of me.

Ron whirled Lana closer through music-shuffling couples toward where I stood locked on the edge of that dance floor strung with colored light bulbs.

Hank's song stopped.

Ron spun Lana through multiple twirls, sent her flying into me.

Her dancer's hands grabbed my shoulders.

Her dizzy face snapped up to mine.

Heartbeats of who and where we were. And weren't. Could be.

"What a great idea!" Ronald said for the listening crowd, for Dee and Terry sitting at that distant table. "*Of course* you should dance with Jim, honey."

A guitar being tuned plucked over that dance floor.

Publicly adoring husband Ron pressed against wife Lana. He leaned close to speak into her ear. Slid his eyes sideways to be sure I heard him too.

"Never say I never gave you nothing, darling," he told her.

What any witnesses but me saw was him giving her a kiss on the cheek.

I saw Ron lick her.

Walk off with nods to those who knew he was a prince.

Strum went the guitar on the bandstand and everyone heard *get ready.*

The band played that long song with the slow dance beat.

The woman who worked in the prison stepped to the mike.

Her husky voice sang the tale's heartbreak and hope.

My arms rose beneath Lana's.

I took her right hand in my left. The velvet of her grip not guiding, not dropping her weight on me, not demanding:

Melding.

My right hand brushed where the small of her back hourglassed down to her hips. I fought grabbing her tight. Pulling the swell of her breasts against my chest. Pulling her clothed body against my surging. I ached to let my right palm slowly stroke down over the bell of her hips. Cup her. *Squeeze.*

We danced amidst the crowd as the band played at the wedding where the vanilla-iced cake topped by tiny dolls of a groom and bride was not for us.

My every breath inhaled Lana. Her musk perfume. Her warm flesh.

Lana's slicked red lips whispered only to me: "I can't stand this."

"Me either," I said. "You're not alone. I'm with you."

We turned with grace. As if we'd practiced. As if we'd always been dancing.

Lana said: "What are we going to do?"

I said: "Tomorrow."

And she said *yes*.

Told her the needs, the *hows*.

And she said *yes*.

The band played. Our bodies swayed. Their heat. The ache of our flesh. The hell of getting to be *oh so close*. Colored lights strung the horizon of the night. All around us danced couples in their own embrace. The night air smelled of smoke from fires beyond the soft lit world of one wedding's dance floor outside Barb's Ribs in my Montana hometown in that *going going gone* moment.

28

The day that was that tomorrow.

Saturday morning.

My watch read 9:11.

Maybe twenty parked cars lined Main Street.

Steam hissed as I stepped up to the coffee service counter in the P.S.

"Hi!" said the woman behind the P.S. counter. "Can we getcha the usual for you and Cody?"

"Make it three today."

She blinked, but with a *one more sale* smile.

"All café au laits," I said.

"Want a sugar for one of 'em?"

"God, I hope not."

That just came out of me. Hope for what I didn't know.

Steam hissed.

She handed me a gray disposable tray holding three lidded tall paper cups: "You need help with the door?"

"I got it."

I hit the sidewalk at 9:17. My black leather jacket hung partially zipped against the chilled smoky morning. I wore my last clean shirt: blue with my cellphone in its heart pocket. The Glock rode under the jacket on my right hip.

Off to my left ran:

The Chat & Chew with its wall of windows where I'd first *seen*.

The locked doors of the sad Roxy where my rental car waited at the curb.

The Lowdown, where on a Saturday like that night, my "local hero" odds for feminine companionship might be both good *and* lonely.

The Western wear plus high school letterman's jackets store that most days couldn't have sold more than three snap-button cowboy shirts.

'Cross the street from me waited the propped-open door to the Tap Room.

Past the Tap, far off to my right, rose the giant sign for the Zanes' bank.

On my side of the street off to my right stretched:

Cody's gun store.

Re-Runs—an *anything used* store, from clothes to toys to silverware that refugees from Sidner left behind on their way to *has-to-be-something-better.*

A state-owned liquor store.

A formerly family-owned drug store that sold *once-was* postcards of our town when snail mail meant more than a quick toss into the recycle bin.

Across the side road into Main Street rose a five-story-tall, faded orange brick building that had been boarded up my whole life:

The Rainbow Hotel.

Grim locals called that ghost "the pot."

As in "the pot of gold."

As in what's really waiting at the end of the rainbow.

From there Main Street ran west towards the highway out of town.

No vehicles cruising or parked on Main Street demanded my attention.

Cody buzzed me into his gun store.

A man I vaguely remembered as one of the older guys back in high school stood across the glass counter from Cody, cradling an assault rifle in his arms. He turned it this way and that. Stroked its plastic and steel.

"Yo, Lloyd," said Cody. "Do me a favor? I gotta talk to Jim here one to one.

"Don't worry," Cody added. "That beauty is only leaving here with a paying customer, and you're the only one who's got eyes on it."

Lloyd looked at Cody. Looked at me. Looked at the assault rifle.

Laid it down on the glass counter. Nodded. Walked out the buzzed door.

"Sorry to cost you a sale," I said.

I put the coffees' gray paper tray on the glass counter beside the assault rifle akin to the Russian people-killers carried by jungle warriors who'd mangled Dale. He was now probably on a Tap Room stool waiting for breakfast he had to eat if he wanted a beer to help fight off the screams.

"Don't worry," said Cody. "Lloyd's almost saved up enough to walk out of here heavy."

Cody said: "We ready?"

"As can be," I said.

Gave him what I had.

Plus one hot cup of coffee.

Set the other two cups on the glass counter.

Cody said: "How was the wedding?"

"You never told me about you and Rose."

Cody didn't blink. Looked straight in my eyes.

"We never got far enough to tell you more than that."

"How do you feel? About her married now?"

"What's gone is gone."

"*Yes* and *no*," I said. "*Gone* is just another state of *going on*."

"I know the physics."

"Knowing isn't all that matters."

His eyes that usually bored through me softened.

"I had to break it," he said. "She wanted me all the way, but didn't want all the ways of me. She was too nice."

"What about you?"

"I'm me. Hell, she started to push before we'd even gotten to where I could tell her enough about what that meant for her to really decide. She didn't want to see enough to know enough and that wasn't enough for me. Plus, the *'wonder if's'* were starting to run into the *'won'ts.'*"

Cody's eyes bored into me: "You've got to face who you are. No matter what something or somebody else makes you want to be. *Right?*"

I took a sip from one of the coffees I'd brought into his place.

"Right?" he said again.

"You know me."

"Down through your bones, motherfucker. You strapped?"

"Yeah."

"You sure you don't want my CS?"

CS—counter-surveillance.

"Thanks, but I'll run clean—and careful, very careful."

"Don't just watch your six: Work the whole sphere. Keep your phone charged. My car's gassed. I'll get to *wherever* like a shot."

We both knew that shot might not be fast enough *if.*

But my nod said *yes*, said *respect*, said *brother.*

The black hands of the clock on his wall pointed to 9:27.

The red hand swept its way toward *when*.

Cody said: "You see your mom this morning? What'd she say?"

"Drive careful."

"*Ha!*" said Cody. "Little late for that. And not just for this."

The clock on his wall read 9:29.

"Now," I told Cody.

He came around the counter—*yeah*, he was strapped, too.

Buzzed his door and held it open for me as I held a coffee in each hand.

Let me walk out into that chilly Main Street morning alone.

29

Saturday morning meant there were fewer potential witnesses to see me standing there on the sidewalk holding two cups of coffee. But the timing couldn't be helped. The red second hand sweeping around the big clock waits for nobody.

I saw no motorcycle parked on Main Street or passing by.

Looked to the east and saw what I needed to see waiting there.

Slowly walked that way toward my car parked in front of the Roxy.

Out of the Tap Room came Gary, looking like my father might have if he'd lived. Gary angled across Main Street toward the Chat & Chew. I figured my assumption of Dale's breakfast routine was accurate. Gary gave me a nod, a smile, slowed his pace so we wouldn't meet in front of the Chat & Chew's picture window with me carrying the competition's coffee.

Out of the corner of my eye, I saw waitress Elly inside her café. Knew she saw me walking past with my hands full of a sale that could have been hers. Knew she witnessed me step off the sidewalk in front of an *everybody knows who* sedan parked right in front of her café and turn toward its driver's door.

That parked car's driver's window slid down.

Lana sat behind the steering wheel.

She looked stunning. Savvy. Determined. She looked scared.

I passed her a cup of coffee.

Asked: "Are you OK?"

"Do we even know what that question means?"

I took a sip of my coffee.

She drank from her cup, pulled it away from her lips. Her red lipstick brightened the coffee's white lid.

"Drive careful," I told her. "Speed limit. Eyes open. You got your phone?"

"Since I was twelve," she said.

"Anything strange, call me. And keep your eyes open for a motorcycle."

Her brown eyes searched me for *why*.

"Don't worry. I'll be right behind you."

"You better be," she said.

I turned, walked toward my ride parked behind her rear bumper.

Heard the hum of her rising window.

I clunked open the door of my rental car and looked around for witnesses.

A mom and her three kids left Re-Runs. Gary came out of the Chat & Chew carrying a white Styrofoam box. Headed to the Tap and Dale again—and again and again.

A man swept the sidewalk in front of a store where I knew no customers were waiting or likely to crowd. He had to know the dust he was pushing off his property would float away in the chilly morning west wind to someone else's land just as sure as that same chilly wind would blow the dust of others onto what was his. And on he swept.

There'd been changes in the parked cars since I showed up on Main Street that Saturday morning. Now some of those four-wheeled people movers had gone and some new ones had arrived, but nothing caught my eye in that usual small Montana town cast of pickups, family sedans, vans. Sheriff Fenton's cruiser was not among them, nor were any other "cop" looking cars or a wedge of darkness Tesla Cybertruck.

No motorcycles.

My black leather jacket unzipped with a rumble. As it came off, I made sure to keep it draped over the gun on my right hip, slid behind the steering wheel of my car, confident, if not certain, there'd been no eyes that saw I was packing.

I slammed the car door. Positioned the jacket with my black nylon attaché on the shotgun seat where no partner waited. Even though my cellphone was 100%, I plugged its charger cord into the car's dashboard. Snapped on the seat belt. Keyed the engine. The satellite radio played the channel for classic jazz.

My cellphone rode the console's cup holder. Jazz is not really me. *I mean*, Coltrane and Brubeck, Mingus, Monk and Cannonball, *sure*, but my soul wants stories made by music *and* words.

Yet I didn't Bluetooth my Spotify or any of the Internet radio channels I'd downloaded and let fill my listening hours. Through the car's speakers that Saturday morning, I didn't want my personal AI programming telling me what to feel. Nor did I spin the channel to any of the rock song channels I'd sampled.

One way or another, this trip around the sun would be jazz.

My fingers flashed my headlights.

They winked in her driver's side mirror.

She pulled away from the curb, headed west on Main Street.

I checked my mirrors: No oncoming vehicles.

Hit the left blinker.

Checked the empty sidewalks on both sides of the street.

Cranked the steering wheel, surged out of the parking place.

Her car filled my windshield as we drove away.

30

An empty four-lane interstate highway lined the rolling fields of prairie and golden and brown chessboard farmlands south of Sidner. I drove that road out of town as I had hundreds of times before that Saturday's paranoia and promise.

Leaving my hometown always flicks my eyes to the car mirrors. I glimpsed my pink high school vanish as the land I traveled rose out of the town's valley.

If you could see yourself now, I thought of those high school days.

Jesus, how did I get here?

Far off to my left was where Lana and I claimed our only kiss.

The prison flowed past on the right. That chain link and razor wire, crime and sorrow factory whizzed past in less than a minute. Every second bled.

My shoulders relaxed as the prison vanished and the shotgun seat's window filled with the saw tooth ridges of the fifty miles away Rocky Mountains.

Off to the right came Doomsday. A chain link and laser-optic caged missile silo burrowed into a prairie field. Some of the Minutemen Intercontinental Ballistic Missile silos buried during the early days of rock 'n' roll in that stretch of Montana had been retired. Not because of wondrous *Global Peace*: 21st century cyber America was spending one trillion dollars modernizing Dr. Strangelove's Armageddon dreams. Martin County still had two missile sites—the one east of town past the *Oily Boid* road sign, and this one south of the prison.

A genius jazz piano'd the morning as I drove past the exit sign to Sidner's Country Club where there'd recently been a banquet.

I wondered what she wore then.

How she'd dressed to show her 'fuckability.'

How no one there could see all the wonders of her.

The highway curved around, dove into the Eve River Valley: a half mile slope down this side of the valley, across that sixty-foot bridge over the river, then a half mile straightaway so truckers could rev their engines to carry them up the quarter-mile steep slope of the other side.

My windshield captured Lana's car gliding up that far slope as my ride hummed down the hill toward the bridge.

Coonskin-caps Lewis and Clark named this river "Eve." They'd been traveling so long and so hard up the Mississippi and then the Missouri that they wanted to believe this mere thirty feet wide in places and in other places wadeable during dry summers was *at last* the mother of their new America's western waters. Naming the river after the legendary first of mankind's mothers seemed only right. They were wrong. There were further waters.

We were nine miles from town when we topped the slope out of the river valley. We'd only seen two cars going the other way, north to Sidner, or more likely, Canada. There'd been two trucks roaring south almost in tandem when Lana and I looped onto the interstate, but all I could see of them then was a puff of black smoke over the rise of a hill. My mirrors showed the empty road spooling away from my rushing wheels.

We each passed a minivan full of grade school kids whose jerseys implied Saturday morning soccer. A zombie-faced mother muscled that steering wheel. Kept her eyes locked on the road ahead of her clown car of chaos. Lana and I were both back in the right-side lane when a tan van blew past both of us.

The radio played but I didn't really hear the jazz trumpet. My windshield fixated on Lana driving the gray snake we rode.

The interstate bypassed another small town, one that when both shrinking bergs could field a team was a high school sports rival of Sidner.

The road hummed on for twenty-one minutes.

White letters on a green metal EXIT sign read REST STOP. Lana's brake lights glowed. I watched her turn off the highway and onto that exit loop. She parked outside the alpine-styled, cinderblock square building of restrooms. Was waiting in her car when I pulled in to the rest stop to park beside her.

We weren't alone at the rest stop.

Four soccer jersey kids cavorted around the family sedan that had loosed them. A dad leaned on that car and watched his cargo of kids stumble into the restrooms where they'd been told they belonged. The tan van that passed us sat parked at the far end of the lot facing the road we'd left.

My rental car shut off. I stationed my cellphone in my blue shirt pocket. Contorted my way into the black leather jacket covering the gun on my hip as I stepped outside. Lana beat me into standing in the chilly wind beside her car.

The wind blew her ebony hair around her face. She wore a hip-length red Western jacket with fringe sleeves.

Stood there with her arms crossed over her breasts. That white blouse under her jacket complemented dark slacks free enough on her long legs to not be called tight. She wore the stiletto heels.

Her husky voice said: "Why did you tell me to stop here?"

My eyes broke away from her gaze.

From her red lips.

I forced my eyes to stare at *'no vehicles'* turning off the highway to where we waited at the rest stop.

Lana got it: "Motorcycle."

"*Yeah.* And *no.* None around. And that's good."

"You'll tell me later." She brushed her wind-blown hair off her face. Looked around. Looked back to me. "What should we do now?"

I wanted to scream words I didn't dare let myself think.

Responsibly said: "Check the restrooms. See if anyone we know is there."

She frowned, but nodded.

We walked side by side toward that blockhouse. Our hands dangled between us. Almost touching. Almost.

Damn that rest stop MENS room stunk! Pine disinfectant and a wall-mounted odor eater lost to the yellow acid smell of urine.

The soccer jersey boy jiggling in front of the urinal wasn't helping things with his machine-gunning aim. I eased past him, deliberately *not* looking. Pulled open the door on the silver metal commode closet. Stepped in and used the toe of my shoe to lift the toilet's horse-collar seat. Unzipped my pants for the other reason I'd wanted to visit the MENS room: The coffee from the P.S. And nerves.

I came out of the stall. I was alone. I hadn't heard the boy flush his toilet like I had mine. Was *not* going to grab the handle of his urinal to do so.

The white sink mounted on the yellow cinderblock wall worked—or at least the cold faucet did—and there was still soap in the dispenser. As I washed my hands, I realized this tax-paid-for facility was piping in mindless "soothing" music for travelers that none of the musicians in the jazz station I'd been hearing would play for anything short of a gun to their head or true love in their bed. The polished metal mirror above the sink distorted the face it said was mine.

Lana leaned on the hood of her car as I walked back from the MENS room. She stood as I came close.

"A bunch of soccer girls laughing and giggling and *oh-my-God*-ing," reported Lana. "A mom I didn't know got away from them into the stall after I—after me."

She shrugged.

"We better go," I told her.

She waited.

I didn't move. Didn't reach for her.

Her hair floated in time's breeze.

Her slick ruby lips said *yes*.

The slow roll of her black-slacked moon hips carried her back to her car.

I got back into mine with the same slip-off-the-jacket/hide-the-gun ballet.

As I hooked my phone back into my charger, she backed out of the parking space, followed the EXIT arrows for the road south.

I followed her.

The hell with jazz and random fate.

I Bluetoothed my cellphone into the car's speakers.

Watched Lana's car racing ever away from me beyond my windshield. Tapped my Spotify playlist hoping for songs with words to tell me where I was going.

31

I was riding Lana's rear bumper as we reached the airport exit. Followed close behind her as the airport road took us past a state Air National Guard base. The chilly October sun glistened off the shiny metal of swept-back-winged warbirds waiting, waiting, waiting to take off. I faded back as Lana followed the SHORT-TERM PARKING signs. Drove as slowly as I dared past the ground-level, tinted-glass walls of the airport terminal. That delay let me see the white lined spot where Lana parked her car.

RENTAL CAR RETURN signs led me to a parking lot positioned right next to the terminal's side door. I found a spot—47—parked. Filled out the rental form mileage statement and didn't give a shit about how much that cost.

Sitting behind the wheel of my rental return. Scanning the rooftops of motionless cars and the parking lots around me: Nobody close. No shapes looking like hostiles filled the nearest tinted-glass wall of the terminal.

Somewhere not far away had to be the prison caging Irma.

My barroom bruises made me wince behind the steering wheel through awkward contortions to unsnap the holstered Glock from my black jeans' belt. I unzipped my soft attaché, pushed the polymer gun in there. Intellectually knew it was *absolutely* safe against accidental misfires due to being dropped or banged against, *say*, a car outside a heavily policed airport.

Sometimes you've gotta go *old school.*

I tore a fingernail-sized strip of paper off the rental agreement.

Positioned the paper strip in my bag's zipper's tracks.

Pulled the zipper clasp over the silver metal rails it mated. Held the tiny strip of paper so the clasp ran it over and lodged it half in, half out of the attaché.

Someone would either notice it or not if they unzipped the attaché. Most people who noticed it would *fo'get about it*, a dumb scrap of paper, probably from what's inside the attaché. But savvy people . . . We all take our shots.

I got out of the rental car. Shrugged into my black leather jacket. Tucked my cellphone charger into a jacket pocket. Put my cellphone in its obvious shirt pocket. Held my attaché in my left hand. Slammed the rental car's door. Walked away. Raised my right hand like a movie hero and zapped the provided key fob. From behind me came the *beep* of the rental car's locks.

But I left that lot heading *not* into the terminal where the rental car counter was, but instead into short-term parking where Lana waited.

Her mirrors showed her me walking toward her. She was halfway out of her car when I got to her, worry wrinkling her brow: "What . . . Is everything—"

"We're cool," I said.

I handed her my black nylon attaché case. Saw her gauge its weight.

Told her: "I'll be right back."

Felt her eyes track me through the terminal's sliding-open doors.

The man at the rental counter looked like he was barely out of high school. The well-mopped terminal played piped-in mindless music.

He tapped in the payment with my credit card.

Told me: "Have a good day!"

Directed me toward a bank of phones with direct access to local motels that had pick-up/drop-off service "from just right outside there on the sidewalk."

"Don't worry," I lied.

Told the truth: "I've got a ride."

32

Lana drove.

I rode shotgun.

We wore our seat belts like the law said.

Her musk perfume filled every breath I took.

We kept our eyes staring through the windshield at the road looping us out of the airport. Passed the Air National Guard base. Drove over the bridge across the four lanes of highway from where we'd come.

Lana gripped the steering wheel so hard her knuckles paled.

She wore no wedding rings.

No music came out of our cellphones or her car radio.

No words came out of either of us.

Our wheels rumbled the road we drove.

She checked the rearview mirror. We refused to lock eyes. She hit the left blinker to pull us off the two-lane blacktop headed into a dirt road running into bare prairie. She could have turned right. Pulled into the truck stop with a dozen pumps and three charging stations built into the white-walled convenience store. But she took us left, a 180-turn down into the parking lot of a well-cared-for three-story gaudily painted complex with a giant neon sign:

DREAMLAND MOTEL

She parked the car in a white-lined spot.

Looked hard at me. Found me looking hard back at her.

We opened our doors. Got out of the car. Both reached back in.

I lifted out my right-weight attaché:

YES, the white paper scrap was still lodged in its zipper!

Lana retrieved the black-clasped purse to dangle from her shoulder on its golden chain amidst the blowing fringes of her red jacket.

We walked side by side through the sliding glass doors into the lobby.

The glass doors *whunked* closed behind us.

From the open doorway behind the registration counter came a bouncy woman who could have been one of my high school's pale-skinned powdered-pink girls.

"Hi, folks!"

Her eyes clicked on Lana.

Blinked.

She gave us a professional smile: "Welcome to Dreamland, now under franchise with BAM—*B*est *A*merican *M*otels. What can I do for you today?"

Lana stepped to the registration counter: "We'd like a room."

"Certainly! Do you have a reservation? No?"

The clerk frowned and made a point of showing us she was looking back over her shoulder at the old-fashioned analog clock mounted on the wall.

The two black hands on the clock read high noon.

"Well," she told us, "checkout is 1:00 P.M. That works with most of the airline departures. But that's also the official check-*in* time. So technically, right now you'd be checking in for yesterday *and* today. Two days' rates.

"But . . ." she said, "given what time it is now, let's forget about technicalities and say you got here today and forget about yesterday."

Lana spoke her name for the desk clerk to keyboard into the computer log.

I inserted my credit card into the proper slot.

The clerk gave us our computerized third-floor key cards. Directed us around the corner to the elevator. We had to walk past the wall of windows to the small indoor pool where no one splashed in the turquoise chlorine water.

The silver elevator doors opened when I pushed the button.

I got in first.

Lana walked in. Stood shoulder to shoulder with me against the back wall.

The button to 3 got pushed.

Lift-off like a rocket to the stars.

Landing like a train on a subway platform.

Those silver elevator doors slid open and sent us into a comedy movie.

We stepped toward the open doors at the same time—stepped back.

Tried to leave the elevator again—lurched to the same near collision.

My nod chose to watch her march out of the box.

The walking-away tremble of her black slacks moon hips.

I followed.

A maid's cart piled high with fresh white towels and washcloths waited down the hall the other way by the open door into another room-for-rent where I heard a vacuum cleaner sucking up what other travelers left behind.

Lana and I stood facing the closed door of the motel room that fit our keys.

We looked at each other.

Saw we were both there.

She slid in her key. The computer lock clicked. Its screen glowed green.

That brown door with a round peephole swung inward with her push.

She walked inside the room.

I came in behind her.

Pulled the door closed.

33

The two of us alone in that motel room.

She's staring at me from only four steps away.

The queen-sized motel bed stretches out behind her.

My gun bag drops itself on the luggage rack beside her black purse.

The heat of her. The smoke of her musk perfume.

I can hear her breathe. The shallow quickness of her exhales, her inhales.

We both heard the *Click!* of the closing door.

"You don't have to do this," she said.

"If I don't, I'll go crazy," I told her.

Told the universe: "Hell, I already am.

"Most important," I said, "it's all up to you."

Sunlight beaming in through the open-curtained window of the outside wall lit the big bed with a soft glow. That glass portal to the real world muffled the sounds of a jet taking off at the nearby airport.

Lana's eyes held me.

She threw off her red fringe jacket.

My black leather wrap fell crumpled to the floor.

She took a step and I was more than halfway there. She cupped my face, I pulled her close. My palms pressed the warmth of her back. She wore no bra. Our hips ground together and told her about me—

—and I didn't.

Our mouths wet and slick met like this was our millionth, not our second kiss. Her soft lips burned, crushed mine, opened. Tongue lightning.

Pull back, we pull back.

Stare at each other like boxers.

The heat scent of our flesh.

My hands race through the buttons of my blue shirt. I almost forget to be careful of my cellphone in its heart pocket. Toss (carefully) the shirt onto a chair near the bed. I turn back to see her.

Black hair brushing her white blouse. We'd messed her war paint lipstick. Her smeared red lips curve a hungry smile.

She kicks off her high heels.

Her bare feet claim the motel carpet.

Red-fingernailed hands dance the buttons on her white blouse.

The blouse drapes open all the way down yet still hides the true of dreams.

Lana looks up from unbuttoning herself.

Looks me straight on.

The white blouse floats away.

Heaven's curve of heavy flesh. Centered nipples swollen like top hats.

Lana takes my hands. Fills my grasp with her breasts. Holds my hands on her as they cup her *oh God* smooth heft.

Comes her whisper: "Any way you want me. Every way you want me."

"The only 'way' I want *is* you."

We slam into kisses. A mash of embraces. *And I didn't.*

I pull away—her face blinks to *why*.

Had to tell her: "I'm—Forget about the apps. I haven't been with anybody for way more than a year, two physicals, and if you want, *yes*, sure if you—"

"You know me," she said. "That file. What it said. I trust you. Want just you."

Kicking off my shoes. Stomping free of my black jeans/kicking them away.

Standing on one leg and pulling off a stocking/staggering—catch myself. Stand on the other leg. Throw the last stocking away. Claim my ground with both my bare feet. My arms swing out *Ta-dah!*

"You knock my socks off!"

Lana laughs as she slides her arms around my neck. She folds herself against me slow yet strong—

—and I didn't.

My mouth moving with hers. Kissing her cheeks. Her hair. Her closed eyes. Past her panting mouth. Her neck. Her moans rise to gasps as my kisses wet her breasts. As my mouth sucks in her swollen nipple, as my tongue—

She gasps/shudders. Holds my face on her breasts.

Kneeling naked in front of her.

Fumbling off her black slacks.

Black bikini panties. Slide them slow down to her ankles. She raises first one foot then the other to let them go.

The warm ocean breeze of her.

The kiss of her *there.*

Push her down on the bed. Kneel between her spread-wide legs.

Lana cups my face. Bends down to pull me up to deep kisses.

Vampire her neck. Her mouth panting on my cheek slides away as I press my weight down on her. The bed sinks. Kiss her breasts, *oh her breasts.* Kiss my way down to her stomach. Down to her belly button. Kiss just below that, her *t'an tien*, her center. Kiss lower, lower still. Kiss her *Oh God yes!* Tongue her *there.*

I jerk the whole of her to the edge of the bed.

My tongue fills with the taste of her.

Her naked back slides along the bedspread as she cries *Oh!* Her legs bend and spread. Her heels grip the edge of the bed to thrust herself up to my mouth.

Lana cries out/jerks, then again, again—

—drops off the bed onto me. Her hips on the floor between my splayed-open thighs. Her legs circle over mine and behind me. One of her arms wraps around my neck to pull her hips off the carpet. Her other hand finds me, wraps around me I don't *oh I don't* she guides me up into her—

—she yells *flashes/squeezes* around me *don't I don't* our arms wrap around each other like look-at-me yoga lovers grinding into each other on Dreamland's carpet surging *oh oh* Lana *flashes/squeezes* cries out my name I *oh I!*

34

What happens now?" said Lana.

She stares at me, her right cheek pressed on the motel pillow.

My left cheek lays on the pillow beside hers as I stare back at her.

We're naked. Front to front. Legs that could run instead stretch out nearly toe-to-toe. Her black hair webs on her pillow and the white sheet beneath us.

"I'm with you," I told her. "Not just now. Not just here. Not just for this."

Her hand slid up the bed in a clutch of shy sheets over her smeared smile.

Then her brow wrinkled as she frowned.

"Why doesn't a guy like you have someone?"

"Why doesn't everybody have someone?"

"Yeah, but you're a semi–hot shit author—"

"Yesterday's news," I said.

"—and far more important, you're getting good at being a man. Respectful. Smart. Handsome—if you like the lean coyote look."

She raised her head off the pillow: "I happen to dig coyotes."

Our faces came together for a soft kiss. Settled back on their pillows.

"Plus," she said, "you've got guts. And some kind of true. I trust you."

"You trust me," I said.

Don't tell her! screamed in my skull.

"I trust you enough that I figure you planting that scrap of paper in the zipper of your bag was for a good reason."

"You are so smart!"

"If you were me you'd have to be smart, too. Try to be. Fight to be."

My right hand held her left, the bridge of our bare arms connecting us over the white sheet's sea.

"Are you going to tell me what I think I already know?" she said.

I turned away from her and swung off the bed. Walked around it.

Lana turned to lie on her back to watch. One foot slid up the inside calf of her other bare leg. Her breasts curved on her ribs. Her eyes never let go of me.

My attaché lay on the luggage rack beside her purse. I picked it up. Retraced my route to my side of the bed. Swung back onto the sheet in the same groin-to-groin position with her.

Plopped the black attaché with its bulge onto the white sheet between us.

She rose on her right forearm. Used both hands to take the bag. Pulled the zipper down. Her red-tipped left forefinger and thumb lifted the freed fleck of paper off the sheet. Turned on her back toward the nightlight table on her side of the bed to put that scrap there. That stretch expanded her chest up and forward. Her bare breasts rose toward the sky beyond our motel room ceiling.

Lana turned back to lie on her right side.

Her left hand slid into the attaché.

Came out holding the holstered Glock.

She sat up.

I did not move as she claimed the covered gun.

Lana flipped her hair from side to side. Snapped the Glock free. Tossed its holster away. Cradled that lethal wonder in her right hand. She lowered her spine toward the bed. Used her left hand to flip her long black hair out from under her head so it fanned out on the white pillow. Used both her hands to hold the thirty-one-ounce black gun above her naked breasts.

"One in the chamber?" said her voice in the motel room.

"Locked and loaded. Wouldn't be much use any other way."

"Glocks don't have a safety. But don't fire unless they're gripped."

Bounce! The bed jerked. Her arms shot out from her chest. Her red-fingernailed hands zeroed the gun to kill an image only she could see on the motel room's white ceiling.

She relaxed on her back. Stroked the gun in her hands.

"Why do you have this?" she said. "Why did you bring it with us?"

I told her about the motorcycle.

I told her about WhORe.

"Nice to know I have fans," she said.

"I'm not sure that's about you. Doesn't feel right, soaped on my window. Hell, in . . . this thing, that fits me as much as you."

"But nobody . . ." She read my face: "Who'd you tell?"

"Cody."

Her eyes closed around that lost secret of her life. Opened.

"So then, *who*?" she said. "Who else knows? Who cares? Who's the motorcycle? Doesn't make sense for Ron or Terry to . . .

"*Well*, unless they soaped that there to cover up what else they did. But you said the *who* got nothing from your stuff. Plus, they're not hands-on guys . . ."

She corrected herself:

"*Well*, Terry is. He's Ron's make-it-happen guy. Terry can get pretty kinky about that. He's quick through the changes. Could keep up with you. Follow you and not let you catch him. But either of them on a motorcycle? *Naw*."

"Plus the timelines don't match," I said. "And either of them out in the streets like that, somebody'd see and eventually, everybody'd hear."

"Maybe they hired it out." She let her eyes rest on me with her flat *here it is* stare. "Like other things."

I ignored 'other things.'

Said: "For what? To keep tabs on me? On us?"

Her right hand set the Glock on the white sheet between us.

She kept her grip on the handle.

The gun barrel pointed between our bare feet.

"So what's our plan?" said Lana. "This. Now. We've . . . done it. We even left a *guilty* trail for their divorce team to find when we registered here."

"Did you notice the funny look the front desk clerk gave us?"

"Wasn't *us* she gave that look."

"Yeah," I corrected myself: "Was that some kind of woman-to-woman look?"

"Wasn't about her and me both being women."

Lana pressed her hand on the gun beside her.

"Was about me being Indian. Native American. Indigenous."

That global room closed in on us.

"Every breath I take," said Lana. "It's like the smell of smoke outside now—only always there. It's what you hear even when it's not said out loud. It's being *one of them*, not one of *us*. It's '*how good she does for being one of You Know*.'"

Tension rose in her with the haunting of a thousand evils.

I ached to hold her. To work some miracle and destroy the specters who shimmered through our closed motel door. But I knew I couldn't.

Knew that the best I could do was *Shut Up And Listen*.

"It's doors that didn't open," said Lana. "Sometimes with a *not-me* private '*sorry*' from who slams them shut. It's that *oh-oh* look from the desk clerk. The second look at your credit card and your driver's license or when you're in a store. The red lights spinning in your cousin's mirrors for driving down the wrong street at the wrong time, which is any time the White badge says it is.

"It's hearing '*Injun*' and being expected to laugh or at least let it pass, you learn how to let it pass and hate that every time. You hear snipes like that all the time. Ignorance. Fear. Hatred. All those and maybe more and you *Walk On By*. Battle with yourself for doing that just so you can get through the day without blood on your hands—or your blood on their hands.

"It's hearing how '*you people*' are *loaded* with big-time government checks and welfare on the Rez. Funny how all those millions never seem to be visible in the trailers and crumbling family homes and worse on those lands."

She shook her head.

"College, that year that my mom worked her ass off to help me working my ass off to afford. I had a professor, Acting 101. He called me 'easy money.' Couldn't figure out why, finally asked. He said: '*You know, all the money you get from your tribe and the government to go here—easy money for being you.*' Hell, my allotment from the tribe that year was less than $200. '*Easy money,*' my ass."

Couldn't stop the paranoia in me from blurting: "He might have meant more than . . . You know, that there was a way for . . . for you . . ."

"Don't you think I figured *maybe* that, too?"

The eyes of the naked woman lying beside me narrowed like a caged tiger.

I felt my dreams burning in a hell I desperately didn't want to deserve.

Lana shook her head. "Hard enough being any woman out there. Being a target for somebody else's . . . *expectations*. But being not White . . .

"It's being *a good one*. It's being here but it's not you who really *gets* to be here. It's being whipsawed in your own mind. It's walking down the street on land stolen from your great-greats and having a carload of White guys drive up slow alongside you: *'Hey, squaw, wanna go for a ride?'"*

Her voice rose, her volume roaring through all the years of her life.

"It's being so sick and angry of being a less-than. Like a minus sign on me to brand me not just *an American.* Not just a *person* like everybody else. It's being so proud to be Indian—by the way, that name's fine with me.

"My sister Grace disagrees. Wants *native* to be our *who.* Or *Indigenous.* Younger generation, right? She works so hard just to get really seen. If you aren't a star athlete—or when you're done with those high school basketball games—the boys she goes to school with, that's all they get judged by and the girls, *well*, we know how they're ranked."

She zeroed in on me.

"You want to hear the worst one I ever got?"

"No. Yes."

"Prairie nigger."

That smack of hateful shit rocked me deeper into the pit of what was.

"Just when you think creativity is dead in America," said Lana.

I felt helpless. Angry. Ashamed. All of that all at once. And powerless.

Had to ask and felt like a selfish fool for doing so: "What about me?"

Lana LaBuff stared at the naked man she lay with.

"I know *now* that you're not like that," she said. "But I had to learn that. Why should I have to live not knowing what to expect from a stranger just because of the color of my skin? Why can't I be just *Lana*?"

Steel filled me: "You know I punch at that every chance I get—and that's not about you or just for you. It's about and for me and all of us."

Her soft smile to me was hundreds of years old.

"You *know* and *care*, try to *do*. But you don't get a medal for that. That's what you're *supposed* to do. That's what we're *all* supposed to do.

"But you'll never know how it feels. You can't, *White boy*."

Our foreheads pressed together. Our fingers touched each other's cheek.

I felt no tears on her flesh. Sensed the lines of a thousand such scars.

Dreamed that somehow, someday, maybe I could fight. Beat that monster.

Didn't kid myself. I could only do what I could do. Refuse. Resist. Hope.

And walk on with the burdens of truth.

Somehow we moved on without moving.

We pulled back and away. Again lay face-to-face on side-by-side pillows.

The Glock lay between us.

Lana said: "What if this is all about you?

"Not this," she said, waving her hand at our motel room. "But you.

"*You* you," she added. "The motorcycle. Your home invasion. Even . . . *whore*."

"I shouldn't have anybody who cares about me like that. At least, not anymore. And nobody up there in Sidner."

"What do you mean: *shouldn't* and *anymore*?"

Only Cody knew. And he only knew the outlines. I knew how to keep secrets. He had to know I could if I was to expect him to keep mine or share his.

"Was a time back after my first novel. Cops. Spooks—spies. More beyond that. Ghosts. Cartel guys with suits and ties and Uzis. 'Respectable' Wall Street *dudes* with their earbuds bodyguards. New mafias most Americans don't know exist.

"Internet freaks gearing up with guns to fight the whacked-out conspiracies they helped make up out of their own hates and big bucks' manipulations like the insurrection rioters who stormed our Capitol and killed cops. Private contractor soldiers carrying out covert ops for Uncle Sam but really for profit and to pay their lobbyists, so go figure who makes 'policy' that gets people killed. I walked into bullet alleys with my dumb eyes wide open. Told myself that if I was going to write fiction about such things, I better know their realities."

I shook my head. "That's what I told myself. But *reality* is I liked the edge. *The life*. Figuring out how to stay clean and vertical in the meanest streets. Me learning and knowing in my bones what prestige-educated, more sophisticated, more powerful, maybe smarter and definitely more acceptable members of society only know in theory or screenshots."

Lana glared at me: "We're not some theory or hashtag or YouTube post."

I took her hand in mine. Held it on the bed's white sheet between our hearts and above the gun. Met her brown eyes' gaze.

"This is as full-on real as I've ever been," I said. "It's all me and I'm alive."

Her bare shoulders and arms holding her on top of the bed relaxed.

"Stay that way," she told me. "Me too. That's why we're here."

"I'm here about more than just staying alive."

Her lips tightened over words she wouldn't say and I dared not guess.

Until she said: "What happened? About *anymore*?"

"I got out. Carefully. Diplomatically. Left behind no enemies. Nobody who'd want to come after me—especially not come all the way to Sidner."

"You got any law on you?" she said.

Up shot her hand before I could answer.

"Speaking of which," she said as she turned her back to me, the line of her spine, her curved bare butt—

—and then she whirled back on to the bed, her black purse opening in her hands as she took out a cancer stick lighter and a joint she put between her lips.

"Ah, the times that have changed," I said. "But beyond dope being legal now, his is a No Smoking room."

She lit the joint. Took a drag. Let it out. Handed the joint to me as she turned again on her side to watch me take it.

"Look at it this way," said Lana. "Us getting busted works for Ron's plan."

"The hell with Ron," I said.

Took a drag and handed the joint back to her.

Coughed as she said:

"You must have freaked out the government with *Mirror Man*."

"How was I to know that what I made up was so real?"

"Try saying that *without* a grin," she said, took a deep drag.

"*Naw*."

"Good!" she said. "You're honest with me."

My smile stayed steady.

I broke away from her gaze to take a drag.

"Save the rest for later," she said as she snubbed the joint out on its metal tube in her black purse she snapped shut. "We might want a second round."

She brushed ashes off the white sheet where the gun lay between us.

Her palm touched my chest where she'd sent that smoke.

Turned over to let the backs of her fingers brush my ribs.

Kept their touch over my heart like the backhand part of *Taiji*'s press.

"How did *Jimmy-Jim-James* from Sidner, Montana, with no connections, barely out of college and no experience *back then* come up with *Mirror Man*?"

"The *what-ifs*," I said. "And the *what-would-I-do*'s."

She gave me a slow smile.

Got my stoned grin:

"I've been a writer since before I could read.

"Our generation is 9/11. Columbine. Terror out of the sky. Getting shot in class. We grew up in the first houses to have computers and lots of us didn't see the houses that couldn't afford that. We thought we knew *what's-what* because we could Google it. Too many of us thought the good we got worked for everybody.

"But the reality is you damn near already had to be somebody for a chance to be anybody. We got trophies for participating. Too many of the lucky kids with high-earning parents never got to work blue collar summer jobs to learn and love their fellow Americans who wear those blue collars and are just like them—and lots of times are more savvy and realistic. Lots of our dreamers carried labels like ADD or HD or non-neurotypical *on* them and little white pills *in* them. I said *yes* to my crazy and *no* to the meds. Even now, we're just realizing 'our time' was before we got here. I wanted to write about us. Not some costumed superhero. A *just-starting-to-get-it* guy like me. Like millions of us."

My smile was nervous: "Did you read the book?"

"And your other books. Saw the movie, too.

"The woman," she said to me. "They did better with her in the movie than you did with her in the book."

"I didn't know much about women then," I said.

Touched her chin and made her smile, said: "I don't know much now."

Her hand stroked my cheek: "You're learning."

We leaned together for a soft, friendly, affirming kiss. That lingered.

"But now what?" said Lana. "Are you in your own book? A dreamer trapped in a reality of motorcycles and black bag jobs and a dangerous woman?"

"A dangerous woman." I smiled. "Is that who you are?"

"Yes," she said without a blink.

"I'm taking that risk," I said. "Going to where I imagined."

My right hand on that white sheet inched closer to her and the Glock.

Waited. Trembled.

"What you imagined," said Lana, "is that what you want?"

Her sunlit black hair on the pillow. Her dark eyes. The smile of her swollen rouge lips. Her left arm curled in front of her astonishing breasts. My eyes traced the slope of her hips, her soft hips created to hold, to caress.

My right hand trembled across the white toward her.

Stopped near the Glock.

She read that aching reach.

"Touch me," she said.

My gun hand covered her ass as she pushed her damp groin to mine.

Our hips pressed the Glock into the mattress beneath us.

Her arms snaked around me. Our faces slid along the white pillow. Our mouths worked *together.* Her lips pushing mine. Her tongue.

My hand stroked down between us. Caressed her damp half-moon.

She pulled me down her as she lay pressed against me on her right side. Pulled my face to her neck. Pulled my mouth to her breasts. To her swollen nipples. I kissed her stomach.

Felt the Glock beneath the ribs near my heart.

Lana twisted beneath me, pulled me up onto her, up to her kiss as she shifted her hips under me and spread her legs to curl around me.

The Glock lay under my bare thighs.

She hugged me tight onto her. Her hands pulled my face to her kisses—pushed my face away from her, stared straight into me with her eyes of fire.

Her panting breaths carried words: "I want you! I chose you! *Choose* you!"

She reached down/pulled me inside her.

Bed rockin' 'n' rollin' and we cry out and the Glock . . .

The Glock platforms my balls as I slam myself again and again into her.

"Yes!" cried Lana. "*Fill me! Fill me!*"

35

We lay between the white sheets of our room in the Dreamland Motel.

Lana curled on my chest, her body molded to mine from her feet to her gently resting-on-me hips to her face pressed to my naked flesh above my heart.

My left arm circled her there as she wanted. As we wanted.

My right hand lay open-palm touching the white sheet near the Glock.

"If we don't go soon," said Lana, "I'll never leave here."

"We can get on a plane and just go."

"You got seats for my sister and my mom and the *who* you gotta be?"

The window to the October Saturday afternoon trembled with a landing jet.

Lana said: "So we gotta go back."

"But don't—we can't play this their way," I told her. "Anybody's way but ours. Ron and Terry or Queen Dee—"

Blink/flash tell Lana about Dee/Don't.

"—and Mr. Motorcycle," I said. "And the soap creeper."

"What does that mean?"

"I don't know. Yet."

She felt me shake my head as she lay on my chest.

"I can't let them move me around like a pawn," I said. "I never was going to."

"But you risked that for me," said Lana.

She kissed my heart.

Whispered: *"Thank you!"*

What I wouldn't/didn't dare say weighed on us with its *what-to-do*'s.

"Can I tell you something?" she whispered.

"Anything. Everything."

"I'm *starving!*"

Now it was laughter that shook our bed.

"I don't know about you," she said, "but I couldn't think about breakfast I was so nervous! We gotta eat before we hit the road. There's the pancake house next door, but they have burgers, too. And milkshakes."

She gave it the sincere drama it deserved: "*Chocolate* milk shakes."

I remembered the wedding where we'd danced.

"There's a new place I want to spend my money at," I said. "I heard the guy say it was called Clyde Packers."

"Do they have—"

"I don't know their menu, but if they don't have chocolate milkshakes, we'll save room and circle back to the pancake house. Take our shakes on the road."

"That will take longer for us to get where we've got to go."

"I know."

Lana burrowed her face into me. Looked up with a grin. Gave me one of her long, slow kisses that were so much more than any I'd ever had.

She sat up straight—yelled back to me lying in the bed: *"I've got to pee!"*

I watched her scamper into the bathroom.

That door closing behind her on the echoes of our laughter.

The door-muffled sound of a toilet flush.

The bathroom door flew open.

She swung into the room grinning at me.

Said: "How 'bout first shower?"

"Go for it."

And she popped back into the bathroom.

Left that door open.

Spraying water turned on in the motel shower.

The sounds of two shower curtains clinked apart . . . clinked back together.

The Glock filled my right hand as I stood up from the bed.

The barrel pointed straight down.

The open bathroom door was behind me as I pawed through the mess of motel bedding and our clothes on the floor. My left hand brushed the flat pockets of her white blouse. Her black slacks held only a few tissues.

Her red fringe jacket had only her cellphone in an inside pocket.

She'd turned her phone's power off. Didn't want to be connected.

Told myself she wanted to be with *just us.*

I put her phone back in her pocket.

I'd seen nothing but keys and coins and cosmetics in her black purse when she pulled out the joint, didn't bother to unsnap it and look for more now.

Found the Glock's holster under a thrown-off pillow, snapped in the gun.

Shower curtains clanged open on their metal rod.

"Hey!" yelled Lana.

Two steps and I'm standing in the open bathroom doorway.

Lana's face grins out to me from the two shower curtains she holds open just enough: "It's lonely in here!"

She disappears into the steam as the shower curtains clanged shut.

I tossed the holstered Glock onto the white-sheets bed.

Shower curtains clang open/clang shut and my bare feet on the white bathtub's wet floor stand me with her. Hot water sprayed down on me. Steam encompassed us. We laughed like dancers under the Dreamland waterfall. Her hair matted and draped far down over her breasts. A toss of her head flipped the ebony locks over her shoulders. She soaped herself: Her sloping breasts. Her groin. Her armpits. Neck. Her wet face.

She turned her closed eyes straight up into the shower spray as I stood behind her. Changed places with me in the tub so I was under the spray.

"Your turn," she said as she wrung out the snake of her hair. Flopped that matted rope over her shoulder. *Screed* the shower curtains open then closed. Left me alone in the waterfall.

How long I stood in there, I don't know. Soaped and from habit shampooed my hair. My mind washed away in the hot water beating down. I didn't want to stop the rain of where I was for where I had to go.

Life is what we do with the choices we get.

My hands turned the faucet shut.

I shook off. Jerked open the shower curtains.

Lana walked into the bathroom with a white towel wrapped around her head and nothing on her body that glowed from the shower and toweling.

She saw me, grinned.

Whipped the damp white towel off her head—tossed it to me.

As I caught it, she said: "What's mine is yours."

She handed me a clean fresh white towel off the bathroom rack.

"Plus," she said, "you get your own, too."

I stood there in the bathtub.

Wiped the white towels over my wet flesh.

Lana turned her naked front away from me to the bathroom mirror above the sink. Her hand wiped condensation off the glass to reveal her face. Her fingers combed through her towel-dried hair enough to pull it out of her way as she looked at her image. I saw her reach in the black purse I hadn't checked *now* on the edge of the sink. Pull something out.

Lana leaned forward over the sink to get closer to the mirror. Her bare ass curved toward me. Quivered as she moved. I watched her reflection. She held a small gold tube. Her fingers made a thick nub of red appear.

Her eyes watched with mine as she used that nub to ruby her lips.

Then her eyes flicked to mine staring at her from behind.

She turned full towards me.

Looked me up.

Looked me down.

Offered me her hand and I stepped out of the tub to the bathroom tiles.

She let go of my hand.

Her soft strong grip closed around my growing.

"We don't have much time," she said.

Her dark eyes narrowed with her slow grin of those reddened lush lips.

"But lucky us," came her husky voice, "I've got plenty of lipstick."

36

We rode in the car they'd given her.

Lana drove.

I rode shotgun.

The Glock owned my belt.

Our smiles faded two miles from the Clyde Packers restaurant where we'd eaten steak salads with fresh local tomatoes. Savored chocolate milkshakes.

There, in public, we'd talked nonstop.

I got to hear how she carried her newborn baby sister Grace home from the hospital after their dad took off. How hard her mom worked so Lana could have that one-year shot at college.

She coaxed stories from me about my dad and growing up watching dreams unfold on the big screen in the darkness of the Roxy. My mom trying to control the world from her living room to keep sister Katie and me safe.

We shared the *onces*. The *did yous*. The *whens*.

Paid our bill.

Gotten my desired handful of silver-coins change from a wedding-ringed rusty-haired waitress who smiled at our togetherness.

Walked out to the parking lot under the wispy smoke sky.

Looked at each other.

Got in that car. Drove towards our consequences.

The interstate highway rolled us north from the big city. Past a corral of brown and white cattle waiting to be slaughtered. Up a slope out of that river valley to the golden prairie stretching toward Sidner and the border of

America. Our smiles were gone and a thick line of billowing dark clouds filled our windshield.

"Might stop the fires in the mountains," said Lana of those October clouds.

"It's early for snow," I said. Like that mattered.

The digital clock on her dashboard read: "SAT—4:10" The machine thought we were smart enough to know if we were in the darkness or the light.

I'd followed her lead and didn't connect my cellphone Spotify to the car's speakers by either wires or waves.

The car's own radio played as our tires hummed the road.

Lana'd made Ron and Terry give her car the previous century's satellite radio. Voices from somewhere besides Sidner's over the air station or the streaming service Spotify algo'd just for her calculated tastes. Radio gave her airwave poems she didn't keyboard. Poems in moments shared with other human hearts. Poems of lyrics and guitar strings in her shared *now* that thus cosmically came alive in the moments she'd hear them.

Even though, *yes*, she'd spun a dial and chosen their channels.

A compromised *clong* is better than no *clong*.

Our cellphones lay near the gearshift slammed into Drive on the console between us beneath where the radio played from outer space. She gripped the steering wheel. Kept her eyes locked on the dark-clouded windshield. Her red-fingernailed right hand spun the radio dial through channels of the decades in our rearview mirror. Spun from channel to channel, song to song, off *no's* to *maybes* and *keep searching*.

My heart beat to hear what song she'd land on next.

I ached to hear her Spotify playlists. Yearned for her to hear mine.

The road rushed us ever closer to what we'd done.

There's a savvy critic for *The Washington Post* named Chris Richards who wrote about *imminence* surging through the best of music, a sensation of *being and doing* rushing you toward some core truth of your own life.

The music river I rode that trip came not from Lana's mystery list nor mine with its souls whose wordsmithing earned my awe, a few rappers but mostly singer-songwriters like Tori Amos. Kurt Vile. Granduciel. CeeLo Green. Joseph Arthur. Sarah McLachlan. Jason Isbell. Tom Morello. Sam Fender. Chuck Prophet. Billie Eilish. And I have to admit grudging admiration for Taylor Swift.

Instead, I rode in the fossil fuel machine of my father listening to his songs. His Springsteen. Richard Thompson. Otis Redding. Fogerty and Chrissy and Aretha. Jackson B. and Joni M. chasing Rolling Stones along the ocean beach with wondrously whacked-out Brian Wilson. The sighs and wise of the Beatles. The generation-older-than-my-dad's deserved Nobel Prize winner Bob Dylan.

Realized:

All songs ride the same highways.

And the destination is always *Please.*

The road rumbled beneath my seat.

"The only time I feel free is driving alone," said Lana.

Like I didn't know.

Or like I needed to know.

She'd spent the last seven years and tanks of gas cruising the streets of Sidner. Main Street with no *do* for her true. Stores with nothing she wanted. Houses where she didn't live. Lawns of laughing kids who weren't hers.

She'd drive north of town toward the last interstate crossroads and the easy turnaround before the Canadian border. *Fuck it.* Rocket the gas. Get sucked back into her driver's seat as crazy rushed her ever forward. Accelerating until the terror of *Too Fast!* Then pushing the pedal further. The fear of crashing innocent travelers'd rev her down. Turn her around. Send her back.

She'd drive west on the two-lane state highway to prairie fields conquered by hundreds of giant invading robot monsters—really, wind turbines, their three white blades spinning electricity out of the wind that never seemed to stop.

Drive south to watch the Eve River flowing away.

Drive east past the *Oily Boid* sign to the next roadside tourist attraction, another weathered redwood tourist info sign, this one about what happened at a bend in the river nine miles south of that rolling two-lane blacktop highway in January 1870. Blue-coated US cavalry troops charged a winter encampment of peaceful Blackfeet—mostly women, children and senior citizens—massacred at least 200 of them into the bloodied snow. The American soldiers gunned down Chief Heavy Runner as he stood waving their peace treaty.

Wherever Lana drove, she'd end up back at her red-doored prison.

Where we were driving now.

Ziggy Marley came on the radio as storm clouds rolled toward us. We heard the reggae of Jamaica on these Hank Williams plains where we'd been born in a dying century that made all that possible. Nodded as Ziggy told *"tomorrow people"* that if you don't know your past, you won't know your future.

A truck blasted past us in the left lane.

"What I know is what I've got to do now," said Lana.

"We chose this *do*," I said with a lie she didn't know.

The miles rolled behind us.

A family car on Saturday errands whizzed past us.

Lana gripped the wheel with both hands to keep it from turning us around.

A tan van whooshed past—

—but this one bore a sign: "Pulaski Electric."

"This isn't the real us," said Lana above the radio music as she stared through the windshield at the black-clouded horizon.

The road hummed.

"Yes," I told her. Told her: "No."

"Would you give a shit about me if not for all of this?" she said.

"I mean," she said, "beyond wanting to fuck me?"

"You lightning bolted me," I said. "All the way down. All the way through. Then you let me see who you really are and I knew your lightning is true."

She faced the windshield so we would not crash.

Whispered: "We can't say certain things until we're not who we are now."

"I know."

A fancy sports car blew past us.

"What about the money?" said Lana.

"*Yeah*, I need it. But *yeah*, mine's going to you."

"What?"

"Use it for your mom and sister. Get them and you really *gone free*."

"What about you?"

"I'll be where I was when I came home to Sidner."

"Just forget about these last five days?" she said. "Forget about *me*?"

"Remembering you is every breath I take. Every beat of my heart."

She faced the windshield full of rolling gray clouds.

A tear trickled down her right cheek.

She drove straight ahead.

37

Raindrops splattered our gray afternoon windshield.

Lana flipped the wipers as we drove off the interstate into Sidner.

Turned off the radio.

We slid our windows down. Cool damp air washed our faces.

Felt great.

We drove past Barb's Ribs. Turned the right corner past the grocery store where my neighbor Debby worked. Made the next left onto Main Street.

The wipers *whumped* on intermittent to clear the drizzle.

"Hit your horn!" I yelled as we drove past the boarded-up Rainbow Hotel.

Honk! came without her hesitating . . .

. . . as we drove past Cody's gun shop where the lights were still on even though the dashboard clock read: "SATURDAY—5:33."

I wondered if he heard the blast of our horn.

If he looked out his storefront window. *Recognized.*

Lana *groked* why we'd honked.

Her blast of *trusting me* brought back the woman who'd popped her head out of the shower curtains to grin.

We felt that change. Let ourselves fall back into it.

Wondered if our blast made anyone on Main Street look up to witness who was driving past.

Drove past the Chat & Chew where we'd met.

The Tap Room's red neon sign glowed. The door was open.

The Roxy's neon marquee held Hollywood words clinging to hope.

The Lowdown stood ready for hope and hookups on this Saturday night.

Rain came down harder.

Our route took us up to First Street and past my family's house with its two pine tree sentinels. I'd chosen the route so I could see my mother before I did what I had to do in this night of that rainstorm.

Lana parked at the curb sixty feet from the Evergreen's glass front doors.

Faced me as I clicked off my seat belt: "When will I see you again?"

"As soon as we can. I don't know when. Tomorrow."

"Come on!" she yelled as she opened her car door.

"You can't—"

Lana was already out in the rain and scurrying around the hood of the car.

My ballet slid me into my black leather jacket as I twisted off my shotgun seat through the opening car door while I grabbed my empty attaché from the back seat to stuff down the back of my pants held up by my gun belt so my hands were free when I landed standing on the sidewalk as Lana rushed to me—to us.

We swirled on the sidewalk beside the car she had then. Spun in heaven's falling tears. Her hair tumbled above wet splatters on her white blouse. Her dark eyes burned. Her crimson mouth curled a defiant smile.

"Fuck *can't*. Fuck the plan. Fuck Ron and fuck Terry, too. This is *me*."

Her whole body sidled against me as she tumbled me into our kiss.

My arms wrapped around her forever and ever.

The rain fell on us.

She pulled back.

Her eyes filled with what she saw of me.

Lana yelled: *"Now go see your mother!"*

Laughed. Ran around the back of her car and jumped behind the steering wheel. Dropped the gear shift from Park to Drive. *Whooshed* away with taillights staring back at me like two burning red eyes.

I flipped the collar up on my black leather jacket as I made sure it was zipped over the gun on my belt and hurried toward the glass front doors.

The castle boogeyman watched me come.

Owl Eyes Mike couldn't wait for me to get there. Shoved the glass door out of his way. Blocked my path in the pelting rain.

Yelled: "*The mark of the beast!*"

Stabbed his finger at the glass door behind him: "See!"

I stepped past him to stare at my reflection in the glass door.

Saw her lipstick's dark smudge on my lips.

Swelled with grateful pride and joy for my luck.

Wiped it off with the back of my hand for my mother to *not* see.

Stared into the foggy thick round lenses of Mike's glasses.

Deadpanned: "Good eyes."

"Maybe I can't see what's in front of my face, but I saw you with her!"

"Who *her*?" I asked from my reporter's bones.

"Just now! Another Godforsaken, Goddamned Zane woman!"

Owl Eyes Mike uncurled from his bent-over old man. Rose like a Pentecostal preacher pounding me with righteous anger.

"And I saw you before! With the other one! *Dee*, she'll let you call her *Dee* then drive nails through your heart. Your hands. Your feet. Pound you right where she wants on her cross. No matter how hard you try, you'll never pull off. Never get away. Never be gone from where she wants you to be. You kiss her, you're caught—and all of those Zane bitches are the same! I warned you!"

Blink.

"You," I whispered.

He shrank back under the rain pattered patio roof.

And I flashed on my family home's unlocked front door. An old man's two-block after-dinner shuffle from the Evergreen. His knock that no one answers. A turn of a knob. Self-righteous intoxication from busting into where you're not supposed to be. A chance to scream what no one ever hears. To leave your mark.

"*Whore*," I said. "That was you."

"They all are! They make you give them what they want. Make you take what they leave you. Get you so tied up in knots you can't get away."

Owl Eyes Mike shivered but not from cold that anyone else could feel.

Is he having a heart—

His charge startled me.

Made me jerk back with a stunned look on my face.

Flash on history's black and white picture of the white cowboy hat Texas cop jumping back from the thrust gun of a Mafia *moke* who squeezed a killing shot into the guts of the handcuffed official assassin of President JFK.

Owl Eyes Mike's breath smelled of the Evergreen's *'tastes like chicken'* gravy and crushed-up meds.

"I seen her brand you! I seen her mark on you! Too late now. Too late for you. I tried to tell you. You didn't listen. Nobody ever listens to me!"

"You got something to say, *say it*. But back the fuck off of me."

His retreat came like backing down was what he knew. Raindrops tapping his balding head made him flinch.

He shuffled into the corner of the patio.

"Gonna come a day," he muttered. "You'll see."

"Maybe," I said, "but I'm not going to wait."

Left an old man standing alone in the rain.

Walking into the Evergreen sent me past the open greetings and security counter where again, no staffer sat on duty.

Lights glowed in the dining room even though only a few of the "residents" lingered there. A handful of their comrades were shuffling or walker-clumping or wheeling their way out. Hell, it was coming up on six o'clock and most everyone who wanted to *and could* had already eaten dinner. Time to get back to their rooms. Where else could they go?

The silver elevator doors slid open and I stepped back to let the nurse's aide from the cemetery roll out a silver cart of empty dinner trays.

"Hi!" I said. "How's it going?"

"Better." She stopped to catch her breath. "Or maybe I'm just getting used to the hang of things now."

"Seems like you got a new job here."

She looked around where some people who were lucky enough to grow old ended up.

"Is that what all this is?" she said. "A job? *My* job?"

"Not if you do it right."

She nodded and I knew she got it.

My hand raised between us: "My name's Jim."

She blinked. Gave me a firm shake.

"I'm Jen," she said. "Your mom is Mary, Mary Traven. 229."

"Glad to say we'll see you around, Jen."

The elevator carried me up as she rolled the metal cart of trays away.

My Aunt Bev sat beside the bed to face her sister whose legs and an arm were trapped inside white casts.

"Well, hi there, kid!" said my aunt as I walked into that hospital room.

Images filled the screen of the muted TV mounted above the bed. Mom turned her head to see me coming to her. I gave her shoulder a squeeze and she smiled. I saw her relax as my aunt pulled up a chair for me.

"We were beginning to wonder," said my aunt as she tossed me a white hand towel to dry my hair. "Did your ride drop you off?"

Could they have seen Lana and me swirling in the rain?

"It took longer at the rental car place than I expected."

"You're here now," said Mom.

I'd told my mom "a friend" was picking me up at the airport and driving me back. She didn't ask *who*. That meant she thought she didn't want to know.

Now she said: "Take good care of my car."

"I don't think that will be too hard."

My aunt reported: "She ate a good dinner."

"Don't talk about me like I'm not here!" snapped Mom.

"Nobody's ever stopped you from talking but yourself," said her sister.

"Used to be it wasn't so hard to get a word in edgewise."

"The older we get, the more *used to be*'s we got," said my aunt. "*Used to be*'s, *once was*'s, *back when*'s, and *did I ever tell you*'s. But we aren't givin' up—right?"

"Right," said Mom.

They nodded together as sisters do.

I thought of Katie in Chicago. Wished she'd seen them then.

"So how was dinner?" came out of my mouth.

My aunt said: "Was a nice girl who brought it."

"Wasn't Irma," whispered my mom.

That moment held the room.

Then Mom said: "She wasn't bad, though."

"Which nurse's aide?"

"She said her name was Jen. Isn't that right?" said my aunt.

"Yes." Mom's eyes narrowed. "She doesn't have a boyfriend."

"Or enough years," I said. "If you can, let it be Jen who's on your duty."

I saw my aunt start to ask *Why?*

Cut her off, said: "We know her."

The wind blew rain against the evening windowpanes.

I settled back so I could watch the faces of these two *senior citizens* who'd lived their whole lives in this town.

"So why did Owl Eyes Mike bust on me again just now about Queen Dee?"

"What?" said my aunt.

"Like before?" said Mom.

"Seems like he's getting more pissed off by the day."

Mom said: "He spent his whole life working for her at the hardware store. That'd piss anybody off."

She nodded with pride: "Your father knew what that would be like. That's why he quit the theater and went to Mason Trucking. Well, that and they paid more. And Mason was a good man. A good boss. Let your dad be one, too. Queen Dee would have jerked him around. Like she did to Owl Eyes Mike."

My aunt leaned in to our triangle: "*Well* . . ."

And I knew I'd found the right source: "*Well* what?"

"Some people say there was more to it than that," said my aunt.

Mom frowned: "Like what?"

"Like that maybe they used to screw around, Mike and Dee. Starting back when Mike was in high school, Dee older than him, married, but hot as hell and hungry for all she could get. Her creepy husband was always working the rigs."

"Why the hell don't I know about this?" said Mom.

"You never wanted to hear nothing about Dee since she took over the theater and the best husband you could have asked for quit so's not to be around her. Maybe he knew she wasn't just a bad boss. Maybe he didn't want her hitting on him. Giving her the paycheck power to do so."

"Why the hell didn't he tell me?" said Mom.

"Probably he didn't want you to worry. And you never had to."

Mom shook her head on the pillow: "She should have married up with Mike after her weirdo husband bought the farm."

"Then she'd have to give up being Queen Dee," said my aunt. "Be just a regular woman with a good guy husband, even though she had all that money. And when she was—hell, long past your age, Jim."

"—looking hot. No man's ring on her. Bet she used all that to make a bunch of hotshot men jumping through hoops to get her where she wanted to go."

"She stuck around here," I said.

"She stuck around where she could show everybody who knew her coming up that she wasn't a knocked-up, trailer trash, slut loser," said my aunt.

"The hell of that is, nobody thought like that until she put it in their heads," said Mom. "She's spent her whole life fighting what she made up in *her* own head."

My aunt said: "Poor Mike. He's spent his whole life just being where she wanted him for whatever she wanted him for."

"Damn," said Mom. "The things you find out when you're laid up."

"Poor Mike," repeated my aunt. "Poor stupid Mike."

"Goes to show," said my mother, "gotta watch where you put your dick."

My aunt's jaw dropped.

She fled my eyes by looking out the window with my mother.

I sat frozen in the darkening hospital room.

The muted TV played a commercial for a car none of us would ever own.

"But," said my aunt, her eyes still staring away from me. "But nowadays, you kids, you got matchmakers on your phones. Swipes and such. You can see what you're getting into. There are a lot of great women out there."

"So I hear."

Mom whispered: "Be careful, Jim. Just be careful."

"Yeah," was my answer.

Rain beat on the windows

My aunt finally said:

"What you got going on tonight?"

I told them the truth: "I haven't had dinner yet. And I've got things to do."

"Oh well," said my aunt. "That's good. Good to be busy."

"I better go now."

Stood—

—turned away from my mom in the bed and my aunt sitting there.

Walked to the dresser and the pile of library books.

The two old women who'd watched me grow couldn't see what I was doing beyond straightening the library books I'd brought earlier. They chatted about something, didn't notice I pulled out the quarters I'd gotten in my change from the milkshake restaurant with Lana. I reached into the gaping open purse. Pulled out Mom's red wallet with one hand, snapped the change compartment open and slid five quarters in there to reinforce Mom's one lone silver quarter for any potential vending machine foray. Snapped the change purse shut—

Saw the money in the wallet.

There was only one one-dollar bill where there should have been . . . *What was it?* . . . Oh yeah: four. And I knew there should have been more than one five-dollar bill.

"Is everything alright?" mumbled my mom's tired voice.

My aunt hid her pleading nodding *yes* face from her straining sister as I turned to look at the two of them.

Don't drop worry bombs on them! Not now!

I walked to the bed and stood there until Mom looked me straight on.

"Will you come see me tomorrow?" she said.

"You know I will."

I squeezed her left shoulder, and her unbroken right hand covered mine.

My aunt turned from saying goodbye to telling my mom something about nothing that mattered. We all heard that. We were supposed to. We were moving on even if the two of them were staying in that room.

I was a dozen steps on the green carpet in that white mineshaft hallway beyond Mom's room when an apartment door up ahead on the left opened.

Backing out with soundless steps came the recycled nurse's aide Denise.

She pulled that door closed with nary a click.

Turned to walk away and saw me standing there watching her.

Like it was casual, I unzipped my black leather jacket.

Held its two sides out to *obviously* flip away any *wet* from the rain.

Green smocked Denise stared at me and my revealed Glock.

Said it cold, said it loud: "I've got one of those too."

My smile wrapped her in sunshine as I said: "Good to know."

We waited. Watched.

She walked away toward all the tomorrows where she knew I wouldn't be.

38

What brings you two to the Tap Room on a stormy Saturday night?" said the tattoo-armed bartender as she wiped the bar with a rag and moved a bowl of peanuts down between the stools where Cody and I sat.

"We're just looking for a place to be," said Cody.

"Aren't we all," she said.

We ordered beers.

When the bartender turned to get them, our out-of-sight hands exchanged what had been tucked into our jackets' inside pockets. Our hands were empty by the time she turned around with our glasses filled with cold gold.

Nobody in the bar noticed our switch.

No one there cared.

Probably.

We sat at the middle of the bar. No one sat near either of us. No one could hear us if we whispered. No one could see the guns under our jackets.

But hell, every local knew Cody had to be packing.

The bartender's playlist fed the bar's speakers a mix of generations' songs.

The pool table in the back clicked balls toward the holes desired by two couples holding cues and laughing.

Two rust-haired women sitting at the end of the bar hovered past their quarter century mark. Their cellphones lay beside two glasses of beer. They looked like they belonged across the street at the Lowdown. But maybe they wanted a change of scenery. Like they wanted their tomorrows to be more than their yesterdays. Their reflections in the bar mirror *didn't* watch Cody and I, two *not too old* unmarried men on stools waiting for What's To Come.

We all wear masks when we face the world.

And when we face the mirror.

Or when our screens face us.

My slight nod keyed the two women to Cody: "Looks like you've got fans."

"Possibly," he said. "But you're the come home—"

"Don't say it."

Cody took a pull of his beer.

Ignored playing it cool.

Let a smile come off him as he turned to his right to face those two women.

They smiled back. The one with short red hair sent him a small wave.

"She's Isabel," said Cody. "The other one is Clarisse. They're sisters."

"We all gotta be somebody."

"And you didn't see any *maybes* today. Nobody on your trail."

"Nobody and everybody."

"Least you nailed Mike."

I took a swig of my beer while the jukebox played on a Saturday night where I sat on a barstool with my buddy and not anyone else.

"When's the blow up going to happen?" said Cody.

"That's not up to me." Added: "Not *just* me."

"Told you about that," said Cody.

Short redheaded Isabel scrolled her cellphone.

Long red-haired Clarisse's hunter's eye watched the visible in the neon bar.

"Tell me this," I said as we drank golden brew. "Ron's whole *'Dee hates gays'* thing. Do you buy that? In this day and age? Even here in Sidner? Our generation? Most people here aren't like that, are they?"

Cody shrugged and saw Clarisse's reflection catch that in the bar mirror.

"You don't know what you ain't seeing," said Cody. "I've seen Billy K pass nasty smirks. Shelly, too. Bad jokes. Folks changing where they sat *because*. Once had to stop a *just because* beat-down. Still, it ain't as bad as it used to be.

"But Ron hiding who he is fits more with Dee's needing a kid for the *dynasty to outlive her* thing," he said. "When we were together, Rose working at the bank, she'd tell me stuff she'd hear Dee say that fits with that *gimme a grandkid*. Beyond that . . .

"Dee runs with the big-time politics crowd. Ones who—to get votes—throw their saddles on all the old fears and sidle up to folks who say Jesus doesn't love everybody and that no way could evolution be how God makes things work. They hate trans and gays—*'perverts'*—or say they do. Now out here, there's another carpetbagger billionaire who's running for Congress. Anti-gay though he doesn't say it that way. He's given a few hundred thou' to a museum of the Bible in the state's biggest town. They got wall-sized dioramas that show cavemen riding dinosaurs after they left Eden, so that proves all that.

"So Dee having a gay son *and heir*, she might have to disown him and his sinful ways to stay tight with that tax-breaks and no-rules-for-them crowd."

I raised my glass and Cody met it with his.

"To America," I said. "Free to be you and me and whoever we want to be."

Clink!

Our gesture found the eyes of the redheaded sisters Isabel and Clarisse.

Cody sent them a nod and a raise of his near-empty glass.

Isabel sent us a smile.

Clarisse didn't flinch.

"I gotta get out of here," I said.

"In a minute," said Cody.

He called the bartender over. Placed an order. Dropped dollars on the bar.

"I'll cover you home," he said. "Check your crib."

We drained our glasses. Stood and zipped up our jackets.

From down at the end of the bar, through the music of the jukebox and the rumble of an 8-ball on the pool table, Clarisse called out to us: "So you're leaving."

The bartender set two fresh beers down in front of Isabel and Clarisse.

"My friend's had a hard traveling day," Cody told those two sisters.

"I'm going to ride him home," he fibbed, not mentioning my mother's car parked outside in the rain on Main Street. "I plan on being back before those new beers of yours are gone. If I'm not, know it wasn't up to me. If I am and you're not here, figure that's on you. Either way, the rain's gonna fall."

He flipped his rain jacket's hood up like a monk.

I flipped up my jacket collar like a hatless fool as we reached the door and opened it to sounds of falling water.

Cody's hood hid his face as I said: "Who the hell are you?"

39

You're never sure what you feel when you're home alone in the rain.

Cody's drop-off security check was thorough but fast. He played it cool when he flipped his hood up in my living room to go back into the rain.

I wondered where and how he'd end up that night.

Thunder rumbled outside my white walled, blue shingled A-frame cottage in Sidner, Montana, USA, Planet Earth, twinkling darkness of expanding space.

Lightning and thunderstorms were unusual in October for that part of the globe, but *usual* wasn't what it used to be anywhere on our earth then.

I felt relief as the rain beat against the house, the windows.

I was warm. I was dry. I was safe.

But.

There was no one there but me. No one in the closets. No one had climbed through either of the two windows in my boyhood room and then sidled on their back under the bed. Suppressing giggles. Patient. Eager. Waiting.

There was also no one there for my smile to hold.

Opening the refrigerator bathed me in light.

But I wasn't hungry—or at least the doggy bag of my double cheeseburger and cold French fries didn't appeal to me. After leaving my aunt and Mom, I hadn't wanted to eat dinner but thought I should. Caution and wanting to stay dry drove me to the drive-in hamburger stand by the highway out of town. I parked on the street. Let the engine idle to let the intermittent wipers whump my windshield view. Watched other cars *whooshing* by in that evening's tears.

And I wasn't thirsty—one beer with Cody took care of that and promised a wake up in darkness. I'd have to sit up in bed. Swing my bare feet down to the carpet. Make my helpless ankles visible from under the bed. Pad to the bathroom. I always pee sitting down when I get up in the night so I won't need to turn on the lights and let that blare wake me up to see what was there.

The refrigerator door closed.

I stood there in the kitchen.

Thunder rumbled and rain beat against the picture window to the night where Owl Eyes Mike'd soaped his monsters.

Had to be him, right?

My belt held the weight of the gun. I was as ready as I could be. What I'd done, what I was still going to do, that was me being smart. Cody had my back. Had my whole sphere.

That made me smile.

And relax. As much as I could in the rainstorm I'd chosen.

My laptop lay closed on the dining room table, done for the night.

My black moleskin journal lay closed next to it by a fountain pen of my father's that my mother made sure bled ink and . . . *AND—*

Surge up my spine/my skull filling/muscles tensing *go, go, go!* I huddled over the black journal. Popped the cap off the fountain pen.

Two pages of cross-outs and scribbles later, I sat at the table.

The doorway into the kitchen was behind me.

Rain battered the window of darkness in front of me.

That blue-inked poem breathed on its own white page in the black journal.

What if this is the last thing I ever get to write? flashed through me. *How will they know I kept trying to do it true right up until my very end?*

Every act of writing is hoping to be read. Every song is played to be heard. Every painting exists to be seen. Every movie is made for an audience. Every social media post is made to be clicked, liked, or better still, loved and shared. Even if trolls from Russia, China, Iran, Big Hate and Big Money are the clickers.

But even if no one ever found or read that haiku after they found my corpse, I'd helped it exist in infinity.

We carve what we can into the river of time as the river rolls on, not caring we rippled it. But we did, we do.

I sat alone at that table I'd come to. That precise moment.

Mark it.

I wrote it all down below that haiku. October 3. Saturday. 2024. The time of night on the kitchen's old-fashioned clock. The rain pounding my hometown.

Closed the black moleskin journal by my resting laptop and—

Bzzt!

My charging phone buzzed a text message . . . from *her*.

Tomorrow morning when the
church bells ring. Walk west
on Main Street, Roxy side.
Wear your sunglasses.

40

Sunday morning shone bright with a vast blue sky. Saturday night's storm washed away the forest fires' smoke. The air smelled fresh and clean. Cool but not chilly came through my open driver's side window as I sat parked in Mom's old car at the east end of Main Street.

The black metal hands of my wristwatch clicked 10:47.

The Methodist church bells chimed loud and clear to summon the faithful.

My car door opened and I stepped out onto the street.

Main Street held a dozen or so cars strung out along both sidewalks further up the road from where I started walking.

The sidewalk held only me.

Up ahead and across the street I saw the door to the Tap Room was closed. The law didn't let any bar open until after the official church hours. The Low-down on my side of the street was closed, too, another Saturday night swept away. Everything was closed as far as I knew. Elly's Chat & Chew was never open on Sunday. The P.S. opened after church when Sunday savorers might replace some of the weekdays' caffeine customers.

I walked past the picture windows of the Western wear store.

Up ahead by Cody's closed gun store, a parked car I couldn't see clearly because of a pickup truck slumped behind it opened its driver's door.

Out stepped Lana.

Her crimson dress clung to her curves. Long sure strides carried her towards me. Her midnight hair flowed with every step.

She wore sunglasses.

So did I.

My black leather jacket covered the Glock and my pocketed cellphone.

We marched towards each other like sly lovers in a French movie.

She got to the glass doors for the Roxy before I did.

Waited for me to meet her there.

Her ruby smile dazzled my morning as she said: "We're here."

"Where?"

She took off her sunglasses. Tucked them into my jacket's outside pocket. Pulled off my sunglasses and put them in there, too.

Lana pulled one of the Roxy's glass doors—

—and it opened.

"Come on," she told me. "You know where to go."

Where to go.

Heartbeats pounded my chest. Answers. Questions. Visions.

Once upon a time movie theaters like the Roxy helped create our *Shared Reality*. Didn't matter if you bought a ticket for the movie proclaimed on the Roxy's Main Street marquee. You knew something about it, even if it was only that the theater showing it was real. Thus you were part of the universal "*us*" that knew so and so you shaped your life within that *Shared Reality*.

That year of 2024, our *Shared Reality* . . . wasn't.

Once upon a time French movie creator Jean-Luc Godard noted that the difference between going to the movies and watching the TV screen in your living room or as you lay in your married couple's bed was that the TV screen beamed its programs into you while the movie screen rising beyond you beamed its story from behind you, that 24-frames-per-second vision sweeping you up in it and carrying *you* into the story—not nailing *the story* into you.

Like a novel pulling your seeing eyes with its lines moving you ever forward word by word, letter by letter, to reveal the wows in that prose.

You own your role reading a novel and watching a shared reality movie.

A TV or cyber screen like a cellphone owns the role it gives you.

Like the title of a whacky slim paperback published in 1967—the year my dad graduated from high school—says:

"The Medium Is The Massage"

Godard was two years gone from us that autumn morning in 2024. He wept in his beyond knowing how right he'd been.

For the world he left behind—

—the world we live in now where step-counters walk through city parks staring at the cellphone in their hand and not seeing savvy black crows on the tree branches above where an urban coyote shelters and a mugger watches.

Now until bullets, bombs, plagues, climate change's wildfires or poverty intervene, "reality" is created by cyber screens of cellphones, laptops, iPads, desktop computers and TV screens streaming into us as data entry points—DEPs. Each DEP is linked not to its own beating heart, but instead to the digital flow created by the screens—

—and thus we have no *shared reality* beyond gravity or the smoke from distant fires that we can tell ourselves doesn't matter.

That Sunday morning as I stepped into the foyer of that haunted palace of my childhood dreams my beating heart sensed Lana walking behind me.

A tired woman in a sweatshirt and saggy jeans waited at the door into the theater's lobby. She nodded to Lana. Walked past us. I heard her lock the door.

Soft lights lit the theater lobby where everything was the same and everything was different. The red carpet had been replaced by a durable green. Stairs still led down to restrooms I'd cleaned with a strong stomach, brushes and bleach. Downstairs was the office my father once filled six days a week—but only a few hours on Sundays.

To the right as Lana and I came in waited the candy counter. A glass display case for almond Hershey bars and candied marbles that a clumsy purchaser or some smart-ass watching a movie often dropped onto the sloping-down-toward-the-screen floor. Their rolling clatter made the audience chuckle or groan. The popcorn machine was silent, but a heap of yellow kernels sent their smells our way as they waited to be scooped into handheld cartons. The soda machine was emblazoned with the red and white swooping colors for Coca-Cola.

Lana smiled at the sweatshirted woman.

"Do you two know each other? Lorraine, this is Jim. His dad used to have your job," said the woman whose husband's family owned this theater now.

"Modern times," Lana told me. "Lorraine can do it all from out here. Tap a few commands into a keyboard. The disc of the movie plays itself."

Lorraine said: "*Well*, more than that with previews and—"

"Today has no previews of what's to come," interrupted Lana.

The Roxy's manager's answering smile carried some shared secret.

Lana told her: "Give us a few minutes to find seats."

Lana turned us around toward one of the two propped-open doors into the shadowed auditorium.

My heart pounded.

Probably you've been in far grander movie theaters than the Roxy. The auditorium held around 500 seats. They'd been upgraded from the push-down cushioned metal planks from the JFK days when my dad was a kid, but were still less comfy than the button-reclining padded thrones most big city movie theaters installed before the end of Obama's presidency. The main floor sloped down to a stage with stairs leading up to the same red curtain from my boyhood hanging over the giant white screen far bigger than American living rooms' "reality" TV screens that created the Trump presidency. The balcony's twelve rows of chairs led up to the closed door of the projection booth and the glass portals through which the magic beamed and that an Eisenhower-era horror movie filled with mushrooming-out-to-the-audience red killing goo called *The Blob*.

"What are we doing here?"

"Finding our marks," said actress Lana.

Behind us, Lorraine closed the propped-open doors. Left us alone.

Lana led me to the center of the perfect row slope for a perfect view of the screen. She sat me down on her right side. Sat down next to my heart. She dumped my black leather jacket on the seat beside me. Showed the world my gun. Her clinging crimson dress rode up her bare tan thighs.

This woman who brought me here turned and kissed me with a deep fire.

Snatched my cellphone from my shirt pocket and turned it off, her voice an official monotone as she said: *"Please remember to silence all cellphones."*

Grinned: *"We hope you enjoy the show."*

She snapped my cell in her black purse and put that on the sticky floor of the movie theater.

Sat back in her seat. Took my hand.

Darkness fell on us.

The red curtain cranked up to reveal the giant white screen.

A beam of light passing over our heads from behind filled the screen with the famous logo of that Hollywood movie-making corporation. Music swelled in the auditorium's speakers as another production company's name appeared.

My heart pounded my ribs.

Lana said: "Whatever you've imagined doing at the movies. *Whatever.*"

Her perfect grip filled my hand.

I held on with my whole life.

Pleaded: *"Just be with me!"*

Whispered: "*Thank you! Thank you!*"

Trembled for what was coming that I'd seen dozens of times but never in my hometown dream factory that helped make me. Colors fill the screen. Sounds.

FADE IN:

An aerial pan: Washington, DC. Capitol. White House.

Swoop down to street level. Morning rush hour.

Cars. Traffic. Drones in suits and ties and proper dresses.

MIRROR MAN

ROBERT, 25, blazer, no tie. Strides through commuters.

Starbucks cup in his hand. Smiling. Eyes observing.

Big Brother lenses everywhere. On poles. In stores.

ROBERT passes statue of slaveholder Confederate general.

Credits roll: Director. Actors. Producers. Screenwriters.

ROBERT steps onto a subway entrance escalator.

Flowing across ROBERT riding the escalator down:

Based on the novel by James Traven.

ROBERT rocking in moving subway car.

Aerial pan: CIA headquarters.

Interior shots: Wide corridors. War rooms. Guards.

Elevator descends. Factory floor of cubicles.

ROBERT's work cubicle. High tech. Taped to wall:

A downloaded photo of Marilyn Monroe reading a book.

His computer screen: *Five days/no response*—"Fuck!"
Next cubicle, his buddy MAX: "You OK?"
These two young CIA programmers banter.
MAX: "Got us those tickets." High-fives.
ROBERT: "You always know how to work it."
CUT TO: The boss named CLIFF's office.
ROBERT confessing his rebel move:
Off-task keyboarding national security's Big Grid.
His hustled plan: *Grok* hostile infiltrators—INFILTS—
by inputting known bad guy tactics + personal data
mirror man cogs like himself to create a PP:

"Possible Profile"

Version 1.0 based on him programmed as test.
Automatically zapped to the Wise Wonkers first.
But no response from Upstairs. Nobody must care.
CLIFF: "*Full stop. You are exceeding your program.*
Obey system parameters. Work the Grid."
Sundown reddens the ivory-monument city.
Subway rumbles ROBERT going home.
Bzzt! Tinder match.
Cut To: A hip bar. ROBERT and a cool blonde woman.
FAYE: gig work graphic artist. All the right *sames*.
Strokes his hand. But she won't. Maybe next time.
The next morning.
ROBERT's CIA screen: *No response/six days*
After work.
Second date with FAYE. Outdoor café. Dinner before dark.
A neighboring table with Married Couple on date night.
Another table holds Hipster Duo making the scene.
White tablecloths. Smiles. Jokes. Eyes full of—
Crack!
ROBERT'S red wine glass shatters! Waiter crashes onto their table!
ROBERT & FAYE jump. A customer's head explodes!

Two Quirky Masks killers *cough-cough-cough* machine-guns.
ROBERT & FAYE dive to the floor.
Surprise gun blasts from Hipster Duo—*targeting Masked Killers!*
Masked Killers *cough cough cough* at Hipster Duo!
Bullets crash over ROBERT & FAYE on the floor!
They're trapped in the middle of a gunfight!
Hipster Duo bloodied down.
Hipster Man skims his gun across café floor to ROBERT & FAYE.
ROBERT grabs Glock: *Bam! Bam!*
Masked Killers flinch. ROBERT pulls FAYE inside café.
A chase to the kitchen. Bullets fly. Cooks flee. Plates clatter.
ROBERT spots open shiny metal door in wall—a dumbwaiter.
Shoves FAYE inside. Fires cover *Bam!* Punches button.
Jumps into dim red bulb lit box. Slams door shut.
Crammed in with FAYE like a romantic tangle.
Dumbwaiter lifts off. Bullets ding its metal door.
Rooftop cafe. Chaos. Dumbwaiter pops open.
ROBERT & FAYE stumble out.
Masked Killers racing up the fire escape.
ROBERT & FAYE leap to building across the alley.
Tumble safe landings.
ROBERT looks back/down. Masked Killers reversing.
Rushing off fire escape. Now charging building
where ROBERT & FAYE are on the roof.
ROBERT grabs FAYE'S phone. Tosses it off roof with his.
Phones bounce onto roof of passing Amazon delivery van.
A beat. Masked Killers whirl to chase van.
ROBERT: "They're tracking our cells!"
He and FAYE race down other fire escape.
Busy night sidewalk.
Rando Man checking his cellphone screen.
ROBERT & FAYE fleeing through crowd.
ROBERT spots Uber waiting at corner's red light.
Sees Rando Man watching his cellphone screen.

Charges Rando as traffic light about to change.
"Sorry!" Knees Rando in groin. Grabs his phone.
Pushes gasping Rando to stunned FAYE who spins him away.
Uber pulls up. ROBERT & FAYE dive into it.
ROBERT waves stolen phone ID.
Uber drives them away.
Uber lets them off near Lincoln Memorial.
Mom and two impatient kids waiting on sidewalk.
Mom consoling them: "He's coming. He's on his way."
ROBERT leads FAYE past family. Trashes cellphone.
"If we call anybody, we call everybody."
Security cameras on light poles. They board tour bus.
Get out at Arlington Cemetery.
Find a quiet spot amidst evening graves.
FAYE: "This is all wrong! They shot our cover team!"
FAYE is CIA. She lied to him. She tricked him.
But she's not an agent. She just taps a keyboard.
A geek the CIA's Grid matched to his Tinder profile.
His rebel program algo'd smart—and profiled him
as Probable INFILT. FAYE and cover team detailed
to clear or corner him. "But not to kill anybody!"
Then who are the Masked Killers?
ROBERT: "The ones who want us dead."
"Not me," says FAYE: "You."
Plus: Now FAYE missing and her cover team killed.
The Grid will upgrade: ROBERT is CONFIRMED INFILT.
Now it's CIA sanctioned OD time: Overwrite & Delete
Night.
Burglary into suburban taxidermy store.
Strategy amidst walls of stuffed animal heads.
Masked Killers = hitters for a real INFILT.
ROBERT's rebel program spotlighted him—
he's a savvy threat to the bad guys—
so INFILT spotlighted ROBERT. With crosshairs.
INFILT knows ROBERT's profile. What he'll do.

Plus the Grid is running predictive scenarios.
Masked Killers *and* Agency TDBZ—Take Down BoyZ.
Both will shoot to kill target ROBERT.
FAYE: "If we're going to die tomorrow, let's live tonight."
She's facing him from in front of the store's counter.
FAYE flips open her white blouse. FOCUS ON:
FAYE from behind. Her hands unsnap her bra.
Her naked back. ROBERT's face over her shoulder.
They embrace. She whispers: "Unzip my skirt."
He reaches behind her. Obeys. She pulls skirt
and panties down. The counter blocks full view
of her naked butt. Kisses we see from behind her.
ROBERT's hands flow between them.
FAYE whirls her back to him. An R-rated glimpse
of her naked breasts. She bends over the counter.
FAYE: "Take me! Take me now! Come into me!"
Pan ROBERT standing, lunging into FAYE
as she bends over, grasps the counter.
They groan. They pant. *"Yes! Yes! Yes!"*
The walls of stuffed animal heads watch.
Dawn rises over DC taxidermy shop.
FAYE stands at counter as dead animals watch her.
Presses shop's antique landline telephone to her face.
Buzz of call.
ROBERT'S buddy MAX stands at his DC bathroom sink.
Buck naked. Shaving. Lifts cellphone to his face: "Yes?"
FAYE: "I'm coming now for those tickets you got us."
MAX *realizes*: "Be careful. I hear traffic's murder out there."
FAYE hangs up.
ROBERT nods from under a wings-spread stuffed condor:
"My profile says I'd never put a friend in danger."
FAYE: "So now you've glitched the system. Again."
ROBERT: "And now I'm following you."
Riding a packed city bus.
ROBERT hides face under taxidermist's leather cowboy hat.

FAYE wears stolen taxidermist's baseball fan jacket, cap.
Holds a handkerchief. Forces a sneeze. Sprays spittle.
Other people on bus try to turn away/thus not see her.
Capitol Hill. Shops. Cafes. Bars. Pedestrians.
ROBERT & FAYE stalk off the bus.
Slide into the stream of commuters and shoppers.
Man in a red hoodie. Walking toward them. Past them.
Store window reflection: Red Hoodie spins after them.
FAYE spots reflection—
—pushes ROBERT away from Red Hoodie's thrusting knife.
Idiot careening on rent-a-scooter crashes into Red Hoodie.
Red Hoodie flips/stumbles into the street—
—in front of a screeching bus. *Splat!*
ROBERT & FAYE run away from screams and sirens.
A rat runs across the alley behind MAX's townhouse.
ROBERT & FAYE sneak in MAX's back door.
Conspirators huddle in the kitchen.
Excitable ROBERT babbling, recapping the whole thing.
MAX trying to get him to calm down. To have coffee.
FAYE listening to ROBERT riffing unfolding logic.
She's scanning as the two men start *mansplaining* to her.
Pours them cups of coffee from pot on stove.
Gets milk from fridge. Opens drawer looking for spoon.
Spots five pre-paid cell phones in back of drawer.
Stares at soft bulge in MAX's front pants pocket.
Walks close to give MAX his coffee. He takes it.
ROBERT riffing: ". . . so INFILT has to be, *like*, a clone of me . . ."
FAYE jerks killers' Quirky Mask out of MAX's pocket.
MAX grabs at her.
FAYE swings wide with a black iron frying pan.
MAX ducks back—she misses—hits ROBERT!
Numbed ROBERT crashes back against wall oven.
FAYE swings frying pan—
MAX dodges—stomps her in the stomach.
FAYE crashes into ROBERT. They fall to the floor.

MAX stands on left leg/snaps right knee up high.
Grabs the gun in his pants-covered right ankle holster.
FAYE rolls off ROBERT with his gun in her hand.
BANG! MAX's forehead blooms a bloody red third eye.
Oops. Another Op lie: FAYE is *not* just a CIA office geek.
Later. The alley behind where MAX was deleted.
Inside the battle zone house. Searchers. Suits. Techs.
ROBERT stares at FAYE: "Who are you?"
Version 1.0—a keyboard dreamer like me?
Version 2.0—an algo'd upload of my best fantasies?
Version 3.0—a spy who says she isn't?
Version 4.0—a programmed shooter who doesn't miss?
FAYE: "Does my *who* matter if the Grid makes us work?"
He looks around the spy scene: "But it was me who got this right."
Shakes his head: "And it was the Grid that got me wrong."
FAYE: "All that's a null set now. Deleted. System secured."
She leads him out the front door.
FAYE leads him to a car. Opens his door: "You ride shotgun."
She walks around. Opens driver's door. Sees him hesitating.
FAYE: "Come on. Don't you want to see what's next?"
ROBERT stares at the open door of the car to *where.*

FADE OUT.

41

Imagine your teenage bedroom.

How many times did you lie there aching for someone?

How many times did you fantasize a lover there with you?

Lana's car sat parked outside my house for everyone to see.

"That plus what we did here," she'd said as we blinked out of the Roxy into Sunday's sunshine. "So much for the *'secret'* of the affair."

"I hope so."

She grinned.

Pulled her sunglasses out of my black leather jacket's outside pocket.

Slid them on. *Tres cool.*

Reached into my jacket's heart pocket.

Found and fitted my sunglasses over my eyes.

Our rides took us to my family home.

I parked Mom's car in the driveway.

Lana parked in front of my family's house.

I jogged to meet her at the curb—

—saw her wave to the west.

Ten-year-old Brett Petersen shuffled outside his house like he was looking for anywhere else to go. He saw Lana pull up. Saw her get out of her car. Saw her wave at him. And froze.

I walked up to Lana. We took each other's hand.

"Hey, Brett," I said. "How you doin'?"

He shrugged. Sort of smiled.

"Dude," I told him from my heart, "may you get this lucky someday."

Then I led Lana away from him. We walked up to the Traven family's front door for all that after-church October Sunday to see.

"Are your parents home?" Lana whispered from every teen adventure.

We laughed. I worked the locks. Let us inside. Closed the door.

The person who'd changed my life stood in the living room of the house that graduated me to a life of my own.

Yes, my eyes swept for hostiles, but what I saw was her. Seeing me.

"You were so lucky to grow up like this," she told me.

"Even more." I stepped right in front of her: "Lucky to grow up to *this*."

My jacket landed on the sofa my mother liked to sit on and watch TV.

Thunder and lightning. A cloud caressed us. We were where we were supposed to be in the soft electric. We held our kiss for five seconds. For five years. Didn't matter. This was us. Every push of her body told me it was her. Every burn of her mouth said it was me.

Lana stepped back. Pulled my hand from her face. Kissed my palm.

She turned around.

Flipped her long black hair off the back of her crimson dress.

My grip slid her zipper down—the best direction.

She stepped out of her shoes.

Afternoon sunlight from the living room windows lit us as her hands slid the crimson dress off her shoulders and let it fall to the carpet.

She wore nothing under her dress but her pride and scents. The straight tan river of her spine to the valley between two half-moons. The long smooth of her shaved legs standing her there where she chose to be. *With me!*

Turned and glowed as she watched my eyes devour her.

Her husky voice said: "Where's your bedroom?"

Her face follows my eyes snapping toward what waits at the end of that hall. Her grin beckons as she steps away, walks backwards to see me following—

Tripping on her shoes!

Laughing, I caught my balance as she caught me.

Kicking off my shoes. Shifting legs to throw off my socks: "You beat me!"

I jerked my belt loose. Pulled my jeans down.

"You look ready to me."

Laughing, we kept laughing, and wasn't this how it was supposed to be?

I was in the hall from the living room when my pants hit the ground with a *clunk* from the belt-holstered Glock.

Leave it where it lies.

My shirt flew off. The hell with my turned-off cellphone in the heart pocket. Let the shirt and all that be a heap on the floor where I grew up. She backs through my bedroom door as my kick snaps away my white jockey shorts.

Then we were there.

Where I'd spent thousands of *Shh!* teenage hours staring at porno screens.

Where I'd slept with secret dreams for thousands of nights.

Now wide awake sunshine fills that room. The window blinds are up. We can see what's real. We see each other.

"You made your bed," she said. "You're a man who makes his own bed."

"Every day," I said.

"Now," I said.

Our cloud floated us to the bed we had. We knew just what to do. Our parts fit. She arched to be kissed by aching-to-kiss-her me. Every touch a wanted caress. Our bare legs entwined on the rumpling bedspread.

We followed her lead. Her choice. Her desire. Trusted her.

Conflicting desires propelled her.

Broke her away from our deep kiss. Pulled me kissing my way down her body. Let me kiss the flesh we both knew covered her heart. We both knew what I meant there and then *oh there*, she pulled me to mouth over her breast *there*. Let me slide to the other side and *oh!* Pushed me down past her belly button that had connected her to everything that came before. Pushed me down between her oh so wide spread legs. Let me *oh she let me* oh let my lips and tongue kiss and lick her all *there*—

—until her shudders shook the bed beneath her and her screams startled the cowboys pictured on my wide-open boyhood bedroom curtains.

She pulled me up onto that bed we made.

Turned me so my back pressed against where I'd so long slept. Swung her leg over me. Straddled me. Smiled down with a hungry grin. Her breasts swung forward and free as she leaned down for our kiss. Her right hand claimed me. Drew me into her. My hands clasped her trembling hips as she rocked back and forth, pushing harder and higher and her black hair waving in the air of her open-mouth gasps/shudders—

The mirror.

The mirror on the inside of my bedroom's closet door.

I saw our reflections surging together on my bed. Saw Lana riding me. Her breasts bouncing. Her flowing long black hair. Her face tilted to my ceiling. Her open mouth panting.

Are we who we see in the mirror?

But I turned to see and caress the flesh of her above me *and and and*—

AND.

Lana curled down on me. Held me tight yet soft and free. Her face bent down along my right cheek. Her hair lay around us like a cobweb we'd spun. I brushed strands off my face. Saw down the curve of her spine toward the foot of the bed and the wall past it. Saw her eyes draped, her lips smile.

I angled my face to the closet mirror framing us to stretch and give myself more space to turn towards her. To find the courage for all I had to confess.

My shift back toward her slid my gaze off the mirror. Took my focus along the wall toward the foot of the bed. Let me see the framed-by-open-cowboy-drapes window to the Petersens' house next door. Let me get a glimpse of blue sky.

The black rectangle of a cellphone rose like a periscope above the bottom sill of my bedroom window.

42

My hand slid up Lana's spine under her long hair.

Gripped the back of her neck like a vise.

Strangled her gurgle.

Trapped her ear against my whispering mouth as I pinned her on top of me: *"Shut up! Don't fucking move!"*

She chose to trust. To not to fight. To obey. To listen.

"There's a cellphone watching us from the window behind your ass!" I whispered. "Foot of the bed. Odds are the camera's running. There's apps to make it work like a listening device. Up the sensitivity of the microphone."

Her whisper thrilled my soul: "How can we get the son of a bitch?"

She flowed into the moment. Flowed into *warrior.*

Listened to me whisper the script:

"We're happy. Carefree. In the middle of a Sunday afternoon lovefest. Fucking our brains out. We're going to roll around so my back is to the door. Only look in my face. See only my face. Don't even *think* about the window. Do not look at the window! Or the other window that's to your left now—my right. Don't look at that window either. It'll be behind you when you roll off and over. On the north. The backyard side. Above the patio."

My hands lifted her head but kept her face turned down to mine.

Her naked back blocked the view of her face from the cellphone's window.

She stared down at my phony *just-in-case* half-moon smile.

I pulled her heavy breasted beauty down for a *like-we-mean-it* kiss.

Her lips lifted off mine.

I whispered: "Now!"

She rolled off me to her left as I turned under her to my right. We were groin to groin. Heart to heart. My prayer hands cupped her face. Her top hand rested on mine.

My whisper: "I've got to get out of the bedroom *and* make him think I'm coming straight back. And you've gotta stay safe."

"So do you," she whispered. "You."

We grabbed a breath.

"I've got the skit," she whispered. "Drop your hand to my breast."

"He might not be able to see this."

"He'll know what's happening. Now hurry! Never lose the audience. Stroke your hand on me down there. Yes. Like that. Now on the way back up to my face, poke me in my belly—and keep facing me no matter what!"

My poke jerked her back laughing hard and gleefully facing me.

Lana charged!

Instincts jerked me back toward the edge of the bed.

She pounced on me. Grabbed me/held us together. Her hands shifted us so my body was between her and the window to my back. My legs naturally had to angle toward the floor. She shifted to sit in front of me. Whispered: "Tickle time!"

Her fingers arced around my body as they dive-bombed my armpits.

And I jerked up off the bed like anyone *literally* in my position would.

Her hands gripped my hips for viewing from behind.

Her hair wildly fanned out from my silhouette.

She slid her naked front up mine to whisper in my ear: "I've got to buy you time. Keep him occupied. Make him certain that you're coming right back."

That west window watched her beyond the flanks of my flesh as she flowed back from me.

Can the window see her face off to the side of my naked ass?

Is the spy still there watching us?

Lana's whispers flicked through her lopsided lying grin: "Tease me! You're coming right back! He's gotta know that! Make me stay right here!"

My hands pantomimed: *Back off. Stay put.*

The window behind me framed me as I pointed up: *Wait one minute.*

One step towards the open bedroom door—

—Lana turned with me to slap me on my bare ass!

"Hurry up, cowboy!" she yelled. *"We gotta talk about what's going on!"*

Maybe her words vibrated the bedroom window's glass to be heard outside.

Maybe they didn't.

I stepped toward the bedroom door and she rose off the bed to face my going. Her back was to the window. I glanced over my shoulder.

Naked Lana was dancing to music only she heard like this was a moment of joy. Lana danced *obviously* to celebrate what was coming back to her.

She danced that October Sunday morning as I charged from my bedroom of dreams. She shucked and jived like the groomsmen shuffling down the aisle at last Friday's wedding. She filled the view from the window with that show of how everything is *cool*. Her black hair swayed on her bare back. Her curved moon hips trembled with rhythm.

All that pane of glass could see was her celebration from behind—

—blocking my leaving and where I'm going/what I'm doing.

My glance back *groks* the dancer's hidden face contorted in grim fury.

Three steps through the hall—scooping up my gun belt jeans.

Lana dances her heart, her soul, her savvy.

Her bare ass stares at the pane of glass.

I surge through the living room.

Pull the Glock from the holster.

Drop everything but the gun's cold black weight.

Lana plumps and straightens the helter-skelter pillows.

My bare feet race across the living room carpet toward the kitchen.

Lana schoolgirl leaps *Ta-dah!* onto her back on the white-sheet bed.

I slide on my bare feet across the kitchen floor. Naked. Gun in my hand.

Lana beams at the ceiling and crucifies her arms on the white bed sheet.

I sneak past the kitchen table.

She arches up from the mattress. Her breath pumps her breasts toward the ceiling. Her eyes close as her lips kiss heaven. Her stretched wide open palms face the stars that will nail her.

Back hall and the heavy inside door opens without a sound—

—shows me the screen door facing the empty backyard.

Lana folds herself up in a yoga sit-up to her toes.

My left hand frees the screen door's latch.

My lover jerks my bed's top sheet up and over her head. Only strands of hair on the white pillow identify Lana as the body under the sheet.

Obviously, she couldn't see anybody or anything.

The storm door opened without a squeak.

Cold air reached into the house to claim my naked body. I stepped out onto the back porch with a black metal railing around its top slab and four steps down. Turned around and gently let the screen door close.

The latch *clicked*.

Nobody gunned me down.

My back pressed against the house as I slid down those steps past our kitchen's rear window once wounded in action by WhORe. My face locked on where the patio would appear. Where the north-facing bedroom was. Where a wide gap waited between the northwest corner of our house and the Petersens' garage. Through that gap waited the window where the cellphone surfaced.

Rocks jabbed my bare soles.

On the cement path running below the kitchen window. Solid ground.

The Glock snapped above my thundering heart in a two-handed combat grip.

My aim scanned across its short black barrel.

Crouching quick, swinging around to face the backyard window—

There! He's there now!

Black motorcycle helmet. Brown leather jacket. Cellphone raised to the second window into my bedroom.

Quick steps on the cold October lawn to box him on the patio slab—

—maybe he hears me coming, maybe my reflection shines in the bedroom window, maybe it's time to go or killer instinct HE'S TURNING AROUND!

"Freeze, motherfucker!"

The helmet's black visor reflects naked me zeroing it with my gun.

43

My gun-aiming naked image filled the motorcycle helmet's black visor.

"You move one fucking finger and I'll blast you full of holes!"

One thundering heartbeat. Two. Three.

Muffled voice: "Do you think your gun's big enough?"

"I've got thirteen chances to find out."

"You don't want to do that."

"*'You're right, Sheriff Fenton. I didn't want to shoot the son of a bitch but he gave me no choice. I was in fear for my life.'*

"But hell, this is Montana. You're trespassing. Throw in stealing naked pictures of us, *well*, anybody would shoot to stop that from happening to them."

"I got lost looking for my bike."

My grimace at his alibi couldn't be contained: "*Really?* You'd try to float some weak-ass shit like that? *Lost* in my backyard? Give me a break."

The muffled voice inside the helmet said: "What do you want?"

We both heard Lana's voice from the back door. "I'm coming out!"

I yelled back to her: "Watch it! Where and how I say!"

Told the black visor: "You're going to give me what I want."

The screen door slammed.

Lana stalked into my field of vision.

The black visor mirrored her naked body on the October lawn.

Butcher knife in her hand.

God, I was proud of her! She charged to help NOW, naked or not!

My nod directed her beside me.

She crouched like a nude ninja ready to thrust the knife.

The Glock's death hole zeroed the spy's brown leather jacket.

The black visor reflected us posed there side-by-side naked.

"You two make a hell of a sight," said the muffled voice inside the helmet. "Don't you worry what the kids next door might see?

"*Oh my*," said the muffled snide voice as the visor focused on my naked groin. Or on Lana's bare breasts. Or both. "Looks like it's chilly out here."

"Take your helmet off! You throw it, I'll blast you before it hits the ground."

Those black gloved hands popped off the helmet's snap.

Left the dark visor down as they lifted the helmet up and off the head of—

The woman at the end of the bar the night I fought Darrell!

She wore her blonde hair chopped short.

Shook her helmet-freed head.

Lana whispered: *"You're the woman from the rest stop bathroom!"*

The reply sent a grin my way: "I'm just a girl trying to earn a buck."

"Two lies in one line," I said.

"I'm good at what I do."

"What you're going to do now is shut the fuck up. Don't say one word until I tell you to. No yelling for help."

"It's called *backup*."

"You call anything, you're done. Now shut up. Roll the helmet across the grass to Lana."

Lana checked it inside and out: "Just a helmet."

She tossed it out of our way. Held the knife high and ready.

"Now," I told the shaggy blonde, "slowly—and I mean *slowly*—unzip your jacket. Let it fall to the ground."

She did.

No visible weapon on her belt or in her armpits. Possibly something could be holstered beneath the bulge of her breasts under her sweatshirt. I ordered a slow-turn and saw nothing tucked by her spine.

Lana grabbed the brown jacket: "Wallet. Cellphone charger. Another cellphone. Small spiral notebook and a pen."

"Leave it. We need our hands free."

I shifted Lana and me until our prisoner was between us and the back door.

"Keep facing away from us," I told the shaggy blonde.

Lana and I combat-shuffled behind our prisoner as we marched her across the lawn to Mom's white garage.

"Hands and feet out wide," I ordered the caught blonde. "Stay back far enough to lean against the wall. Assume the position."

She leaned forward enough to need to spread her arms out wide and press her thin black-gloved hands against the garage's white wall.

I kicked her feet wider apart to show that I could.

"Now turn your hands on the wall. Turn them thumbs down. Press the back of your hands against the wood. Lean there like that."

She did.

I pressed the bore of the Glock into her spine at her waist.

My free hand stroked down each of her arms from fingers to pits. I felt the muscles across her shoulder blades straining from the arm-twisting lean. Found a blue and white bandana folded in her right rear jeans pocket. Her left pocket held a lock-picking kit. What felt like a roll of bills was in her right front pocket. Both front pockets bulged with sets of vehicle keys. My hand patrolled up her blue jeaned groin, across her stomach, up to the bulge of her bra.

"Oh baby," lied her whimper.

My Glock jammed her spine: "Not on your luckiest day."

My hand stroked her left leg down to her ankle—nothing but cloth, flesh, bone. My fingers checked as far down in her low boot as I could reach.

The double-edged and needle-pointed dagger was in her right boot.

"Where's your gun?" I said as I tossed the dagger.

"It's Sunday."

I backed her off the garage wall. Made her drop her thin black gloves to the ground. I wanted her fingerprints everywhere. We moved her toward the back steps into the house. Made her freeze, dip her head, hold it facing down.

Lana took the gun from me. I took her butcher knife.

I choreographed a spin where our prisoner and I were in the same line of fire at the bottom of the steps for only a heartbeat. Propped the screen door open. Backed buck-naked into my house. The prisoner obeyed orders to follow me. Chosen-nude Lana walked rear guard. If bullets had to fly, I'd made myself the one downrange in the line of fire.

We marched the prisoner into my mother's living room.

Sat her on the couch. Her bare hands on her knees.

Lana and I shuddered with the house's warmth on our blued skin.

She kept the gun pointed at the sitting woman while I scurried around the house. Slid into my shirt with my clicked-on cellphone in the pocket. Shut the back doors. Pulled on my jeans. Socks and shoes (and underpants) would wait.

I took the gun back from Lana.

Raised it toward the prisoner: "You got a name?"

"*Oh come on!*" she said. "You thought my line was weak-ass? You know better than this. Ask a question with an answer that gets you past the obvious."

"What's your name and where are your vehicles?"

The prisoner near my age had a face you couldn't label. *Intriguing* to *harsh* in a blink. Long clean jaw. Arctic blue eyes.

"Shawn. My motorcycle's parked a ways up the alley out back."

"Give us your last name . . . *Shawn*," drawled Lana.

"If you hadn't dumped my wallet before checking, you'd already know."

"And your IDs and docs would all be real, right?" I said.

Our captive shrugged: "Whose ID is really real these days, huh?"

Sighed. "But since we're all so intimate now . . . Bradley. Shawn Bradley."

She stared straight into the bore of the Glock I held on her.

I said: "Where's your tan van?"

Shawn made a smile: "Around the corner of the block past the Evergreen. Magnetic Pulaski Electric signs are in the back. Along with the ramp for the bike."

She shrugged: "You never know how you gotta go."

"How you've been going is what you're going to tell Lana and me now in full and glorious detail. How you're an out-of-town spy somebody sicced on us."

"I prefer the term *investigator*. That's what it says in the books of the out of town lawyer whose papering this show under *legal privilege*."

"Who's the client that's paying both of you?"

She stared at me.

My face set stone cold behind the dead-centered Glock.

I told her: "If you get it wrong, then you're making an aggressive move. I might get the shakes and stain my mom's couch. I don't want to do that."

Lana blinked at me.

Prisoner Shawn said: "You think you're that savvy and tough?"

"I know I'm that crazy. And I've got my confirming witness for the law."

Shawn spoke the name of her client—

—and was right.

"What?" said Lana.

"Get dressed," I told Lana as she realized she'd unconsciously stayed naked to not miss a thing. To be my backup with a butcher knife. "Then Shawn's going to call her client. Find out where *this* settles *now*."

44

The front door to that ultra-modern house stood a hand's-width open.

Lana started to push that dark wooden slab—

I grabbed her forearm.

She wore her red fringe jacket over her crimson dress on top of *naked*. She'd left the jacket in the back seat of her car that chilly October Sunday morning when she'd stepped out wearing sunglasses for drama and dreams.

Now she stared at me with unshaded killer eyes.

I pulled my unzipped black jacket wide and nodded to my holstered Glock.

Nodded toward the angled door's narrow shaft of *open*.

Yelled loud enough to echo through the gap into the quiet house.

Loud enough so maybe the neighbors could hear.

So maybe they'd look out their windows and witness us standing there.

Maybe cellphone video us being patient. Respectful. Lawful.

"Trespass is a crime!" I yelled. "You have to invite us in!"

The wind blew past us standing on the landing for the slivered-open door.

A voice inside the house: "Invite you in. Like vampires. How appropriate."

That voice fell silent amidst small town sounds on a Sunday afternoon:

Pro football TV from other houses in the forty-year "new" development that commanded the valley rim on the north side of town. You could taste the beer.

A screen door slammed. I remembered Dad's favorite song.

Someone called for their mother. I knew it wasn't Carrie from the Evergreen assisted living facility where my mom lay chained to a bed.

A distant car alarm.

Dust devils swirled in the street.

The voice inside the house said: "Come in."

I edged Lana behind me as I pushed the door wide open.

A hallway shaft ran from the door toward a room's wall of sunny windows.

We saw furniture. Stuffed armchairs.

The edge of a TV screen mounted through a doorway on a wall to the left.

The wall running down to our right arched into a room that held two chairs probably facing a desk.

The hallway propelled us down its rifle barrel of rippling colors.

Dozens of paintings covered the walls leading into the house.

Original paintings, not prints.

Paintings as big as a desktop.

As small as a book.

One painting framed in a circle like the top of a drum.

Another was framed like a red playing card's diamond.

All of the paintings swirled color.

And all of them envisioned Sidner.

Streets. Buildings. Houses. Cars driving down Main Street. The county courthouse and city hall. The library and the Evergreen. The Coyote Hills over the town's rooftops. The Big Pink. The cemetery of stones. The roads stretching from the mountains and the prairies to end here. The trains. Blurred figures of citizens trapped inside the frames. Men. Women. Children. A dog.

The backroom voice said: "Are you coming or not? I haven't got all day."

Queen Dee'd had time from her private eye's phone call to make sure her makeup was perfect. She wore a Wall Street boardroom power suit.

The hallway rifle-barreled Lana and me through blotches of color to two chairs facing Dee's cushioned high-back throne. We entered her lavender fog.

I took a stand in front of where I was supposed to sit.

Lana stood beside me.

"We got you, Dee. Mrs. Deirdre Zane. Queen Dee."

"I know who I am. And who do you think you are, *Jimmy*?"

"I'm the man with the criminal complaint and the lawsuit.

"And *boy*, won't that get you a lot of publicity!" I added. "Because that *James Traven*, he knows how to work—*What was it you called it?*—those new things like Twitter, Insta, Tick and Tock. And even though he technically isn't part of it, he also sure knows how to swim in what you call *mainstream media*."

"My lawyers would crush you. And why would I care how you *swim*?"

"Because the only thing you care about is what ghost you'll leave to haunt these streets you never could escape."

"I never tried to get out," snapped Dee. "I took over instead."

"I get offering me a bribe," I said. "But hiring a private eye to hawk me?"

"I don't give a shit about you," said Dee. "Not now that you've done what you're supposed to."

Her pinked lips curled a smile when she saw our stunned expressions.

She turned her palm up—

—and damned if we didn't both sit down across from her.

Dee leaned closer: "Do you really think I'd trust *little Ronny* to *not* screw up the plan? His ego's so fucking big he can't conceive that you two might have been smart enough to double-cross him. Not provide proof of adultery. Come back at him with the threat of divorce that even with a prenup could drag on for years and a whole lot of dollars."

"This doesn't make sense!" said Lana. "The plan was to get around you. Fool you. But if you know . . ."

Rattlesnake eyes locked on Lana: "The whole plan was to get rid of *you*."

The old woman snaked a smile at the younger woman sitting across from her, and with some whiff of genuine regret said: "You should have played the baby card right away, dear. Your gig needed savvy that you obviously don't possess. Or for you to lose your qualms."

Dee looked at me as she said: "Too bad you didn't have a hunk like Jim here to help you out with that back then.

"But when you came selling your affair idea instead of Ron's wild schemes, the road smoothed out—*if* Ronny didn't let you fuck up our plan."

"Wait," I said: "Who's *our*?"

Answered my own question: "*Terry*. Ronald's—"

"Bitch," drawled Dee with all the vile bile of that insult of those days.

She smiled.

"Terence is a smart man. Who's tired of being Ronald's fetch-it dog."

"That's how you're going to do it," I whispered. "The whole plan. To grab your whole Zane family empire. Getting rid of Lana makes it easier for you to get rid of Ron—with Terry as your inside man."

I shook my head: "What does Terry get out of it?"

"What he gets is *out* of it," answered Dee. "And a chance to be on top."

She laughed.

I thought Lana was going to throw up.

That made Dee smile even more. She shrugged. "There may have been . . . *extenuating circumstances* in the mix. I'm not a pro with words like you, Jim."

"I'm not here about *words*," I snapped. "I'm here about *whats*. And the *what* of Terry is you got him locked down enough to be sure he uses the big bucks foundation you tried to bribe me with to keep your name alive for all eternity."

"Eternity is a long time," said the shellacked silver haired Dee. "The Deirdre Zane fellowships and art museums, donated do-dads in all the right schools—and I'm told an 'optimized online presence'—all that keeps me alive until at least everyone who's ever breathed with me is dead.

"Hell," she said, "the way we're going these days, there might not be any *afterwards*."

She shrugged: "Still, don't we all want to be remembered?"

"What were you going to do to us?" whispered Lana.

Dee leaned back in her throne.

"I lied to you about vampires," she confessed. "Sometimes, *yes*, they come knocking on your door or window at night. Or maybe they just show up, *yes, James?* Look what the damned wind blew in from out of town!

"But you know all about vampires, don't you, dear?" she said to Lana. "You lived in Hollywood. You know the movies. You know the truth. You know how vampires can slide their way into your house through the tiniest or stupidest cracks. Ride in on some fool. Hang around like a bat.

"But however they come, they don't ask your permission."

She leaned forward: "And if you don't give them the stake, they keep coming back for more of your blood."

As a son of a former manager of the Roxy theater, I said: "You must have seen a lot of bad movies growing up as a kid."

"I never got to *be* a kid!" snapped Dee.

She breathed control back into her. The tension in her small frame lessened. She leaned into her throne. Her blue veined, freckled and pale hand rose in front of her like she was using it to wipe fog off a window, a gesture that ordered us to *look* as she said: "What do you think of all my paintings?"

Lana shook her head.

"It's like . . . like a wall of proof. Images of this town. Locked up and hung on your wall as proof of your realm. Or what it once was."

I shook my head at Dee: *"Are you crazy?"*

"How could you tell? Or should I say: 'It takes one to know one.' What difference does it make? We're all where we are. My house. My town. My life."

"Like the paintings," said Lana.

"More than that for you, James," said Dee. "They all came from the foundation that would have given you a generous check."

"Doug *Something* from Wyoming," I said.

"After he painted Ronny, I thought it would be . . . *interesting* to keep him around for a while. And it was. He took the money like you should have. I told him what I wanted, left the rest to him. You would have had a free hand, too, Jim.

"And obviously other things, too," she said, nodding her head to Lana.

Lana and I shot to our feet with the same breath of rage.

Dee blasted her voice to stop us cold:

"Do you know what's important about all these paintings of this town?"

She grabbed a deep breath, blared:

"You're not in any of them!"

45

Give me your phone!" I yelled to Lana as we raced to Mom's parked car.

She blinked but snagged the cell out of her fringe jacket's pocket—

—tossed it into my fumbling catch as we split apart to run around the rear end of the car.

My left hand jerked open the driver's door as my right hand—

"Your security code!"

I slid the phone back to Lana across the roof of the car.

Dove behind the steering wheel. Slammed the door shut as Lana jumped into her shotgun seat—thrust her phone back to me.

And I pushed it back toward her. "Call Ron's cellphone!"

My hand cranked the old-fashioned key to roar the car's engine to life.

She swiped, tapped. I grabbed her phone to my face.

One *Bzzz!* in my ear. Two. Th—

"What do you want, Lana?" snapped her husband.

"It's me! Traven! Where are you?"

"Don't you want to know what I'm wearing?"

"*Shut the fuck up!* Tell me!"

Dee was right. Ron was not a dullard. He told me.

"Are you alone?"

Ron hesitated.

"Well—in the room where I'm standing—yes. But . . ."

"Stay that way!"

I tapped End Call.

Tapped the keypad icon.

Tapped in the one phone number I forever knew by heart.

"Running hot! I need backup and The Man, *now!*"

I told him where and why.

"On it!" replied Cody.

We punched out. I threw her cellphone back to Lana.

I slapped the gearshift into Drive.

Shouted: "Buckle up!"

46

We raced my mom's old blue car through the small town's streets.

I slammed the car to a katty-whompus halt in the rich man's driveway.

Lana charged the house: "I've got the right to—"

Stopped dead in her tracks.

Shot up her hand: HOLD!

The house's windows vibrated shouts inside.

Lana slid her key in the red door. Swung it wide but swung it silent.

Terry's voice: "—so just listen, listen to me! They're going to be here any—"

Ron's voice: "I know! But what the fuck are you—"

They were so intent on each other that they didn't realize we were there until we halted side by side several paces from the steps down into the sunken living room where they shuffled like boxers in a ring. Terry waved placating hands out from his sides as Ron fixed on him with a killing stare. The wall of windows past them held the three Coyote Hills.

The light of that day flowed in on *yes*, again: a Montana standoff.

Four corners. Four chess pieces of flesh and bone and blood.

Terry jerked his head at us: "They only think they know the whole story!"

"What story?" snapped Ron. "What, that—*Are you fucking me?*"

"Just calm down, Ronald! Just stand . . . Stand there!"

"You don't tell me where to stand! Why would you fuck me over?"

"Because I KNOW!" shouted Terry.

Terry shot an accusing finger straight at Lana: "Because of *her!*"

Terry's hand blurred under his cardigan sweater—

—snapped out/up straight toward Lana and me and *GUN!*

"Stop!" yelled Terry to us. "Just stop right fucking there! Stand there!"

My right hand tensed alongside my hip covered by my black leather jacket.

My unzipped black leather jacket.

"What the fuck!" Ron yelled to Terry. "Now what? *Ooo*, big man with a gun!"

"Is that my gun?" whispered Lana.

Ron ignored the silver pistol locked on us.

Yelled at Terry: "What about Lana?"

Terry's eyes whipped back and forth—us to Ron and back to us again.

The silver gun's bore stayed pointing at us as Terry ranted at his lover.

"I know how your mind works. All these years, don't think I don't know. Once you get rid of Lana, you're going to get rid of me. Use me one last time to put your mother in a box on the shelf. Then dump me on the side of the road. *'Bye-bye, Terry, you drag me down.'* All the parties and bigtime and cock you can buy. I should have known my days were numbered after what you did to Doug!"

"What the hell did I do to Doug? He wanted it."

Lana whispered to me: *"Terry has his own gun. Why does he have mine?"*

Terry snapped at his lover, his cousin, his boss:

"You conned your mother into using Doug. Contract him to stay around for you sneaking on the side from me and he was just a . . . he was real and sweet and could have been, wouldn't let me—But you broke him and drove him away!"

Time ticked bloody cuts on me: *How long have we been here?*

"So you decide to sidle up to my mother and sell me out? Be part of a coup by her after Lana's gone!"

Terry glared at Lana and me over the barrel of his gun.

"All you two had to do was go along with the fucking plan and that would have worked!"

How long do we have?

"You idiot!" said Ron to Terry. "Whatever deal you made with my mother, don't you think she'll fuck with you just because she can?"

My eyes flicked to my left. Glared back toward the hall where the poster of Lana hung. She saw the boldest flicks of my head I dared to make.

Does she get that she should dive there for cover?

Ron laughed at Terry: "If Dee was going to *maybe* fuck you over before all this, now she *has to*. And you know you're numero uno on my *do* list."

"Yeah," said Terry.

He shook his head: "Sometimes total clarity hits you in a blink. *Like that.* I saw this whole movie when she called a few minutes ago to tell me that you two . . ."

He waggled the gun at Lana and me.

". . . that you two had busted our play."

Breathe. Breathe. Breathe.

Terry held his left hand up in a command to steady us.

Kept us in his peripheral vision as he smiled at R—

BAM!

Terry shot Ron in the chest!

Lana's silver gun in Terry's hand whirled—

—caught me catching myself from moving!

Terry shifted his aim back and forth between where Lana and I stood on the landing above the sunken living room where Ron flopped on the floor.

"Congratulations, Lana!" snapped Terry. "You murdered your husband. Shot him dead. You came up here after busting Dee and her hired slut. Went berserk at your husband over the affair you're having with Mr. Local Zero here. Things got loud and things got bad and you shot Ron. Right in front of me. The corporate attorney who's also the executor of his estate put there by law that even Dee can't beat in the time she's got left. Now it's all about what *I* say."

"Wrong gun!" I yelled.

Terry blinked.

"You can't shoot us with that gun!"

Ron flopped on the floor beside Terry.

Who laughed: "I'm a good shot."

"But that's the wrong gun. Remember who the fuck you're talking to!"

Eyes on me. I've got to keep Terry's eyes on me! Not Lana.

"I'm James Traven! I write shit like this for a living! You can't shoot us now with that silver gun—which you were clearly going to do—because you made the classic rookie author mistake!

"You shot Ron with Lana's gun—*right*? Every TV cop show in the world, we all know they've got ballistics. That you can't use Lana's gun to shoot us. The bullets won't let you get away with lying and framing us.

"And then there's this," I said.

I pulled my black leather jacket open wide.

He saw my Glock.

"If you go for your other gun so the bullets will show your story about how you were too slow on the draw to stop us from killing him . . ."

Ron shuddered in a pool of his own blood.

". . . you have to ask yourself if I can get there first with a rewrite."

Ron gurgled.

Terry locked his gun's aim at me standing there poised to draw on him.

He cocked his head like he was reading a legal report.

"Fuck it. Lovers quarrel over the gun while—"

Flash/roar from his hand as I lunged to the combat stance I'd been *learned.*

Zings rip past me as my gun blasts over the explosions from the silver pistol jumping up and down in his hand.

My bullets rip past Terry—

—shatter the wall behind him!

That wall, that glorious window to the outside world. The panorama of my hometown sprawling down to the railroad tracks. My Big Pink high school. The afternoon blue hulks of the three Coyote Hills.

Bustin' glass!

Fragments and shards and crystals crash to the floor of that house of lies.

Flinching, we all flinch and duck for cover.

The cold rush in of Sidner's air.

And I'm scrambling sideways—

—*Lana!* Crouched in the dead-end hall. Frantic. Waving me to her.

Terry stands tall.

A gun now in each hand.

Like a zombie reaching for brains, he thrusts his pistol-filled fists toward me scrambling on the floor and *fires fires fires!*

In charge Cody and Sheriff Fenton—

—blasting his black iron over my scrambling form at a two-gunned killer.

Terry crashes KIA onto the floor of broken glass.

Roaring explosions echo in my whirling skull.

I can't hear myself scream.

47

My ears took forty minutes to stop ringing.

By then, the whole world had rolled out to the Sidner shootout.

Cop cars crammed the street.

Black SUVs from ICE.

Cruisers from the Montana Highway Patrol, its officers bearing badges emblazoned with 3-7-77, the dimensions of the graves dug for whoever the vigilantes lynched back in the good old days.

The Toole County Sheriff from nearby Shelby showed up as a cross-jurisdictional courtesy to assist in the investigation into two corpses lying on a floor of bloody glass shards.

Sidner's volunteer firemen showed up with red lights spinning on their hook and ladder truck. *You know,* 'just in case.'

The town's ambulance waited nearby, its EMT crew drinking coffee some generous citizen brought them from the P.S. on Main Street that was staying open extra hours on this chilly Sunday afternoon to serve and sell.

A voice called out that the hearse was on its way.

There'd only been enough yellow tape to ring the first arrivals on the scene where Sheriff Fenton's car and Cody's SUV targeted the red door that had been open when they screeched to a stop and heard *shots fired* inside.

The yellow tape cut a line across five pre-teen boys lounging beyond it on dirt bikes in their world where something cool *finally* happened.

Past the boys stood three men, arms crossed like they knew what to do.

A woman in a gray duct-taped winter coat raised her hand to her forehead to shield her eyes from the sun so she could see what the hell was going on.

Neighborhood moms 'n' dads and cross-town *let's-go-see* faces showed up to that line and I knew that in our younger days, my thrills-seeking aunt and mother would have been among them. So would have little kid me.

Now I leaned against the hood of a cop cruiser for all the eyes to see.

Crimson dress, fringe jacket Lana leaned beside me on that hard car.

A deputy gave us some space but stood close. He wore sunglasses like those in Lana's and my jackets. Our images never left his black mirror lenses.

Cody stood a quick walk away beside his maroon SUV.

A highway patrolman stood beside him. Maybe officially. Maybe not.

Cellphone videos showing all that hit Instagram and YouTube.

You can see me standing there smelling of gunfire and sweat.

Beside me, Lana said: "Can you hear me better now?"

"Yes."

"I trusted you with my whole life. Tell me again how you betrayed me."

"I didn't. I wasn't betraying you. I was making sure I didn't get fucked."

"By having your cellphone recording everything while we were together."

"Not everything. You took it from me in the movie."

"*Gee*, sorry to ruin your show."

"And later today at the house, I didn't, I left it on the floor in the hall. Turned off. I turned it back on to question Shawn."

"When did you start bugging me?"

"*Us*. After the first dinner. I should have recorded that, too."

"Should have?"

"I showed up not knowing that I needed to have proof of what happened and what I did in case Ronald or Terry or—"

"Or me," snapped Lana. "You didn't trust me. Thought I was playing my own game. Using you for me, not us. You thought I'd break you."

"I didn't know you then."

"The motel. Dreamland. You taped all that. Us having . . . Everything."

"Yes. And when we were with Ronald and Terry. With Dee. Dinner at Barb's Ribs. The wedding."

Her head snapped to the murder house: "And what just happened in there."

"And now the law's got all that. No question, we're innocent."

"We're a lot of things," said Lana. "But not innocent."

She nodded toward where Cody stood with the highway patrolman.

"And he knew. He helped you. He's so paranoid about Russians or whoever hacking his computer, he wouldn't let you use something like WhatsApp to . . .

"To send us to him," said Lana. "Got you firesticks so when you downloaded our private fucking time into your laptop, you could copy all that and give it to him as backup. You two *busy boys* switching sticks back and forth like . . .

"Did he listen?" she snapped. "Did he hear us . . ."

"No."

Her face called me a liar.

Mine pleaded: "None of this changes that I love you!"

Those *Three Big Words* hit her like a bullet on a brick wall.

"Yeah?" she said. "Well that's your cross."

Sheriff Fenton walked our way. He looked ten years older. His holster was empty, his black iron now evidence. Walking with him came the sheriff from Shelby and a man in surprised Sunday clothes who I'd learn was Sidner's county attorney and criminal prosecutor.

Badge-heavy Ross Fenton looked at us with as much sympathy as his anger and aftershock allowed: "You two can go for now."

Lana nodded at the bustling murder scene. "I got nowhere to go. And when I get there, I got nothing with me."

"The deputy here will walk you into your bedroom. Pack a bag and pack it fast. Clothes, your toothbrush, meds, the *whatevers* you actually need."

Sheriff Fenton pointed at me, told Lana: "Where you're at is with him."

"Do I have another choice?"

"Not anymore."

She walked away from me with a deputy who thought he was in charge.

48

"Thank you all for coming. I'm sure I speak for all of us when I say we're glad to be moving on with this . . ."

The white-haired lawyer in the thousand-dollar suit held his pause perfectly.

". . . with this situation behind us and settled."

None of us knew he was lying.

About that.

The winter-white-haired man took his time. His meter clicked every ten minutes. He sat at the head of the rectangle of tables hastily set up in the "conference room" separated by fire doors from the second floor of the Evergreen.

The room smelled of pine disinfectant and jangling nerves.

Mark it as Thursday afternoon on the big clock.

Four days After.

The winter-white-haired lawyer spread his palms wide to encompass all of us sitting at the wobbly rectangle banquet table: "Shall we begin?"

Lana and I drove away from the red door murder scene. We said nothing. Stared out the windshield at the town that Sidner now was. I parked the car in Mom's driveway. Lana grabbed her suitcase and marched through the front door.

Nothing had changed inside the house since we'd released Shawn.

Everything in the house had changed as we stood in the living room.

"What's downstairs?" said Lana.

"Katie's, my sister's bedroom. The shower. Laundry. What used to be a rec room we never used because Katie had a social life and I hung out at Joe's."

"Your mother would've kept it ready. Just in case of Katie showing up."

Lana announced: "I'll stay down there."

Leered at me: "Don't worry. You'll be safe."

Marched toward the stairs my mom fell down and didn't look back.

Four days later in the Evergreen's dragooned "conference center" the winter-haired 'hired gun' lawyer looked around the rectangle of faces.

Two associates from his law firm in big city Missoula sat in school desks set against the wall, their laptops open and ready. Beside them waited computer laptop briefcases that marched them everywhere.

My lawyer Carole from a bigger town a hundred miles east of Sidner sat between me and Lana. Carole had sharpshooter eyes. Lana's lawyer Clint had come up from the city where the airport and Irma's prison were. He sat on the other side of Lana. His posture told everyone in the room he was eager for a fight.

Nobody else at the table wanted one.

But Sheriff Ross Fenton's face said he wouldn't back down.

Cody sat like a steel Buddha across the table from me and Lana.

He didn't have a lawyer, but I'd told Carole to look out for him, too.

"What if there's a conflict of interest?" she said.

"Then cover him," I said.

The Martin County attorney/criminal prosecutor who'd arranged for this conference room sat fidgeting next to a man who was Sidner's city attorney. That man looked exhausted. He sat beside the mayor who looked simultaneously nervous and excited as hell to be "in the room."

All of us kept glancing toward the end of the table and the suit perched there—yes, another White guy lawyer, the attorney general for the State of Montana, where attorney generals are selected by campaign contributions and elected by voters exercising their informed and programmed freedom of choice.

Yes, that year's AG came from the party showered by Queen Dee's cash.

She didn't come to that Thursday afternoon conference.

Sunday afternoon as Lana clumped downstairs to my sister Katie's pink bedroom, I raced out of the house.

Found the good hearts of us in my mom's room at the Evergreen.

Residents of that assisted living facility crowded into the room where she lay chained in bed. The ex-boxer who'd warned me about Queen Dee. His friend with her walker. Teresa. Mrs. Aikens and Mrs. Malletta. Even Carrie, mumbling about mothers. Two of the Old Farts. My aunt sat in the chair by the bed.

They came because one of their "us" had trouble. So you *show up*. Not like the gawkers at the yellow tape. Like good people who knew that there but for the grace of whatever they called God, that could be them stuck in that bed.

Owl Eyes Mike was nowhere to be seen.

People reached out to me as I walked through the visitors' crowd.

Mom's good hand grabbed mine as I stood at her bed. Her eyes glistened.

My aunt gently cleared the room. Left. Shut the door.

Mom burst out crying. Me too.

"They told me and I was so scared for you!"

My ears still rang but I said: "I'm not hurt. I'm OK."

Mom relaxed on the white sheets. I slumped in the chair beside her. My arm reached across her to hold her uncasted hand.

Mom said: "Is . . . Is she . . . Is she OK, too?"

"Yes. I hope so. I'm not sure." I took a breath:

"She's staying at our house. But . . . She's in Katie's room."

Mom nodded. Took a breath, squeezed my hand: "How do you feel?"

"Like I'm trapped in my own novel and I don't know how it's going to end."

"Are you the hero?" whispered my mother.

"There are no heroes in this one."

I stayed and made her eat the dinner nurse's aide Jen brought. Stayed after and watched her take her pills. Watched her fall asleep chained in that bed as the high-mounted TV bathed her in flickering hues.

Went home to my messed up childhood bed that smelled like sex.

Called "Good night!" downstairs to where lights were on in Katie's room.

Heard Lana softly answer: "Yeah."

Thursday afternoon, the winter lawyer said: "As we've discussed, this meeting is an unusual blend of jurisdictional interests both public and private, criminal and civil, designed ultimately for the greater public good.

"And," he said, "given issues of privacy and standard prosecutorial necessities of confidentiality, we've chosen not to record these sessions."

He formally chuckled. "None of us want to see this on YouTube."

Nobody laughed.

"Mr. Traven," he said, looking at me, "while we are all mindful of your various professional activities, while there are no publication strictures on you about this meeting, libel laws and such are matters none of us wish to get into."

My sharpshooter attorney Carole said: "My client knows his rights."

"And responsibilities, I presume," said the winter lawyer.

"As do we all, I'm sure," she answered.

Never one to give up the last word, the winter lawyer dripped sincerity as he said: "Thank you for that reminder for everyone here.

"Now," he said, "to the facts of the matter."

Monday meant mania.

Lana and I were brought down to the county jail to be interviewed by the Shelby sheriff who was stepping in for the incident-conflicted Sheriff Fenton.

Before that, Lana and I worked our cellphones on our separate levels of the house to find the lawyers we ended up with.

I quarantined in my bedroom. The kitchen table office I'd rigged when I got to town was near the open top of the stairs down to Lana's turf. I didn't want to be able to hear her doing whatever—and I wanted her to realize that. I also bet she didn't want to hear me from her basement refuge. I left much of my work debris on it so I could rush away to give privacy. To make it a neutral place.

We'd met at the kitchen table for Monday morning coffee with no milk.

Neither of us used sugar.

I made us lunch from the last cans of tuna in Mom's cupboards.

Left Lana's sandwich on the kitchen table with my laptop and journal. Went downstairs for my negotiated shower time. She'd washed her plate, left it on the counter when I came back upstairs to dress for our jailhouse rocks.

Lana wasn't there when I got home from my interview with the Shelby sheriff followed by a one-on-one with my attorney Carole. I assumed Lana was with her hunky attorney Clint. Talking law. That's all they were doing—right?

I'd brought home a mozzarella cheese, ground sausage and fresh tomato pizza Carole'd walked into the truck stop to pick up while I waited in the car. I ate three slices. Left the rest on the counter for Lana. She walked through the front door at sunset. Said she wasn't hungry. Later that night from my bedroom, I heard her come upstairs and only one slice of pizza still waited in the cardboard box when I opened the refrigerator at midnight.

Thursday afternoon the winter lawyer sat tall in his chair as sunlight of Sidner flowed in on that conference of conspirators.

"These are the facts," he said.

"One: On Sunday, Terence Ewing, corporate lawyer for Zane Enterprises, related companies, subsidiaries and allied groups of a diverse nature, shot and killed Ronald Zane, his cousin and client, in an act of premeditated murder.

"Two: Terence Ewing then shot at and attempted to kill Lana LaBuff, lawful wife of his first victim, and her friend James Traven of Washington, DC.

"Three: James Traven who was potentially legally in possession of a firearm attempted to defend himself and Mrs. Zane from the attack. He fired rounds. He hit no one and nothing of any significance. Except the glass window.

"Four: Sheriff Ross Fenton, who had been alerted by Sidner citizen Cody Larson as to the possibility of some domestic disturbance at that Zane residence, arrived to find the premise open and, upon hearing shots fired inside, proceeded to make lawful entry. He came under fire. Fearing for his own safety and the lives of others, he shot and killed assailant Terence Ewing. Cody Larson had dutifully arrived to assist the sheriff and has stipulated to these facts.

"Five: As already stated publicly to the press by the ad hoc investigative team of the county attorney, the city attorney, the sheriff of Shelby who stepped in as an unbiased lead police investigator, and the purview of the state attorney general's office, the motive for the crimes was a quarrel over money. And while there may have been . . . personal situations between the two men, all that is ultimately irrelevant.

"Six," said the winter lawyer.

He stared straight at Lana and me as everyone else looked some other way.

"Six," repeated the winter lawyer and then lied: "As of the successful conclusion of this meeting, all aspects of these events will be closed."

Tuesday morning, I had coffee waiting for Lana when she felt it was safe to walk upstairs after I'd walked out the back door into the cool morning. We still didn't have any milk. She brought her cup outside to the back porch. Saw me practicing *Taiji* on the patio. She watched for a while. Said nothing. I flowed from posture to posture while trying to relax in contemplation of reality. I did two extra rounds and the full three minutes of standing in *Huang-chi* 'not-thinking' so she'd have time to shower and *whatever.*

When I came back into the house I called out for her but she was gone.

My heart thundered as I checked the basement. The bed was made. Her clothes were neatly stacked on her open suitcase. The shower and that bathroom felt damp and smelled of herbal shampoo. She was not there.

I hurried out the front door, down the porch steps into the morning sunshine and the gritty smells of just another Tuesday for everyone else.

Brett Petersen stood at the curb by his family car.

"She went over to the Evergreen to see your mom," said Brett.

My startled stare brought a slight smile to his face.

"She said to say so if I saw you. She knows my name."

His mother and sister bustled out of their house.

Brett said: "I told her my mom is looking for a babysitter for after school today 'cause the sewer pipe backed up into the daycare where we go."

"What about me?" I said.

He shrugged.

His concerned-eyed mom Debby said, "How you doing? How's Mary?"

His sister Courtney waved and waved until I waved back and said *hi*.

They went to school and work. I went inside my house. Showered and dressed and sat on the living room couch until Lana came back two hours later.

"Your turn," she said.

Walked downstairs.

Thursday afternoon, Lana and I kept our eyes on the winter lawyer.

"Primarily, Mrs. . . . Lana," he said, "how we proceed is up to you."

Tuesday morning I was out the door and headed to the Evergreen before Lana reached the bottom of the basement stairs after ambushing my mom.

"I like her," my mom said after nurse's aide Jen had taken her vitals and left us alone.

"She sat there and looked me straight in the eye," said Mom. "She told me about her mom and her sister. Girl's a teenager now. That must be a lot to handle and even more to be afraid for. What she told me about all your other shit played like what you told me."

"What did she say about now?"

"She asked if she could sleep in my bed when Katie gets here. She *asked*."

"No, I mean . . ."

"I don't think she knew what to say about anything else. I don't think she knows about now more 'n' that she's putting one foot in front of another.

"Do you?" said Mom.

A thousand feelings swirled through me.

No words came out of me.

"I told her you were a good kid who nobody including me ever got."

My smile made her happy.

"And *oh*," said Mom, "I told her Aunt Bev is dropping by with a load of groceries so's you two don't have to go out. God knows what you've been eating. I told Bev to get milk for your coffee. Pick up some beer. No more than a couple six-packs. You still got a shiner from the Oasis. I'm not sure you got any *wild times* luck left this year. I told Bev where my emergency stash of cash is."

"I'll pay Bev back."

"That's what Lana said, too."

That was the first time my mother ever said the name of the woman who'd asked to sleep in her bed. And who I had lain *with*.

Mom said: "Then she had to say that was a promise. Seems like her ATM cards are frozen."

"Don't worry. My agent said my French publisher bought my new book."

After commissions and taxes in two countries, my net from that sale might be enough to almost fund a month of the life I used to have.

"And my guy's hopeful about the Italians," I added.

"We're all hopeful about the Italians." Mom sighed. "I always wanted to sit in a café in one of those cobblestone city squares they have over there. Drink a little wine. Eat great food. Be alive and feel the world smiling with me."

"At least we're here."

"Yeah." She gave me a nod. "You damn well better believe it."

That Tuesday night, Cody knocked on our family home's front door.

Stood on the front porch and told me: "You and Lana need to get out of the house. Meet me in the backyard. Wear your jackets."

I hurried through to the back door, yelling down to Lana.

By the time I got to the backyard, Cody was arranging the metal table and three of the lawn chairs I'd moved off the patio to do *Taiji* into a social dinner.

"Stop," I said. "Look at me."

There he stood. The man who'd been that boy who showed up in fifth grade. Who'd been there since. Who'd risked his life to save mine and Lana's.

I said: "Thanks."

My vibes made sure he felt all that all the way down to the ground.

"It's what we do."

"*Thanks,*" I said again so he couldn't dodge it.

This time he let it all ride the wind.

He nodded: "Let's hope you never get your turn."

"I'm there," I said.

The chill of winter coming blew through our picnic scene.

Lana'd come out to the back porch behind me without a creak of the screen door. Cody had her in his vision the moment she left the house. I didn't turn to see her standing there in her red fringe jacket until she spoke to him.

"I owe you," she told him.

Meant it. And the way she did made me soar and crash.

Cody held up two white plastic carryout bags for us to see: "Throw in for dinner I brought, I'd say we're even."

"You'd be wrong," said Lana.

That was something Cody seldom heard. And that made him smile.

He smiled again when Lana 'commanded' me: "We need plates, silverware, lots of napkins and one of those six-packs your aunt dropped off in the fridge.

"But really," Lana chided Cody as she walked past me with an inertia that triggered me into doing her bidding: "Barb's Ribs? *Again*?"

"It's the best we could get," said Cody.

What they talked about while I was inside I'd never learn.

We ate together. Sat in the breezy and chilly backyard in defiance of being cooped up. Lana pulled out a joint we shared.

The evening cooled to night. Cody went home. Lana helped clean up.

We slept alone in the beds we had.

Wednesday morning the winter lawyer showed up on our front doorstop before either Lana or I had a chance to go see my mother at the Evergreen. I wondered how he knew we were still there as I let him and his two associates into my home after he identified himself as: "Mrs. Deirdre Zane's attorney."

Vampires don't need an invitation.

You need to let them close and risk their bite so you can use your stake.

All Wednesday morning the winter lawyer and his team talked and proffered and explained and threatened to Lana and me and our lawyers hooked up into video chat Zooms through their laptops.

When the noon whistle blew, the winter lawyer stood up from the couch: "You have until the conference tomorrow to make up your minds."

When Queen Dee's legal team were long gone out of sight and our lawyers had signed off, Lana and I ate leftover cold ribs with only milk so our minds stayed clear.

And talked.

Really talked for the first time since we'd driven away from the murder scene on Sunday, that Wednesday noon. Talked about what to do. Must do's. If thens. I even took notes in my black journal.

Yet we talked around and avoided how we totally felt.

I didn't tell Mom about the winter lawyer's visit when I went to see her. We talked about how glad we were my sister Katie was coming to town the next day.

On my way down the hall, the nurse's aide Denise turned the corner.

She smirked as she walked past leaving-town me and that said it all.

Lana was in the kitchen when I walked into the house.

She rose from the table to face me, her sunlit black hair floating free. A pile of her clothes waited on the chair to her left.

She held my opened black journal.

Turned it so I could see it was open to the haiku I'd written the night before she took me to the matinee of my own movie:

The Road
How can I walk straight
when all my fevered soul sees
is the curve of her ways?
James Traven

One last line waited below the time, date and place of the haiku's birth:

for Lana

She handed the journal to me without apology for opening it.

"I guess I didn't need to bother your mom about moving into her bedroom."

She picked up her clothes and I knew where she was taking them.

"But nothing more," she told me. "I want to trust you, but now that's hard."

Wednesday night we slept on our own sides of the same bed.

That was our first time actually sleeping together.

That was our first time in a bed without making love.

Not with our flesh.

Not with our words.

Came Thursday afternoon we sat side by side at that conference table.

Everyone in the room stared at Lana.

"Intermixed with those facts of criminal matters is a complex web of civil issues," said the winter lawyer. "And I'd be remiss if I didn't mention we all have . . . an awareness of other possible criminal issues like, *oh*, fraud, that while the deaths of Ronald and Terence could be difficult to prosecute, have a secondary cast of potential victims and indictable co-conspirators."

Yet another veiled threat crawled onto the table.

"Lana, simply put: We are talking about your dead husband's estate.

"He died without a will. Evidently that was one of the contentions between him and his lawyer Terence, who probably wanted to be certain who was in it.

"That means the entire Zane family estate and holdings are now under a cloud, given their intermingled status and a series of documented disputes involving both of those men and my client, the . . . the other Mrs. Zane.

"For the record, Lana, you know that you could pursue inheritance claims.

"However, given the . . . tumultuous state of your marriage as has been documented in the course of the criminal investigations into those violent deaths, factors not in your favor in any such claims, you—and Mr. Traven who is also linked through your actions—have instead agreed orally to accept an incredibly generous settlement offer."

"Hah!" snapped Lana's attorney.

The winter lawyer's glance shut him up.

"In exchange for renouncing all claims against the estate of your late husband, any Zane family enterprise or Mrs. Deidre Zane, and for ending any kind of involvement or relationship to those enterprises, you and Mr. Traven—who also agrees to renounce any claims—will receive the following.

"*One*: Rather than your attorneys receiving a customary one-third of your award, the estate of Mrs. Deirdre Zane and Zane enterprise agrees to pay your attorney hourly fees and their costs up to their return to their offices today. Plus a negotiated bonus of $37,000 to each of their firms.

"*Two*: You each receive $10,000 in cash to cover . . . out of pocket expenses."

That was my negotiation.

A junior associate rose from her schoolroom desk against the wall and put banded wads of cash on the table beside Lana and me. We didn't touch them.

"There are receipts for that in your settlement packets for your tax purposes that are entirely your responsibility," said the winter lawyer.

"*Three*: Based on sums previously discussed within that web of issues rendered moot today, each of you receives, upon signing all copies of the agreement today, old-fashioned cashier's checks for $400,000.

"This sum includes all monies conceivably or actually owed you by Mrs. Deirdre Zane, the estate of the late Ronald Zane, or Zane Enterprises.

"*Four*: Lana, in part for their waiver of claims signatures and an NDA covering anything but legal tax need—already obtained—your mother and your minor sister will together receive a lump sum of $200,000 for their time as Zane family adjacent. Also, before they are handed their cashier's check, they and you agree to sign an NDA covering all of this."

The high-priced lawyer turned like a lion seeing me trapped in his cage.

"*Fifth*, you there, Mister *Author* Traven, while you have refused to sign an NDA regarding the elements that brought us here today, any attempt by you to write a stated factual account of these elements will result in you forfeiting and returning, with interest, all benefits given you in this agreement. Plus, as one of your absurd fictional characters might say, the Zane empire will use of course only legal means to put you in the ground."

"Hell," I told him: "Nobody would believe all this isn't fiction."

The winter lawyer took a breath.

"Then there is the matter of the funeral.

"Mrs. Zane requires that the widow of her son, as a matter of propriety, attend the funeral, which, as you know, will be this Saturday. If you do not attend, the terms of this agreement mandate our firm to sue you for all funds disbursed here today. And for the funds your mother and sister will get."

Sheriff Ross had told me that the only claim on Terry's body had been made by his distant cousin, Mrs. Deirdre Zane. She'd ordered it cremated, the fires burning as we sat in that conference room.

"At the funeral," the winter lawyer told Lana, "you will be dressed . . . How should I put this? As befitting a widow of a leading citizen. To quote Mrs. Zane: *'Tell her to look like the hotshot Hollywood star she never was.'* To that end, the county attorney has graciously agreed to have one of his staff—"

The county prosecutor's staff consisted of a part-time secretary.

"—meet you at the crime scene house to monitor while you gather appropriate clothing and materials for the funeral.

"While you are welcome to wear any of the jewelry still in the house and part of the estate to the funeral, it must be returned after the service, *forthwith*."

Lana reached in her black purse. Dropped her marital rings on the table.

"You can keep your diamonds," she said.

The winter lawyer's eyes glistened like the stones on the table he built.

"Mr. Traven," he told me, "Mrs. Zane expects you to be there, too, but does not require it. If you do show up, she insists you wear a suit and a tie."

Then he sent the first genuine smile we'd seen to Lana and me.

"Barring any transgressions on either of your part," he said, "the funeral will be the last time I expect we'll see each other. I'm attending. It's only proper."

And billable to the Zane fortune, I bet.

He nodded at his two assistants. They gave pens to Lana and me. We worked through a chunk of documents under the careful eyes of our lawyers.

The city and county attorneys signed as witnesses.

So did Sheriff Ross Fenton.

I wondered what he got for his ink.

Cody witnessed too.

He'd already accepted a $150,000 cashier's check "to forestall any legal claims for his roles in the covered events."

Sidner's mayor picked up a pen and signed where he was told.

Looked up and saw the attorney general sitting in his seat *not* getting up to sign anything. Fear flashed on the mayor's face as he realized who was now politically on the line and who was not.

One of the young lawyers was a notary public who sealed our signed promises with kisses of steel. When she was done, her colleague handed

Lana and me envelopes with cashier's checks drawn on the Zane-controlled local bank.

And like that, the fix was in.

Lana and I got out of there as fast as we could. Hurried out to the cold October Thursday afternoon. Didn't stop running until we'd circled out of the Evergreen and down the block to stand facing First Street South and the house with its two tall pine trees.

"I feel like we just signed a deal with the devil," I told her.

"We did what we did, we got what we got. Nobody dies with a clean soul.

"Come on," she said. "Your sister should be here from the airport by now."

49

Friday morning sister Katie and I spent two hours laughing and talking with our mom as she lay in that hospital bed. We were there when her doctor dropped by, said she was on track to have her casts removed after Halloween.

"Finally!" said Mom. "I can't wait to get rid of this damn mummy costume! Plus then maybe I can actually walk into the polling station in the grade school gym and vote live and in person!"

We had another family reunion when my aunt stayed on after the Old Farts' coffee klatch at the Chat & Chew down on Main Street came and left.

Nurse's aide Jen dropped by and met Katie.

After she left, Mom looked out at her three family members.

"Guys," she said.

Took a breath and made us all nervous.

Tried to make her voice matter-of-fact. Strong. Determined. Satisfied.

"Guys," she said, "now that we're all together . . ."

Mom blurted: *"I should sell the house and move into an apartment here!"*

Her younger sister, her daughter, her son:

We froze to not shatter this moment into a thousand pieces.

"Hell," said Mom, "living in a place like the Evergreen is a lot safer than *falls-down-the-stairs* me living alone. *Right?* I know the people up here. Most of them are OK. They remember me. I remember them. We know the same songs.

"Angie up in the county commissioner's office, about your age, Katie, she's always had an eye on our place. She knows I've kept it great. She said something to Halle up to the library last week 'n' Halle visited here told me and I think Katie

"—you're the smart one, hon, no offense, Jimmy—I think you should call her, see what's what. If she wants to buy it, we won't have to worry about it being stuck maybe forever with one of those damn FOR SALE signs that are all around town."

"You want to sell our house?"

"Think about it, Jim: It ain't been *our* house since you and Katie left."

"That could work, Mom," said Katie. "But let's do this. Why don't you think about it some more, and we'll figure it out over the next couple days?"

Relief flooded the room. Nothing would happen today. Tomorrow would be easier because some decision was already being born. We'd have time to live with it before doing anything.

Katie and I left the two aging sisters alone together.

Sucked in cool fresh air as we stepped out of the Evergreen's front doors.

"The smoke from the fires is gone," said Katie.

"Something's always in the air."

"Yeah, but it's nice enough today," said Katie. "The weatherman says it's going to be a picture postcard perfect day tomorrow for your funeral."

"Who sends postcards in the mail anymore."

"Come on," she said. "Let's sit a spell here."

Lana was a block away at our . . . *the* house.

This was our first chance at real alone time since Katie arrived yesterday.

We pulled two metal chairs up to the Evergreen's steel patio picnic table. Sat there in the breeze of the town where we'd been born and raised.

Katie said: "*Wow.*"

"Yeah." I shook my head. "Before we get into any of that . . . Thanks for coming back early for Mom. She needs that."

"Like you don't?"

"I don't know what in the hell I need."

"Do you know what you've got? Besides a shitload of money?"

"You want to know what I got?" I shrugged. "Me too."

"I'll be able to help you more with that one later. Lana agreed to let me come with her when she goes to her old house in . . ."

Katie checked her phone: "We're meeting one of the white-haired big shot's women lawyers up there in twenty-nine minutes."

"Why'd you arrange to do that?"

"I want to see where my baby brother's life blew up."

She wiggled her cellphone: "Hell, I might take pictures for your nephews."

My sister looked around at where we were.

"Do you think we'll ever end up at a place like this?" she said of the assisted living facility we both knew was going to now be home to our mother.

"Makes you wonder," was all I could say.

Kate stood—

—frowned down at me still sitting there: "Are you coming?"

"I've got something to do back in there. Then I got some errands."

"We're taking my rental. Use Mom's car."

She rubbed my head like she did when I was a kid and shorter than her.

Walked away to do the hundreds of things she was always doing.

I pushed through the glass doors of the Evergreen and got lucky.

Nurse's aide Jen sat alone behind the greetings/security counter and open office where often no one was on duty.

She looked up from where she sat sorting manila files. Saw me and smiled.

I handed a white envelope across the counter to her.

"That's for you," I said.

She frowned. I hadn't sealed it. She looked inside . . .

Her face snapped when she saw the stack of greenback bills.

"That's $1,000," I told her speechless gaze. "It's all for you. Do anything you want with it. And it doesn't matter what you choose to do tomorrow or the next day. Zero pressure from me or those dollars. If you decide to keep doing the good work you're doing here that needs doing well, that'll make me happy. If not, whatever you decide, if you quit right now, I'll be sad but still happy for you."

"I—what—Why? Th . . . thank—"

"Don't thank me. I'm just the *pass it on* guy."

I left her with what I owed and my smile.

Walked the short block to the library.

Halle hurried out of the back room with an *Oh my!* face of concern and thankfulness to see me walking in alive. She blinked when I turned from her—

—and slid ten $100 bills into the front desk's donations fishbowl.

Halle's *Oh my!* face turned to shock and gratitude at the sight of the Benjamin Franklin bills without even counting them. Tears rolled down her face, and her palm pressed her gold cross to her chest.

"Take care of this place," I told her. "Take care of you."

Walked back out to the sunlight.

The Oasis was open with Brenda sitting behind the bar when I walked in twelve minutes later. Her face said she remembered me: *Good times.*

Brenda saw me slap a greenback on the bar.

Blinked when she saw it was a picture of Benjamin Franklin.

"Bring me that." I pointed.

She watched me stuff a sealed white envelope in the jar for *The First Responders' Benefit Fund.*

"I'll know if all of that *doesn't* get to where it's supposed to," I said about the envelope's $1,000 in ten Benjamins. "Tell Sheriff Fenton where it came from."

She gave me hard eyes.

Put her hand on the Benjamin on the bar.

Vanished it with a nod.

Said nothing to my walking-out black leather jacket back.

The *Ding!* . . .

. . . oh that *Ding!* of the bell above the Chat & Chew's door when I walked in that Friday as the sparse lunch crowd had thinned out.

White uniformed Elly gave me a *glad-you're-alright* smile as I sat at the Old Farts' empty table.

She lifted a pot of coffee off the burner behind the U-shaped counter before I could wave *No thanks!* and walked over to me.

"I won't be staying," I told her when she got there. "I owe you."

She frowned. Set the coffeepot down on the table.

"First," I said, "buy the Old Farts a round of morning coffee on me. And you, *you alone*, not the restaurant, you keep the change."

"That's so—" she started to say before she realized I'd given her a $100 bill.

Dazed, she automatically took the white envelope of $1,000 I handed her.

Opened it only after I said: "That's for Dale's tab."

She looked down at me with tears in her eyes. Hugged me so fast I almost couldn't get to my feet. The steaming coffeepot sitting on the table rattled.

As I pulled away from her, I said: "Now I gotta go to settle up at the Tap."

Ding! and I was walking across Main Street on a Friday afternoon.

Gary wore a blue and white Hawaiian shirt as he shifted cases behind the bar when I walked into the Tap Room. He moved with an old man's determined grace my father never got to experience.

"Great, I caught you!" I said as his lone customer Donna shuffled toward the DAMES restroom.

"What's going on?" He leaned across the bar toward me.

"Put this on Dale's tab," I said as I handed him a white envelope. "I already paid the other half to Elle over at the Chat & Chew, so that all stays here."

"You don't have to do that," he said without looking in the envelope.

"Yes, I do."

He looked in the envelope. Closed it. Looked again. Sped through a count of what the envelope held. Opened his mouth. Had to let it close unused.

Finally said: "Your dad would be proud."

"I hope so."

I walked out into the cool October sun and got buzzed into Cody's shop.

"Are you making trouble?" he said.

"I hope so," I repeated.

Put the spare holsters and magazines for the Glock I'd carried and that Sheriff Fenton'd promised might be returned to Cody "soon" on the glass counter.

Cody nodded.

"You're doing OK so far," he said.

And in case I didn't know so, said: "I like her."

"Me too."

"Don't fuck it up."

"Maybe I already have."

"Maybe is a moving target."

He didn't let me escape that gaze. Let me go only after he knew I got it.

Said: "You can drop my suit off at the cleaners after the funeral."

"I feel like I owe you a new one."

"Hell no! Now that one's got a legend."

"Like you need one."

The man who'd saved my life said: "That gumshoe Dee sicced on you. She as tough as you say?"

"I don't want to find out."

"*Shawn Bradley*," he said. "A smart-ass. 'Bout our age, you said. Blonde."

The second hand swept around the big clock.

"Maybe I better look her up," said my friend behind his glass counter.

I blinked—and caught him doing the same.

"Oh fuck me!" I said, shook my head all the way to the door.

Opened the door and as I walked through it, Cody yelled: *"Not you!"*

The closing door didn't stop our laughter.

I drove down Main Street like I was headed west out of town. Pulled into the mostly empty parking lot of the last supermarket in town.

Those glass doors slid sideways to let me in. Closed behind me to lock me in the grocery store's brightly lit aisles of canned goods and boxes. A meat counter waited at the back of the store with display cases of chunks of red marbled beef slaughtered from cousins of the cattle now roaming behind barbed wire just outside of town. Tables of produce waited past four cashier lanes. Heads of lettuce. Bananas. Bins of potatoes. A tilted box of broccoli and another of green beans. I spotted a "Weekly Special!" display of pink lady apples.

And Debby Petersen.

No customers were at her cashier's lane. She smiled. Gave me a wave.

The manager's office was a low-walled platform overlooking all the cashier lanes. Had a good angle on about half the store's grocery aisles. The bald man who sat there watching me wore a white shirt tightened with a black tie.

Like me, he saw only three customers slowly pushing grocery carts up the store's aisles. A woman older than me wearing a cashier's smock mopped Aisle 3.

Mindless music tinkled over everything.

I walked the wrong direction in the customer lane of Debby's counter. She glanced up to see the bald manager frowning.

"Don't worry," I said. "Everything's OK. I just wanted to give you this when your kids weren't around."

Passed her the bulging white envelope.

"What—"

"Don't show it to anybody. Or tell anybody. Down the road, when they're old enough to understand, maybe tell the kids."

"I don't get it."

"You got it now and it's all yours: $3,000 in cash."

"Whatthehellare—"

"Sorry it's such a big packet."

"I can't take this!"

"You already got it. You and the kids are where it belongs."

"What . . . what do you want?"

"I already got it, so we're square."

Blubbering is a term invented for what Debby did then—

—but just for a few heartbeats.

Her face froze and kept my eyes locked on her.

"I can't cry at work! I'll lose my job!"

She took a breath. Stopped her envelope-free hand from wiping her eyes.

"Do you have a safe place to keep that until you can get it home or—"

Debby reached her envelope hand up under her cashier's smock, wiggled, and I knew she stuffed it down the front of her slacks.

Her tear-stained face showed steel.

"Nobody gets in there unless I say so," she said.

She stood tall as she felt the gaze of the manager in the box above her.

"And nobody better try or I won't be the only one who gets fired."

I walked past her into the grocery store.

Chose a pink lady apple off the display.

Walked back to Debby's cashier lane.

Put the lone red apple on her faded black conveyer belt.

Watched it glide toward her.

She weighed it and gave me change for my wrinkled ten-dollar bill.

Smiled from her heart as her official voice said: *"Thank you for shopping at your neighborhood Good Foods and More store."*

I picked up my purchase.

Waved to the bald manager in the elevated box.

Took a bite of the pink lady as the sliding open doors let me outta there.

It tasted apple crisp and sunshine sweet.

50

Saturday's horror dawned bright and clear with a soft October chill.

Lana and I dressed as our contracts and my sister said we should.

I wore Cody's dark suit and a laundered blue shirt with his silk tie. That was the first time I wore his suit without it hiding a shoulder holstered Glock.

Lana pushed her role of *widow* with a retrieved French designer's suit cut sassy somewhere between the dark of night and the blue of day. Her hair flowed free on her shoulders. She refused a hat, a veil, any of the family's jewels. Wore her war paint, seething blood-red lips of rage and pride.

Us getting ready Saturday became a military operation. Katie coordinated. She'd always been a savvy manager.

"The funeral is at 3:00," said Katie as we three sat at the kitchen table with our morning coffees. "Graveside at the cemetery. Normally it's about ten minutes to there and park, but this is now and you're the *who*. Give yourselves thirty minutes to get there well before 3:00. Just in case."

She insisted we eat lunch. I remember it involved catsup.

Lana took a bath *and* a shower. The upstairs bathroom held the house's only tub and was right next door to my bedroom where our tense choreography meant we slept side by side with as little touching as possible and without ever seeing each other naked.

I sat on the bed wearing my *Taiji* sweats waiting for her to finish her post-shower bath.

The bathroom door opened. I snapped to like a Marine.

Lana turned from the hall to look at me. Her long hair was wet and tangled on her cinched tight blue robe. She held her twice-wet towel bundled over her chest with crossed arms. Her right hand held a razor.

I wondered what she'd shaved.

"You better wait for the hot water tank to recharge," she said.

"There's some coffee left. I'll have another cup in the kitchen, then go down to the shower. Katie's still over visiting Mom."

"Coffee." Lana shook her head. "There's not enough of it to wake me up from this."

We walked out the front door *ready* at 2:21.

Reached the sidewalk and got charged by the Petersen kids.

Kindergartner Courtney whooped: *"Hi! Hi!"*

Wrapped her arms around my legs. Bounced back with a beaming smile.

"Mommy said you did something won'rful for us and 's a surprise and you won't tell me I wouldn't tell and suppose to say *thank you thank you thank you!*"

"Was nothing," I told her.

Lana smiled a conscientious teachable moment to someone else's daughter: "He meant to say: *'You're welcome.'*"

Courtney gave her a hug.

Lana forced herself to let go.

Turned the spotlight of her smile to fifth grader Brett.

He shuffled on the sidewalk. Kept trying to look at the ground. Failing.

She said: "Hi, Brett."

He mumbled *hi* back. Gave me a nod.

Couldn't stop himself. What he dreamt on this street where I'd grown up blurted out of Brett: "You look really pretty!"

Lana crouched to look him straight in his eyes.

"Thank you, Brett. This is the best time anybody's ever said that to me."

He froze when she gently took hold of his thin shoulders.

Lana softly pressed her red lips to his forehead.

Like an aunt. Like an angel.

Leaned back.

Told the boy's beet-red face: "Do good. Be happy. Walk true."

Her red lips marked Brett's forehead like a third eye.

She swayed away with each of the three of us seeing a different her go.

We drove my mother's old car to the cemetery.

Montana's legendary blue sky domed this small town.

We joined a slow-moving line of cars two blocks from the black iron main gates. A uniformed deputy sheriff waved all traffic to the right. Whizzing past on our left came a highway patrol cruiser leading two sedans with the state seal on their front doors.

Another deputy manned the open black iron gates to the burial ground. One of the Big Shots from the Chat & Chew wearing a vest from a local service club and holding an iPad stood beside that badge. Those two gatekeepers waved most of the arriving cars off to the far corner of the cemetery. They glanced through our windshield. Waved us straight down the gravel road.

Queen Dee had hired dozens of high school students as ushers. Those teenage boys and girls all wore white shirts and dark pants as they nervously worked this Big Deal none of them would ever forget.

Then I got it: Those teenagers would remember Dee's spectacle of glory into the days of their own grandchildren. They'd remember her as queen. She'd win.

A white-shirted teenage girl motioned me to where I was supposed to park amidst rows of big dollar rides glistening in the Saturday afternoon sun. Our car was by far the oldest machine of any in those assigned-spot vehicles.

We stepped out into the gentle chill and the sound of car doors slamming.

Walked between the rows of cars with license plates from all over Montana. Plates from Idaho. Wyoming. A tinted-windows machine from Nevada. Rentals from the same company I'd used at the distant airport. Enough electoral votes to swing a presidential election were represented at this event. We walked side by side *not* holding hands into a stream of formally dressed men and women.

Nobody wanted to look at us.

Everybody stared.

Even cemetery ghosts we couldn't see were curious about the ghosts we'd be.

"There's our buddy the attorney general," said Lana about the telegenic man striding ahead of us with his white-shirted teenage usher.

A pimply-faced teenage usher beckoned us to follow him. He pressed his cellphone to his face to let someone know we were coming.

A bagpiper screed the air from our graveside destination.

"You've got to be fucking kidding me!" hissed Lana.

Our usher led us toward the front of the gathering crowd.

Green Astroturf covered the autumn earth near the open and waiting grave. That meadow of plastic grass held rows of metal folding chairs.

Our usher led us to reserved seats in the front row at the foot of the grave.

The glistening black coffin costing thousands of dollars lay across thick straps above the deep grave. The straps were part of the frame that held the coffin above the ground to be slowly lowered by the turn of an electric switch by one of the black suited undertakers.

The black capped, red and black kilted and white-knee-socked bagpiper's music filled the air of the gathering crowd.

Queen Dee sat on a throne near the head of the coffin. She faced the crowd filling the gray folding chairs and standing beyond them. The winter lawyer stood behind her to whisper in her ear or step to her bidding. She wore a somber black suit with her shellacked silver hair under a black half-moon hat that draped a veil over her face. You could see her eyes through the mesh. Watching.

Her veil tracked us as we took the seats perhaps forty feet away from her facing the coffin to our right and beyond it to her throne. Family, *but.*

A carefully spaced stream of select mourners left their metal folding chairs to shuffle up to the graveside throne to shake Dee's white-gloved hand. They spoke words to her that no one else could hear above the bagpipe.

The attorney general and an elegant man in his fifties played *no, after you* for all of us to see. With the coffin at their backs, they faced the rows of folding chairs for voters. Shook each other's hand. Stood shoulder with *obviously* appropriate somber smiles in a photo op for the big city by the airport's daily newspaper photographer, the editor of Sidner's weekly paper, their aides' and dozens of citizens' clicking cellphones posting to social media sites.

"The guy dancing with the AG is the lieutenant governor," whispered Lana. "He needs being here more than the governor, because the LT is running for that big chair in the coming election when the current governor's term is up."

"This isn't Ron's funeral," I said. "This is Dee's dress rehearsal. Better than Tom Sawyer. She gets to see her own death ceremony *and* choreograph the show. And with Ron gone, it's also her coronation as the sole crown in town."

One of the undertakers walked over to whisper between us: "I'm so sorry for your loss, Mrs. Zane. As the bagpiper does his thing, the coffin will be lowered. Then at the appropriate moment, Mrs. Zane—the other Mrs. Zane—"

"The real Mrs. Zane," interrupted Lana.

Her droll aside didn't faze this event coordinator.

"You see that red wheelbarrow?" he told us. "See the florist filling it with red roses? Then he's going to wheel it beside the grave.

"At the appropriate moment, Mrs. Deirdre Zane will rise. Walk to the grave. Choose a flower. Perhaps turn. Say a few words. That's up to her."

"What isn't?" I said.

The undertaker ignored my interruption.

"After she finishes at the grave, she will return to her seat. Then the lieutenant governor and the attorney general will separately walk up to the grave. Pick a flower and drop it in. After they have returned to their seats, *you*, Lana, will rise, go to the roses, pick one and gently, *respectfully*, let it fall into the grave. You and you *alone* will go do that, say nothing, then return here."

"Politics before protocol?" I said though I didn't care. "She's the widow."

"Decisions have been made. That's what protocol is."

He took a breath. His ostensibly soothing whisper returned.

"After she is in her seat—"

Lana said: "You mean *she* is *me*."

"We all know what I mean. After that, I'll motion to the seated crowd and all the people now gathering to form a line at the red wheelbarrow to drop in their roses, too. At that time, Mister . . ."

He glanced at his iPad. We all knew that was a lie. He was a pro. Knew my name. He wanted to let smart-ass me know my worth in the order of the universe.

"Then you can join that line, *sir*. Thank you both for your help."

He gave Lana a consoling pat on her shoulder for watching eyes to see.

Walked away.

My eyes went to the crowd.

Many of the people seated in the graveside chairs were strangers to me, but I spotted the city and county attorneys. The mayor. Their wives. Faces from the Chat & Chews Big Shots' table. The bank president. A priest sat beside a minister as the official representatives of God. A highway patrolman with a gold braid dangling from his epaulet and a state commander's cap.

And in the front row, positioned where he could command us, sat uniformed Sheriff Ross Fenton.

We three nodded.

The ushers formed regular-ticket attendees to this show into a half circle standing around the VIP chairs.

We all could see the prison on the horizon about a mile away.

Faces in the crowd. Elly the waitress. Gary from the Tap Room. People who worked at the bank. Faces from the wedding. There stood the newlyweds.

Cody was out there somewhere. If he wanted me to see him, I would.

I wondered if the blonde private eye Shawn was blended into the crowd.

Nurse's aide Jen from the Evergreen stood beside shaking Carrie.

My mother told me that Queen Dee had "cordially" invited anyone in the assisted living facility where she didn't live to attend the funeral. Dee even hired someone to drive the bus. Threw in the inducement of an invitation for them to come to the private post-reception being catered at . . . Barb's Ribs.

"Dee just wants to show how much better she looks and is doing than the rest of us near her age," Mom told me as she lay chained to her hospital bed.

Subtle glances showed me tufts of gray and white hair amidst the standing crowd that I recognized from the Evergreen. The handsome man and his friend with a walker. Teresa. Mrs. Malletta. Roma Aikens. I saw the multimillionaire trucking tycoon and his wife give up their VIP chairs to two feeble residents of the Evergreen. The ushers knew better than to interfere with that simple act of human kindness. They let him and his wife stand amidst the crowd just like their friends and neighbors.

My aunt was somewhere in that herd. She'd offered to stand by me at the service, but I didn't want her on that bullseye.

I saw Main Street faces and their spouses. I saw Lorraine who managed the Roxy. The accountant who gave my mom a discount. Librarian Halle. I saw ushers keep moving everyone closer together. I saw men in work jackets with patches for Zane Enterprises—

—and *damn*: there stood Bushy Beard Darrell. He refused to look at me.

Those men officially worked for the identity locked in the coffin. Ron would not have known a single one of their names. They clustered together and my bones knew they'd been told to show up and show off their colors.

Him:

A face I knew from my Google searches. Younger than me. A city-hip suit. Lean. Angelic boyish features. Pale skin.

Doug *Something*, the painter from Wyoming.

I wondered what canvas he faced now.

The red wheelbarrow rolled to beside the grave.

The west breeze swept up the scent of roses.

Queen Dee's nod might not have been perceptible to the crowd standing beyond the VIP seating, but I caught it.

An undertaker touched the bagpiper's arm. A loud chord. The bagpiper stopped playing.

That silence cued the crowd to join it.

The bagpiper stepped forward. Stood by the red wheelbarrow.

Pumped the bagpipe. Pushed the bag beneath his left arm. Settled his lips around its reed. Squeezed.

Played "Amazing Grace."

The coffin sank into its grave as the bagpiper piped.

Random voices in the crowd sang the words to the bagpiper's hymn:

"*. . . that saved a wretch . . . like me . . .*"

The straps lowering the coffin loosened.

Only those of us close by heard the *clunk* of the coffin's final descent.

The bagpiper finished with a snap of his right arm down to his kilted side. Turned and walked away from the grave.

Queen Dee lifted the veil off her face.

Rose from the throne.

Royalty in black who clearly needed no one's help to stand tall.

Dee walked to the red wheelbarrow.

Picked up a red rose.

Stood at the edge of the open grave. She held her arm out above that long black hole. Held the rose high enough for everyone behind her to see.

Opened her hand and let gravity float the rose down into darkness.

We all watched it fall.

The rose's flutter meant no one noticed that old man in the crowd.

Deirdre Zane turned to bask in the constellation of faces she'd gathered.

Her arms spread wide to embrace that glory.

They'd mic'd her dress. Were filming the historic event.

Her voice boomed through the October afternoon.

"Thank you all for coming to support me in my time of need! Thank you friends and neighbors and distinguished friends from near and far for—"

Owl Eyes Mike charged from the crowd with the fury that had startled me during the rainstorm days before. He was in her face before any of us realized. Dee's expression snapped from surprise to rage.

The mic on Dee's dress caught Owl Eyes Mike's bellow:

"You stole him from me! You never let me have him! Never told him—"

His lunging grab of her became a bumbling stumbling shove.

Dee flew backwards into the open grave!

Mike crashed in on top of her!

His foot caught the red wheelbarrow. Flipped that fate purveyor into the grave to slam them—unseen but heard on the mic—as they hit their son's coffin.

Lana and I shot to our feet.

The crowd screamed. Bellowed. Ran willy-nilly. Ran to help. Ran to see. Ran to flee. Ran because they didn't know why.

White-shirted teenagers panicked or used their cellphones to film this, *like*, riot in a cemetery that you can now find online. The winter lawyer and undertakers raced to the open grave—

—teetered on the edge as they peered down into that final hole. Men in suits reached down into the darkness that was deeper than any of them were tall.

The highway patrol commander bellowed orders no one could hear.

My grave-digging buddy turned cemetery boss Dave charged through the crowd waving his Stetson hat like a cowboy in a cattle stampede.

And I knew that nobody was coming out of that grave alive.

Sheriff Fenton pushed his way through panicked bystanders to snarl at us:

"Time for you two to get the fuck out of town!"

51

Sunday morning Lana and I woke up before dawn in my *growing up* bed.

We made the Montana big city's daily newspaper my Boomer mom still had tossed on her front porch every morning. Knew it would be online, too.

A bold headline stretched across the top of the front page:

FUNERAL HORROR IN SIDNER

A color photo filled the columns below the headline.

The photographer caught the bagpiper's shock as rescuers raced toward the grave. The shot's background froze Lana and me leaping from our seats.

We didn't read the story in the actual newspaper.

Didn't search our screens for the streaming videos of that horror.

I gave my mind a break by skimming *'real world'* news stories.

Russia and Turkey were probably to blame for the bombing of a town the size of Sidner in the seemingly forever six-sided war in Syria that helped to crush 2011's Arab Spring of hopes for freedom and justice.

A report from a US Senate Select Committee on Intelligence found the Internet "rampant" with lies. False front websites. Fake social media accounts both personal and professional. Phony news sites. Ghost keyboard clickers. Scam artists. Uncredited corporate messaging. Frauds. Hackers and ransomers. Fishers and trolls. Chinese vacuums. Iranian snoops. Political manipulators like Russia's Foreign Intelligence Service SVR spy shop and the Kremlin's mothership for all things Orwellian, the Federal Security Service, FSB.

That morning's news reported more billionaires now walked the earth than ever before. Their number had surged 40 percent in five years.

A species of croaking frogs was now extinct. Extinction claimed earth's species at an average rate of one species every day back then.

A new virus had been identified in China.

A mass shooting at an Ohio small town children's play killed twenty-three people.

Mom's breakfast hadn't come as I stood by her hospital bed holding her hand as she held mine. The room smelled of old people, just like Dee said, but they were still here and she was not. Light filled Mom's window and lit her face.

"Just sell that old car when you get where you're going," she told me. "Hell, let's hope it doesn't break down before it gets you some place good."

"I'll take care of it, Mom. And thanks."

"What the hell was I going to do with it? Go to the grocery store? Hell, they feed you here—though they could use a lot of help in the flavor department! But yesterday I got the last fresh peach."

I knew she'd find the $1,000 in cash in her secret cache after she got her casts off and could walk across from her new home in the Evergreen to our family house Katie was negotiating to sell. Both Mom and Katie refused to let me pay for the old car. The $1,000 wasn't for that anyway. Was not enough of what I owed.

"Don't worry," said my sister. "If bills come that selling the house, Social Security and her savings don't cover, I'll collect the half due from you, *Mister In The Money Now*."

"You better," I said.

"Have I ever lied to you?

"Well," she said, "that time when I told you werewolves were waiting for you outside the house. But you were six. That's what big sisters are supposed to do."

"Besides," I said, "you were right. About the werewolves."

That Sunday morning in October felt real beyond belief as I sat holding my mother's hand in her hospital room.

The door swung open and in hustled nurse's aide Jen, breakfast tray balanced in her two strong hands.

"Sorry I'm late!" she said. "We just got set up for the memorial mixer for Mike and we've only got the guitar player for half an hour and the coffee and the donuts right after serving breakfast and getting everyone down to the dining room—It's a madhouse!"

She fixed the breakfast tray across the bed in front of Mom.

Gave me her worried face: "Is there . . . Can I do anything for you?"

"Just be yourself."

Jen shook her head: "You could have given me something easier to do."

"Sorry."

"I . . . I gotta go, the mixer's starting and . . ." She blinked. Shyly smiled. "You don't owe any *sorrys* to me."

"Wait!" I said. "There is something you can do for me—for us."

Jen nodded.

"Irma's son in the Army."

"Johnny," said Jen. "His name is Johnny. He's a good guy."

"My guess is he's going to show up in town sooner rather than later. So much of her life got left behind. Could you keep an eye out for him? Find out from him where and how Mom and I can send some money to Irma? That's all we can think of to do. And get his cellphone number."

"He'll appreciate that. Bunch of us, that's all we could think of to do, too."

She hustled out the door.

"Here, Mom," I said. "Let me help you with breakfast."

"No," she said. "Sheriff Fenton was right. Time for you . . . for you two to go."

I stood there looking down at the woman trapped on white sheets.

She kept her gaze on my face.

"Lana told me to tell you thanks," I said. "That she wished she'd have come to say goodbye, but she didn't want to take away from my time."

"You'll be lucky for what time she gives you."

I nodded.

"Now get out of here," said Mom. "The sooner you leave, the sooner you'll come back."

She picked up a fork for . . . *yes*, black peppered scrambled eggs:

"I want you to see me doing something besides crying when you go."

I left her door open.

Maybe she'd be able to hear the guitar strumming coming up over the very high-railed balcony to her second-floor corridor from the dining room below.

Guitar strums walked me down that ivory-walled shaft of apartment doors. The green carpet led me toward that balcony and the silver doored elevator.

Three flowers and a flopped-sideways child's action figure of a cowboy on a horse lay on the floor in front of a closed door coming up on my right.

Three steps away from the door:

The sign on that wood that said the room belonged to Owl Eyes Mike.

Guitar strumming soared but never as amazingly as Richard Thompson.

Let it all go. Listen to the guitar.

Two steps away from the door:

The toy cowboy on a horse fallen sideways on the green carpet, *sure.*

Plausible.

Why are the flowers crushed?

Stepping beside the door:

An edge of gray duct tape lined the silver plate below the doorknob . . .

. . . where the door's tongue was supposed to slip into the doorframe's faceplate so the door would stay closed. And/or locked. You could slap the pre-cut gray tape on in seconds when someone else in the room with you was busy looking elsewhere. Then walk out of the room. Pull the door closed behind you.

Officially locked.

A Watergate burglary of a dead old man's room?

My hand pushed that door quietly open as the guitar played.

Nurse's aide Denise crouched in front of dead Mike's chest of drawers. Her back to me. Her hands plowing through his clothes in the middle drawer.

She was quick. She was sly.

Silently closed the middle drawer.

Softly slid open the bureau's drawer that was as high as her heart.

Worked both hands into that old man's mix of clothes and papers and—

I slammed the drawer closed on her fingers.

She choked her scream into a gurgle.

She'd been a sneak thief before. Before she even taped the door, she'd psyched herself not to make any noise doing the job.

I leaned on the drawer. Trapped her fingers in its vise.

Pain contorted her face.

"Go ahead," I whispered. "Scream. Scream loud and long and hard. Maybe you should wait until the guitar pauses. Then go for it. Scream like hell and they'll hear you. They'll come running. Burst in here."

I put another ounce into my lean on the drawer crushing her fingers.

The guitar stopped.

Scattered applause.

"Won't this be a sight for the world to see!" I told Denise. "You caught . . . *Hey*: I gotta laugh! You should, too: You're caught *red-handed!* Your record. Your charming personality. Go ahead. Scream. Tell everybody how I attacked you. Or tricked you. Or hurt you, *yeah*, I'll cop to that—because I was being the cop.

"Why don't we call them?"

I only needed one hand to pull my cellphone out of my black jeans, thumb it to life and hold it up for Denise's wide and wild eyes to see.

"Why don't we see what Sheriff Ross has to say about all this? He and I, we got an understanding. I bet you and he go way back. He'll know all about you.

"Bottom line, *Denise*." I leaned another ounce, crushing her fingers. "You're a known thief. A creep and a creeper. Me, I'm the *local fucking hero*."

Fingers strummed a guitar outside this room.

"This is what's gonna happen," I said. "Stop preying on these people. No more stealing from them. No more being an asshole to them. No hurts on any of them. No more stealing from the company either, this *Evergreen* place. No more being a pain in the ass for your bosses and the people you work with. You do your job. You do it better than your sorry ass ever has.

"And if you hurt anybody, if you go back to stealing from them, I'll know. I'll find out. If I'm standing here calm as can be while crushing your fingers toward being a cripple, *well*, imagine what I'll do then.

"Especially," I said, leaning closer to her sputtering face, "if you so much as make my mother less than safely happy. Remember: I'm your nightmare."

I gave her a smile.

"You know what?" I said. "Moments like this are to be remembered."

My cellphone whirled in my hand as I thumbed on video.

The strumming guitar played background music for the movie.

My black screen reflected her caught with her fingers in the drawer. I panned down for a clear shot of her trapped hands. Held the cellphone high above us for a scan that showed us together as we were. Gave that movie a half dozen heartbeats to happen and then stepped away.

Her face snapped with relief and she pulled her hands free as I tracked back from leaning on the bureau drawer to walking backwards toward the room's open door. Denise held her throbbing hands in front of her anguished, angry face.

My cellphone panned from Denise to the open door.

Zoomed in on the duct tape pressed over the door's tongue.

My free hand peeled the duct tape free.

My thumb and forefinger gripped the corner of the gray tape strip as I held it out toward Denise for the camera: "Fingerprints and DNA!"

The guitar strummed.

I stood in the doorway.

Denise wanted to charge me. We both knew she didn't dare.

"Last thing," I said as the camera recorded. "You were so intent on being quiet when you snuck in here to steal from a dead man, you crushed the flowers on the carpet in front of the door. You knocked over a toy. After you put back what you stole, get out of here. Lock the door behind you. Go back to what you're supposed to be doing. And set the cowboy up on his horse like he belongs."

The video showed me walking backwards out of the room. Denise shrank as I went. The video ended with me walking down the green carpeted hallway.

The elevator carried me down.

That *Ding!* led me to the tiled floor leading past the dining room where I saw residents watching a woman half their average age sway back and forth on a stool as she strummed stories from her acoustic guitar. I saw all the familiar faces. The bus crowd. I saw Jen watching over everything. Smiling.

My mind told all of us: *Mom's got you now.*

The strip of gray duct tape rolled into a ball got tossed into the Evergreen's medical waste box as I walked out those glass doors.

Bullshit works if nobody ever calls you on it.

The first thing I saw when I walked through the front door of my old home was Lana's gear sitting on the living room floor, ready to go:

One hefty battered suitcase.

One medium sized shoulder bag.

That gold chained, small black purse.

A maroon parka for the coming cold times draped on her luggage.

My two bags and computer case/attaché stood nearby.

"She's not here," said Katie. Shook her head.

"When we walked out of that murder house with her funeral suit, I helped her carry three other bigger suitcases. Fancy designer suitcases, not like that beat-up bag. All of them stuffed with clothes. Not cheap but not stupid glitzy. She left a lot of such glitz behind in the closet of the room where she'd stayed."

My big sister knew my question.

"She's next door. She's giving all those clothes to Debby. If they don't fit or Debby doesn't want them, she's supposed to sell them for her own profit on biggest-bid consignment at Re-Runs, the secondhand store. The word gets out that Lana's clothes are there, there's money dying to wear something notorious."

I gave Katie a full report about creeper Denise. Played the video.

"You know she's not going to stop," said Katie.

"No, but she'll cool it for a while. The Evergreen needs her for now. They're hugely understaffed. But maybe that will change."

"I'll be working with the director Mrs. Gage to get Mom moved in. Maybe she'll let me help her with the books. Find a few pennies as an incentive to throw on a nurse's aide level replacement for Denise. Between Aunt Bev, Mom and me, maybe we can find a decent protégé for Jen."

"I hadn't thought of that."

"That's why you need your big sister."

The back door creaked open and slammed shut.

Lana swayed towards us through the kitchen. Her tan rough-out cowboy boots clumped on the kitchen tiles. Her blue jeans were faded. She wore her red fringe jacket over a blue Western shirt with black pearl snaps.

She'd cut her hair.

Her below-her-shoulders, blowing in the wind, luxurious black hair.

Gone.

Chopped short. Uneven. A shag two inches long at the most.

A scissors job. A bathroom sink mirror. A friend to watch.

But Lana snapped and sliced the scissors herself.

She wore no makeup.

Wore courage and challenge on her face.

Told me: "We better use the bathroom before we get going."

We did.

Then Katie gave me a hug.

Saw Lana standing there. Gave her a hug and got one back.

There'd been hugs like that the night before when Cody came to the house. None of us had much to say. We made that time into forever.

Now that Sunday morning we walked down the front steps of my family home to the street and our waiting ride.

I had to say it: "I'm proud of you."

Lana took two steps—

—said: "Thanks."

Lightness flowed into me, a smile on the inside.

The morning chill smelled fresh and clean. The sky rose blue above us.

The trunk of Mom's old car *clunked* shut over our bags.

The car doors *whunked* shut as she took shotgun and I took the wheel.

Announced: "One more time."

I cranked the engine. Spun the steering wheel. Turned the car around. Headed down the hill. Turned left past the old city hall and left again on to the east end of Main Street.

An October Sunday morning.

Before the church chimes rang.

Before much of anything besides the wind moved on Main Street.

Less than a dozen parked vehicles lined this road through town.

I chugged the car westward as slow as I dared.

The Western wear store crawled past on our right.

Halloween decorations filled that shop's window. Black and orange streamers. A friendly ghost going *'Boo!'* Jack-o'-lanterns with toothy leers. Black silhouetted witches on brooms. Zombies reaching out for brains. Costumes.

"I don't have to be anybody but me this year," whispered Lana.

The car pulled over into a wide space of empty curb in front of the Roxy.

"Come on," I said. "Let's see if we can get coffee for the road."

I opened my car door. Stepped out. Grabbed my black leather jacket from the back seat. Swung the black jacket through the air high above my blue-shirted shoulders so the universe could see the belt of my black jeans held no gun.

Lana stepped out to the sidewalk wearing her red fringe jacket.

We stared at our reflections in the locked glass doors of the Roxy.

"*Wow*," I said.

"Yeah," she said. "*Wow*."

Walked west with me.

We passed the closed on Sundays Chat & Chew café where we'd first met. The plate glass windows showed me the tables for the Old Farts and the Big Shots. The pine-scented mopped floor where Elly would walk come Monday.

Across the street stood the closed door of the Tap Room where fantasies and familiars awaited the flesh of its customers.

Cody's locked gun shop faced the world for what it was.

And the P.S. *something more than* coffee shop was closed.

"After last Sunday and yesterday," I said, "I thought they might have started opening up earlier."

"Like the sign east of town says," joked Lana: *"You gotta be an oily bird to catch the woims."*

She *joked!*

My soft grin said: "I guess we don't get caught today."

Our eyes met.

She held my look for more than one heartbeat.

Shifted her chopped-haired head. Glanced toward our feet.

Pointed: "Look! On the sidewalk."

I saw what she saw.

Lana whirled the other direction and I turned with her.

"Our shadows," she said. "They were in front of and now they're behind us."

"It depends on the sun. Where we stand. The shapes we choose."

"And the cracks in the sidewalk," said Lana.

"The shade we leave and the shade we send. They're both always with us."

"And then we're gone," said Lana.

"But the sidewalk got a touch we made."

She shrugged *maybe*.

"*Shadows On Sidewalks*," intoned the actress. "SOS."

"We all need all the help we can get."

We walked to the car.

Lana opened the front passenger's door. Settled in to ride shotgun.

I pulled open the driver's door—

Stood in its gap.

The Roxy filled my vision. My memories. My breath.

The wind blew.

As it always does.

I tossed my jacket into the back seat. Slid behind the steering wheel. Slammed my door shut. Keyed the old engine. Cranked the steering wheel. Pulled out onto Main Street headed west past the old boarded-up Rainbow Hotel.

I turned right at the light and drove the two blocks to the stop sign.

My windshield filled with a view of box cars on the railroad tracks across the two-lane blacktop the town called Front Street and the maps called the Highway 2 truck bypass.

Highway 2 ran east-west across the state below the Canadian border.

The interchange for the north-south interstate highway at the edge of town waited off to the left of the hood of our car at the stop sign.

"Which way do you want to go?" I said.

Took a deep breath.

Let it out with all I had: "Where do you want me to take you?"

She sat there staring out of the windshield.

"I want to see the prison get behind me. I want to cross over that river."

My blinker clicked left.

This was the way to the hour-plus-away airport. Planes to my DC lair. Planes to LA. Planes to separate destinations. Planes to Gone Forever.

Lana kept her face glued to her window as we rode the highway.

The chain link fence surrounding the cellblocks flowed past as we drove in silence. She watched until her neck could crane no more. Turned and watched until even its hint vanished in the mirror on her side of the car.

Blink and the last of my hometown left my rearview mirror.

The chain link fence surrounding the underground nuclear missiles site slid past Lana's window. She faced that Armageddon.

We'd rolled maybe a mile more when she flipped her visor down and found a mirror catching her chopped hair image. I tried to keep my eyes on the road as she snapped open that small black purse. Pulled out a thumb-sized gold tube. Glowed her lips a slick ruby red.

Snapped the visor back.

Told the windshield: "War paint works for me."

"I like what works for you," I said.

Risked saying: "I like what works for me, too."

The road hummed us ever forward beyond our windshield.

The river waited dead ahead.

Lana said: "My mom and sister need to meet you."

"Tell me the way."

And she did.

Caught my smile in her eyes as I said: "It'll be a long trip."

She said: "I hope so."

The End

DUE THANKS

A novel is a river fed by many streams. This work owes gratitude to hundreds of sources over decades—interviews, inspirations, encouragers, editors, authors, agents, critics, chroniclers, confiders, fans, family, friends, teachers. These few listed here represent so many more and are due my humble, fervent thanks:

Ahmet Altan Rick Applegate Rich Bechtel Kai Bird Jackson Browne
Albert Camus Michael Carlisle Janet Dante Eric Dezenhall Bob Dylan
John Fogerty Debby Gage Lily Gladstone Bonnie Goldstein Jane Grady
Nathan Grady Rachel Grady Desmond Jack Grady Granduciel Chris Harvie
Gary Harmon Alia Heavyrunner Jeff Herrod George Howe Kendrick Lamar
George Kipp Len LaBuff Sidner Larson Sinclair Lewis Ron Mardigian
Marsheila Mariotte Dan Moldea Marilyn Monroe Tom Morello
George Orwell John Prine Alan Pulaski Chris Richards Arnold Schwarzenegger
Yvonne Seng David Hale Smith Bruce Springsteen John Stewart
John Steinbeck Roger Strull Taylor Swift Tecumseh
Richard Thompson Nicholas Von Hoffman
Kurt Vile Paul Vineyard James Welch
William Carlos Williams Josh Wolff
You
Us